# THE MARY-ALICE FILES BOOKS 5-8

THE TWO-BODY PROBLEM | BLACK WIDOW VALLEY | THE NO-TELL MOTEL | VAMPIRE BILLIONAIRE OF THE BAYOU

FRANKIE BOW

# CONTENTS

# THE TWO-BODY PROBLEM

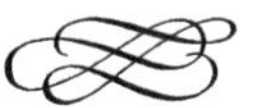

This story is based on a series created by Jana DeLeon. The author of this story has the contractual rights to create stories using the Miss Fortune world. Any unauthorized use of the Miss Fortune world for story creation is a violation of copyright law.



Stock art: Pixabay, Freepik, Vecteezy

# CHAPTER 1

Retired part-time bookkeeper Mary-Alice Arceneaux, recently-arrived resident of the town of Sinful, Louisiana (population 253), was having breakfast at Francine's Diner. Sinful is a small bayou town, and Francine's is the only restaurant in Sinful. But it would be a mistake to write off the tiny municipality as a place where nothing ever happens.

Mary-Alice was finding Sinful to be quite interesting indeed. She had purchased the old Cooper Place, right in town on the edge of the bayou, and the restoration of the historic building had been keeping her agreeably occupied. Mary-Alice's cousin-by-marriage, Celia Arceneaux, had recently been elected mayor, having won an impressive number of votes from the deceased (a recount was underway.) Mary-Alice had made a few new friends in Sinful, and together with them had fallen quite by accident into investigating a local murder or two.

And when Mary-Alice tired of real-life intrigue, there was Harriet's Books, just a short walk from her house, to supply the murder mysteries she loved.

But Sinful had hidden depths of which even Mary-Alice was unaware.

The young woman sitting across from her, former pageant queen and current children's librarian Sandy-Sue "Fortune" Morrow, was, in fact, an undercover CIA operative in hiding. Fortune had annoyed an arms dealer by killing his brother, and the agency had parked her in Sinful, which was the most out-of-the-way hiding place they could find. Fortune kept her mind active and her skills sharp by helping to solve local crimes.

Mary-Alice did not know Fortune's secret. She thought that Fortune, with her detailed knowledge of weapons, warfare, and spycraft, was a very peculiar children's librarian indeed. But then Fortune was a Yankee, and Yankees were a bit odd.

So when a stranger paused in Francine's doorway, glanced around the crowded dining room, caught sight of Fortune, then sped over to their table, Mary-Alice was fascinated, but not surprised. The stranger wasn't from around Sinful, of that Mary-Alice was certain. The woman's hair was short, and its texture was natural. Behind enormous black-framed glasses was a round, pleasant face devoid of makeup. She wore an oversized black t-shirt with a picture of a spaceship on the front (the U.S.S. Enterprise from *Star Trek,* Mary-Alice found out later), dark gray leggings, and black high-top sneakers, a most un-summery color scheme.

"Professor Jackson!" Fortune exclaimed, and half rose out of her seat.

"They told me I'd find you here." As soon as the woman spoke it was obvious she was from up north. "I tried to call ahead, but I only had your address, not a working phone number. Please, call me Gwendolyn. I'm sorry to intrude. I know it seems strange, my dropping in on you like this. But I was hoping...oh, hello."

The stranger had just noticed Mary-Alice.

Despite her bright red hair, colorful flowered t-shirts, and the bejeweled reading glasses that hung from her neck, people tended not to notice Mary-Alice Arceneaux. Mary-Alice was not offended by this. To be inconspicuous was to be ladylike. It was a sign of good upbringing.

And it had turned out to be quite an advantage during Mary-Alice's recent forays into sleuthing. Mary-Alice had come to think of her near-invisibility as her very own superpower. Naturally, she kept this observation to herself.

Fortune moved a syrup bottle holder from the empty place setting next to her and Professor Gwendolyn Jackson sat down.

"Professor Jackson—I mean Gwendolyn, this is Mary-Alice Arceneaux. Mary-Alice, Dr. Gwendolyn Jackson. Gwendolyn taught that computer class I was taking out at Mudbug Tech."

"I'm still teaching it," Gwendolyn said, with a smile. "Too bad you had to drop."

"I did enjoy the class, but things got kind of crazy."

"I know," Gwendolyn's smile faded. "That's why I'm here. I heard you saved a woman's life out in Mudbug. Is that right?"

"Why that's absolutely correct," Mary-Alice said cheerfully. "And I can tell you that for certain because I was that woman. This young lady and her friends happened to be passing by at the time. I must say, I'm as thankful as I can be. Things might have gone quite badly for Celia and me."

"I driving home from your class," Fortune explained. "We saw an orange glow in the sky, figured out what it was, and drove over to help. We called the fire department on the way."

"Well it's an awfully good thing you pulled us out when you did," Mary-Alice said. "By the time the firemen got there, bless their hearts, my entire house was a pile of ashes, and I dare say we would've been, too."

"That's amazing," Gwendolyn said. "So you live here in Sinful now, Ms. Arceneaux?"

"Well, when life hands you lemons, you make lemonade, don't you? I took the insurance money and bought the old Cooper Place. It's right out there past the trees. It needed a little

TLC when I moved in, but it's a delightful place, right on the bayou. And I owe it all to Fortune, Gertie, and Ida Belle."

Fortune shrugged.

"We were in the right place at the right time. Just lucky, I guess."

"I'm hoping you're still on your lucky streak," Gwendolyn said. "I need your help."

Francine, the proprietor of Francine's Diner, lured from the kitchen by the sight of a stranger, came over with a pot of coffee in one hand and a pitcher of iced tea in the other.

"Good morning, ladies," she said as she refilled cups. Then to Gwendolyn, "What can I get you, honey?"

"Coffee, please."

"Ready to order? Or do you need a little time to decide?"

"I'll just have coffee for now. Thank you."

Francine looked expectantly from Gwendolyn to Fortune to Mary-Alice but didn't get any more information. Finally, she said,

"Well, you let me know if you need anything."

She walked back to the kitchen, glancing behind her several times.

"So how can I help?" Fortune asked.

"My husband just passed away."

"Oh my goodness," Mary-Alice exclaimed. "I'm so terribly sorry for your loss."

"Were the circumstances of his death suspicious?" Fortune asked.

"He was fifty, he smoked, I mean I sure wasn't expecting it. But the thing is…I'm sorry, let me start from the beginning. If you don't mind. Do you have a few minutes?"

Fortune shrugged. "We pretty much have all day. Go for it."

"Yes, please do," Mary-Alice said eagerly.

"Mike, my husband, owns a novelty shop. Owned, I should say. Jape & Jest. It's in the French Quarter."

Gwendolyn paused to take a sip of coffee, and her eyebrows raised.

"My goodness, this coffee isn't bad. Wow. Anyway, he had a business meeting with a vendor or supplier or something out near Beaumont a couple of weeks ago, nothing out of the ordinary. I didn't really hear from him when he was gone, but that's normal for him. He's not great at keeping in touch when he's traveling. I finally got a voicemail from him on the morning of July 29. He told me he'd see me the next day. So I went out and did some grocery shopping. I came back, got the mail, and this was in it."

She handed Fortune a sealed plastic sandwich bag with a newspaper clipping inside.

"Make sure to look at the date," Gwendolyn said.

"July 29," Fortune read. *"ORANGE, TX - A 50-year-old Louisiana man was discovered dead in his hotel room Friday morning. The man's body was found by motel staff ... died sometime during the previous night... cause of death appeared to be from natural causes, no sign of foul play. The man's name is being withheld pending notification of family.* So this man passed away the day before your husband called you."

"Fortune, this man *is* my husband."

# CHAPTER 2

Mary-Alice and Fortune both stared at her.

"Are you sure this is your husband they're talking about?" Fortune asked.

"Yes. Of course at the time this item was published they wouldn't put in his name before notifying me, but that's absolutely him. The hotel, time of death, everything is the same. Now, Friday was the 28th. Meaning Mike must have died late on the 27th. How did he send me a voice message on the 29th? And who put this in my mailbox?"

Fortune carefully set the packaged clipping down on a clean part of the table.

"Is it possible the voicemail was delayed for some reason?" Fortune asked.

"Yes. It's entirely possible. The thing that has me worried is this newspaper clipping. The voicemail coming in at the same time, well, that's just icing on the creepy cake."

"Did you report this to anyone?" Fortune asked.

"Not at first. For a couple of days, I was just useless. I mean, I did my job, I taught my classes, but I don't even remember what I said during lecture. And then I thought, this isn't right. Someone's taunting me. Or threatening me. So I went to file a police report in Texas, which is where my husband died. But the police there said because the mail incident happened in New Orleans I needed to go to NOLA PD. And I did."

"I'm guessing something like that wouldn't be their highest priority," Fortune said.

"No. They made sure to let me know that they had murders to deal with, and someone dropping off a newspaper clipping wasn't at the top of their list, even if it was a crime, which they didn't think it was. So then I thought I'd try to report mail tampering to the postal inspector, but again, what am I reporting? Someone dropping a newspaper clipping through a mail slot."

"I'm terribly sorry to interrupt, Professor," Mary-Alice interrupted, "but are you saying you believe there was foul play involved in your husband's passing?

Gwendolyn shook her head sadly.

"Call me Gwendolyn, please. No, I'm not saying that. Honestly, I don't know what to think. I was shocked, of course. Mike was only ten years older than me. But he's been trying to quit smoking for years, never with any success. He's done gum, lozenges, he even tried vaping. I did ask about getting an autopsy."

"What happened?" Fortune asked.

"They pretty much laughed at me. It was like, 'sure, if you want to pay five grand.' Well, I don't have five thousand dollars. We just remortgaged our townhouse to catch up with the store's cash flow, and I haven't been able to find a full-time teaching position. I had to put the funeral expenses on our credit card."

"So you got a voicemail from your husband the day this newspaper article about his death was published," Fortune said. "Did he have any reason to stage his own death? Maybe debts you don't know about?"

"It wasn't staged. I do know that. I identified him. We had an open casket. His family was there."

"And are you sure the message was from him?"

"Yes. Of course. I know his voice. Here."

Gwendolyn pulled out her phone and brought up her voicemail.

"Hey baby," said a man who sounded exactly like a fifty-year-old smoker from the city. He spoke with the hard-edged "Yat" inflection that visitors to New Orleans often mistake for a New York accent. "I'll be seeing you tomorrow. Can't wait."

Gwendolyn blinked back tears.

"It really feels like someone's messing with me, but I don't know who, or why—"

Francine had materialized next to their table and was standing there with a full coffee carafe.

"Just made a fresh pot, and thought y'all might need a refill." She shamelessly took her time topping up the nearly-full coffee cups.

"Anything else I can get for you ladies?" she asked.

"No thank you," Fortune said.

"Thanks ever so much," Mary-Alice added.

Gwendolyn forced a smile. "The coffee's wonderful. Thank you."

When Francine had reluctantly left the table again, Gwendolyn resumed her story.

"There's something else. Things in my house have been disappearing recently. For example, there was a necklace I hadn't worn in a while and when I went to look for it, I couldn't find it. I assumed I'd misplaced it. But then the same thing happened with a pair of earrings, and I've noticed things missing out of the laundry. Mike always claimed he didn't move anything. It didn't bother me, though, until that newspaper clipping showed up."

She laughed nervously. "My goodness, you must think I sound like a lunatic."

"Not at all. Who has access to your house?" Fortune asked.

"Besides Mike and me? Just our cleaning service. But we've had them for years. Anyway, I was hoping you could help me put my mind at ease about all this. I'm sorry to say I can't pay you much."

"You don't have to pay anything," Fortune declared. "We'd love to help."

"That's absolutely the truth," Mary-Alice agreed.

"Just one thing," Fortune added. "May we borrow that newspaper clipping?"

Later that afternoon, Fortune and Mary-Alice met their friends Gertie and Ida Belle at Harriet's Books. Gertie and Ida Belle had been running the Sinful Ladies' Society for over fifty years, which in a way was tantamount to running Sinful itself. The two women had a taste for adventure, a thirst for justice, and a good deal of time on their hands. They never missed an opportunity to help someone in need. The moment Fortune told them of Gwendolyn Jackson's plight, they volunteered their services and would not have taken "no" for an answer under any circumstances.

Harriet, who managed Harriet's Books, had no idea why Mary-Alice Arceneaux and her friends wanted to look through her old newspapers, but Mary-Alice was Harriet's best customer, and pleasant company besides. Tending a bookstore could be a lonely business these days. Harriet let the four ladies use the little round table in her office, cleared all the paperwork and boxes off so they could work, and then brought in a large stack of newspapers. Harriet carried most of Southwest Louisiana's local dailies as well as the *Times-Picayune*.

"I try to take the unsold copies for recycling at the end of the month," she explained. "Fortunately for y'all, I'm behind schedule, so I still have the older issues. I pulled out everything from the last week of July. Can I get you ladies some bottled water? I'd offer you tea or Coke, but I can't allow anything in here that can stain or attract critters."

"No thank you, Harriet," Mary-Alice said. "You're very kind to let us do this."

"Well, I certainly hope you find what you're looking for..." Harriet stared as Gertie pulled a box of purple nitrile gloves from her gigantic purse and set it in the middle of the table. "Whatever it is."

Mary-Alice didn't have the heart to keep Harriet in suspense.

"A friend of Fortune's lost her husband," Mary-Alice explained as the four women pulled on the purple gloves to protect their hands and avoid smearing the newsprint. "He was on a business trip when he passed. She was interested in a learning more about the tragedy."

"Was it murder?" Harriet gasped.

"No," Fortune said, to Harriet's obvious disappointment. "We're just looking for any obituaries or death announcements."

"They say it was natural causes," Mary-Alice elaborated. "No indication of foul play. The man was only fifty, but he was a smoker, you see. That makes a difference."

Harriet nodded to indicate she understood, and slipped out.

"I wonder if she believes that," Gertie said when Harriet had gone. "If I were in Harriet's place, I might wonder why four of Sinful's sharpest minds are investigating a death from natural causes."

"I suppose we won't know until she starts spreading rumors all over town," Ida Belle said. Ida Belle, Mary-Alice had noticed, could generally be counted on to point out the half-empty glass. "We should've told her we were looking for recipes or something."

"Now, Ida Belle," Gertie chided. "Harriet is doing us quite a favor. It would be an ungrateful thing to do, to keep her entirely in the dark. And if we did, Harriet might feel obliged to invent something interesting."

"The problem is, there's no telling what Celia will make of it," Ida Belle grumbled. "As soon as she finds out what we're doing, she'll probably dig up some old law that says you're not allowed to read back issues of newspapers on Tuesdays after three in the afternoon, and then we'll all get fined and thrown in jail. No offense, Mary-Alice."

"I'm sorry, Mary-Alice," Gertie said. "We know Celia is your cousin. But she has rather had it in for both Ida Belle and me for decades. And now that she's mayor, she has the power to make our lives miserable. We're just trying to stay off her radar as much as we can."

"I understand," Mary-Alice said miserably. "Truly I do."

Mary-Alice preferred to think the best of people, and was heartsick at the idea of her cousin feuding with her dear friends. But as much as she liked to say that there were two sides to every story, she was finding it harder and harder to have any sympathy for Celia's side. The more she observed Celia Arceneaux in action, the more obvious it was that the woman was self-centered, begrudging, prideful, and just plain mean.

"Found it," Fortune said. She folded a broadsheet back and laid it on the table. Then she set the clipping Gwendolyn had given her down next to it. It was the same.

"The *Calcasieu Herald*?" Ida Belle said. "I'm surprised they're still around."

"Apparently," Fortune said. "I was wondering if someone had faked this article, or even taken the original and altered the date, but no, it's the real thing. Here's the same date, same ad on the other side, everything."

Gertie took out her phone. "I'll see if there's any follow-up. What was the husband's name again?"

"Michael Mosca," Fortune said. "M-O-S-C-A. Gwendolyn didn't change her last name when she married."

"Here it is," Gertie peered at her phone. "Mosca. It's Italian for 'fly'. The insect, not the act of flying. Oh, I suppose that isn't very helpful, is it? No wait, here's something. I found him. *The man found dead in a room at the McCully Inn died of natural causes, police say. Employees found the body of Michael Mosca, 50, on the morning of July 28. The Calcasieu Coroner's Office found that Mosca died as a result of his pre-existing medical conditions. Foul play has been ruled out in his death, a spokesman said.*"

"Did that newspaper clipping Gwendolyn gave us identify her husband by name?" Mary-Alice asked.

"No." Fortune handed the plastic bag to Mary-Alice so she could see for herself. "Whoever it was that dropped the clipping into her mailbox, knew it was about her husband before anyone else did."

"Do you suppose it's possible to get fingerprints from this?" Mary-Alice asked.

"I doubt it," Fortune said. "The paper looks like it's been crumpled. We can try to find someone who'll do it for us. I really don't want to ask Carter, though."

"No, we should leave the good Deputy Sheriff out of this as long as we can," Ida Belle agreed. "If he thinks we're investigating something, he'll try to shut us down."

Mary-Alice's phone rang.

"Why, what a coincidence. It's Professor Gwendolyn herself. Hello, Professor."

"Put her on speaker," Fortune urged. Fortune, for some reason, had been reluctant to share her phone number, so Mary-Alice had given Gwendolyn her own contact information.

"You're on speaker, darling," Mary-Alice said. "So Fortune can hear. And two other ladies have joined us as well."

"Oh, that's right," Fortune said, "Gwendolyn, meet Gertie and Ida Belle, lifelong residents of Sinful and pillars of the community. Gertie and Ida Belle, Professor Gwendolyn Jackson, who tried to teach me something about computers. Before I dropped her class."

"It's nice to meet you," Gwendolyn's voice replied. "I'm so sorry to bother all of you. Fortune, I was just wondering if you'd found anything out yet about that newspaper clipping."

"We determined that the newspaper article wasn't faked. It was from one of the local papers. Have you thought of anyone at all who could have known that the unidentified man in the story was your husband?"

"Believe me, I wish I knew."

"Professor Jackson," Gertie chimed in, "This is Gertie Hebert. I want you to know we're happy and honored to help. Is there anyone you know who has a grudge against you? Who might have dropped that clipping off with malicious intentions?"

"Not really. I mean, there are always the students who are unhappy with their grades. But they just go complain to my department chair, and when that doesn't work, they go online and post nasty reviews. I'm not sure any of them is clever enough to figure out that the unnamed man in that article was my husband. If I didn't know better I'd say this was Virgil's handiwork."

"Who is Virgil?" Fortune asked.

"My ex-fiancé. We didn't part on great terms. But that was years ago. I'm sorry I'm not giving you anything useful. I still feel like I don't quite have my head on straight. I mean, I still can't bring myself to unpack Mike's suitcase. But I don't want to just abandon it at the Goodwill either..."

"Will you be able to come out to Sinful again, Professor Gwendolyn?" Mary-Alice asked. "To make the acquaintance of Miss Ida Belle and Miss Gertie in person? And perhaps you can bring out that suitcase if you're so inclined."

"Oh, that's really kind of you. I feel like I'm already imposing on you enough, though."

The door opened a crack, and Harriet peeked in.

"Ladies? It's after five."

The women stood, mumbling apologies and thanks.

"Would you like us to take these newspapers to the recycle for you?" Mary-Alice asked.

"Why thank you, that'd be ever so kind. Oh, and Miss Mary-Alice, I'm getting in a new large-print edition of the complete Amelia Butterworth stories. I expect it'll be coming in next Tuesday."

Mary-Alice lit up. "Well, now, Miss Harriet, you make sure to set aside a copy for me."

# CHAPTER 3

Gwendolyn Jackson showed up in Sinful two days later.

She found Mary-Alice, Fortune, Gertie, and Ida Belle in Francine's Diner, enjoying a late lunch. Francine, seeing the stranger again, hurried over with a fifth chair. This time Gwendolyn ordered coffee with a slice of mud pie.

"I think I'm going crazy," Gwendolyn said when Francine had taken her order. "I told myself I wasn't going to come by and bother you again, but when I was getting dressed this morning..."

She looked around.

"My favorite bra was missing," she whispered. "I know I saw it in the drawer a couple days ago. And now it's gone. I can't think anyone took it. I mean, who would steal an old bra? But with everything else going on, it's kind of shaken me up. Anyway, I had some time before my class at Mudbug Tech, so I thought I'd come by."

Francine came back with coffee.

"Honey, you sure you just want coffee and pie? We got fish and chips. Catfish is fresh."

"The fish and chips plate is really good," Fortune said. "You won't regret ordering it."

"You talked me into it. Fish and chips it is."

"Fortune's right, honey," Francine declared. "You won't be sorry."

"I don't think I've eaten yet today," Gwendolyn confided after Francine went back to the kitchen. "And it smells so good in here, I just realized I'm starving."

"Have you given any more thought to who might want to mess with you?" Ida Belle asked.

"Do you have any of those spoiled millennials in your class?" Gertie chimed in. "I've been reading about them. They think of themselves as customers as in 'the customer's always right' and they just want everything handed to them. They sound absolutely dreadful."

"Gertie," Fortune said, "*I'm* a millennial."

"You're not so bad," Ida Belle chuckled.

"I really can't think of anyone who would have it in for me," Gwendolyn said, and then fell silent as Francine set down the steaming plate of fish and chips. Gwendolyn thanked her with a smile, picked up a piece of fish, and quickly set it back down again, it was that hot.

"You okay there, honey?" Francine asked.

Gwendolyn grasped Mary-Alice's glass of iced tea to cool the burn. "Yes, I'm fine, thank you."

"Professor Gwendolyn," Mary-Alice asked when Francine had left again. "You mentioned a disappointed suitor named Virgil. Is it possible he's harbored a grudge all this time?"

"It's possible, but he can't do anything about it. He's in prison."

"Prison?" Fortune's eyebrows shot up.

"Oh my," Gertie exclaimed. "Whatever did he do?"

"Nothing exciting," Gwendolyn assured them. "Mortgage fraud. I actually was engaged to the guy, hard as it is to believe now. Although I can't say I was particularly looking forward to marrying him. He was good-looking, he was charming, he seemed to have his act together, and I thought, well, why not. Then he decided to go to Florida for some real estate opportunity, which of course turned out to be a scam, and he expected me to follow him. I used his move as an opportunity to break it off. Honestly, I didn't think about him again until he showed up at my wedding. Uninvited, of course. He'd had a few drinks, and demanded to be introduced to Mike."

"What did you do?" Mary-Alice asked.

"Well I did introduce them, and it was clear Mike had never heard of him. Because I'd never mentioned him. Well, that really ticked Virgil off. He stormed out, which was fine with me since he hadn't been invited to begin with. Anyway, if there's anyone with an alibi for this stuff, it's him. I wish I knew what was going on. I'm starting to suspect everyone. My neighbors, the mail carrier, the guy who reads the meters, I mean seriously, how does an old bra disappear?"

"Perhaps you'd like to get out of the city for a bit," Mary-Alice suggested. "I have room in my place, and I've just remodeled my kitchen."

"Or you can stay with me," Fortune put in. "Mary-Alice, it's nice of you to offer, but my Aunt Marge's house has plenty of room."

"You're both so kind. I really do hate to impose."

"It's no imposition at all," Fortune assured Gwendolyn. "Just come back here after you teach your class. It's less of a drive for you than going all the way back to the city."

Gwendolyn sat up a little taller, as if a weight had been lifted. "As long as you really don't mind. It's been hard staying in the townhouse by myself, even without all the other weirdness."

"Where are your husband's things?" Ida Belle asked. "You said something about having his suitcase."

"It's still in my trunk."

"Why don't we go have a look?" Ida Belle suggested. "Everyone's done eating, right?"

"Oh, the fish and chips were delicious," Gwendolyn exclaimed. "I'm so full now I'm not sure I can move."

Francine came to clear away the dishes and drop off Gwendolyn's mud pie.

"I forgot I ordered that," Gwendolyn groaned.

"And four more spoons," Francine announced, placing the extra silverware on the table with a flourish. "'Cause, honey, when your friends want to help you out, you just got to let them."

Later that night, after Gwendolyn returned from her class at Mudbug Tech, the women gathered in Fortune's spacious living room. They were going to open the beat-up burgundy suitcase that had belonged to the late Michael Mosca.

Mary-Alice was secretly relieved that Gwendolyn would be staying with Fortune, rather than with her. As proud as Mary-Alice was of her bright new kitchen with its white appliances and its Italian sunflower wall tiles, she wasn't eager to let the world see her yet-to-be-remodeled dining room. The windowless space was inadequately lit by a wrought-iron chandelier that hung from a low cottage-cheese ceiling. The ambiance was made even glummer by putty-colored walls and a depressing gold shag carpet.

Gertie handed Gwendolyn a pair of gloves from the box in her purse, put on a pair herself, then handed the box around.

Gwendolyn unzipped the suitcase and flopped it open. Tears filled her eyes as she gazed at the jumbled contents.

"It smells like him," she whispered.

"He wasn't exactly a neat freak, was he?" Ida Belle observed.

Shirts and boxer shorts were tangled up with shiny plastic beads, oversized sunglasses, and green, purple and gold knockoff Rubik's Cubes sealed in plastic wrap printed with Chinese script.

"What's this?" Fortune reached in and picked out a small, dark gray cylinder. "it looks kind of like a pepper shaker."

Gwendolyn peered at it and shook her head. "It doesn't look familiar to me, but Mike was always getting these weird new toys in."

Mary-Alice, overwhelmed with curiosity, plucked the object out of Fortune's hand.

"It does look like a pepper shaker. Only I can't see where the pepper comes out-- Ow! Goodness gracious, it bit me!"

Mary-Alice dropped the object and clutched her wrist.

"Nobody else touch it." Fortune produced a plastic bag and gingerly dropped the offending object into it. "Mary-Alice, go wash your hands with soap and water. Make sure to irrigate the wound thoroughly."

By the time Mary-Alice returned, someone had lifted the open suitcase onto the coffee table for easier access.

"Do you recognize this?" Fortune was asking Gwendolyn, holding up a receipt.

Gwendolyn took it from Fortune and smiled. "This is that hosiery shop out in Beaumont. He always buys me the mocha fishnets when he has a chance. They're so impractical, but they really do make your legs look fabulous. I know it might be hard to imagine, but I do like to get dressed up now and then."

From behind her big glasses, a tear rolled down Gwendolyn's cheek.

"I'm sorry. Thank you for being here with me. I don't think I could do this by myself."

Gwendolyn started to dig through the suitcase.

"Careful," Ida Belle said. "We already had that thing attack Mary-Alice."

"Buying those stockings was the last thing Mike did for me before he passed," Gwendolyn's voice cracked. "They must be in here somewhere. I know he'd want me to have them. Where are they?"

Then Gwendolyn reached down and, in slow motion, pulled out a blue box. It was not a hosiery package.

The room became quiet.

"Maybe those were for the store," Gertie suggested, sounding unconvinced.

"No," Gwendolyn said, a hard edge to her voice. "This isn't for Jape & Jest. The box is already open. And there's nothing funny about it."

# CHAPTER 4

Gwendolyn stepped backward and sank onto the couch.

Gertie rushed to Gwendolyn's side and produced a small bottle of Sinful Ladies' Cough Syrup.

"Here, have a little sip," she urged. "This is our own recipe. It's handcrafted, brewed in small batches, and very invigorating."

Gwendolyn lifted the bottle to her lips, took a gulp, coughed, and stared at the table with watering eyes.

Mary-Alice sat down on Gwendolyn's other side.

"Are you okay there, darling?" she asked.

"Am I okay? Sure. Fine. You know, considering the fact that I just found an opened box of condoms in my dead husband's suitcase."

Fortune showed Gwendolyn to the guest room and got her set up to spend the night, then returned to join Gertie, Fortune, and Mary-Alice in the living room. When they heard the shower go on, they knew it was safe to talk.

"That poor woman," Mary-Alice said. "Did you see her face? She was absolutely stunned by...by what she found."

"I'd figure she's the prime suspect," Ida Belle said. "It's usually the spouse anyway, and he was cheating on her."

"I disagree," Gertie declared. "Suppose she did kill her husband and they ruled it natural causes. She sure wouldn't come to us and stir things up."

"No indeed," Mary-Alice said. "I'd have to agree with Gertie there. And in any case, I believe Professor Gwendolyn's surprise was genuine. You could see on her face how betrayed she felt."

Gertie leaned over and whispered something to Ida Belle. Ida Belle nodded.

"Fortune," Ida Belle asked, "can you call Deputy Sheriff Carter LeBlanc for us? We need to check something with him."

"You want to bring Carter into this?" Fortune exclaimed. "Mister *Leave the law enforcement to me, little lady*?"

"You can tell him my work in progress is a romantic suspense novel," Gertie said, "and we're calling because I want to check some technical details with him."

"Why Gertie," Mary-Alice exclaimed, "that's a marvelous idea."

"Oh, you can get away with anything when you tell people you're writing a book."

To amuse herself in her spare time, Gertie had started writing risqué romance fiction, in a genre she called "seniorotica," because why should young people have all the fun? Harriet had ordered a few paperback copies of *Passion's Promise,* Gertie's debut, for Harriet's Books. *Passion's Promise* had languished on Harriet's shelves until Mayor Celia Arceneaux caught wind of it and denounced it as disgraceful and scandalous. The book sold out immediately, and Harriet hadn't been able to keep it in stock since.

"Do I really have to call Carter?" Fortune asked. "I don't like lying to him."

This earned her astonished stares from Gertie and Ida Belle.

"What if he hangs up on me?" Fortune persisted.

"He won't hang up on you," Ida Belle declared. "He's sweet on you."

"Us, not so much," Gertie added. "I don't believe he trusts Ida Belle or me."

"Fortune, darling," Mary-Alice suggested, "why not call your young man and tell him Gertie has a question for him? That's the absolute truth."

Fortune shrugged.

"All right. I'll call Carter and tell him you have a question for him, Gertie. Then you can handle it from there."

Fortune made the call, and Carter answered within half a ring.

"Good evening, Deputy Sheriff LeBlanc," Fortune said quickly. "Do you have a minute?"

"It depends. You gonna make it worth my while?"

"You're on speaker. Gertie has a question for you."

Fortune slid her phone over toward Gertie.

"Hello Carter," Gertie said "Thank you ever so much for your help. You see, I'm writing a new book, and it has an element of suspense in it. My plot is at an important juncture, and I need to know whether the situation is one where law enforcement would get involved."

Gertie then described Gwendolyn's plight (with names omitted), up through the discovery of the evidence of infidelity that the widow had discovered in her late husband's suitcase.

"You say the authorities have already ruled out murder?" Carter asked, all business now.

"That's right."

"Is it possible the man died as a result of foul play, and it was overlooked?"

"Well, the man was a fifty-year-old smoker."

"And you say the wife was unaware of the infidelity prior to his death."

"Yes, it seems so."

"It seems so? Isn't this your story, Miss Gertie?"

"It seems so to the *reader*," Gertie clarified. "The way I've written it. *That's* what I meant."

"Is there anyone in your story who had a motive to kill your character, or at least wanted him dead?"

"Well, my heroine does have a man in her past whom she jilted. But she hasn't seen him since her wedding, and he doesn't show up at the funeral, and anyway he's in prison for some boring financial thing. So I don't believe we suspect him."

"And this is just for a book, right, Miss Gertie?" Carter asked. "You're not bothering some poor widow, trying to turn her husband's death into a murder case or anything?"

"Honestly, Carter LeBlanc," Gertie said in a tone that reminded everyone that she was once his teacher. "If I were up to mischief, would I call you and tell you all about it? Besides, do you know anyone in Sinful whose situation resembles my plot in any way?"

"No, I suppose I don't. I guess the only things about the story that seem suspicious are the voicemail and the obituary. But the voicemail might have gotten hung up in the network, although I don't know enough about cell phone networks to say for certain. And the newspaper article did have the name of the hotel, so an acquaintance who knew the husband's travel plans might have thought the wife would be interested. That person may not have even had malicious intent; they might have been unaware that the decedent was actually your character's husband. So, no, I don't see that law enforcement would have a reason to get involved in something like this."

"So my fictional heroine is free to go poking around on her own," Gertie said. "She wouldn't be obstructing justice or anything like that."

Carter paused for a long time.

"Your *fictional* heroine, yes. Why do I feel like this is a trick question?"

Gertie grinned.

"Thank you so much, Carter, you've been ever so helpful."

Fortune picked up the phone from the table, left the room briefly to say her good-byes to Carter in private, and returned.

"Sounds like we just got the green light," Ida Belle said. "You ladies up for a road trip tomorrow?"

"Are we going out to Beaumont?" Gertie lit up.

Ida Belle shot her a severe look.

"This is business, not pleasure, Gertie."

But Gertie was still beaming when they all went their separate ways that evening.

# CHAPTER 5

The next morning, Mary-Alice picked out some of her favorite mystery books, hopped into her Oldsmobile, and drove over to Fortune's house. Mary-Alice worried that Professor Gwendolyn would be bored out of her mind if she only had Fortune's library to keep her occupied. Fortune had nothing but nonfiction in her collection, and all of it was about dry topics like wars and weapons.

Gwendolyn thanked Mary-Alice for the books, then thanked Fortune again for her hospitality. The poor woman really was in a state, Mary-Alice realized. She hoped they could get to the bottom of things as quickly as possible so that Professor Gwendolyn could move on with her life. Even though widowhood had been a blessing for Mary-Alice, she understood that some folks took it very hard.

After getting Professor Gwendolyn set up, Mary-Alice and Fortune headed over to Francine's Diner to meet Gertie and Ida Belle. Mary-Alice listened eagerly as the other three, apparently far more experienced than she in the art and practice of snooping, made their plans for the day.

The first stop would be the Beaumont Plant Nursery and

Café near the Texas-Louisiana border. There they would drop off the little pepper-shaker gizmo so that someone named Tran could examine it. The puncture that Mary-Alice had sustained on her thumb had completely healed, to her relief, and she hoped that this Tran person would find that the device was not some kind of dispenser of exotic, delayed-action poison. Afterward, they would make the short drive up to the hotel where Michael Mosca's body had been discovered, and see whether they could pick up any additional information.

The drive out was relatively uneventful if you didn't count the squabbling over the sound system. Ida Belle had a collection of rowdy driving music that Gertie tolerated until Ida Belle replayed the Dropkick Murphys' remake of "Fortunate Son" for the fifth time. Then Gertie insisted on playing the rough cut audiobook of *Passion's Promise,* which she claimed she had to review minute-by-minute before it was released to the public.

Fortune, who was driving, then announced that she'd permit *Passion's Promise* to play until such time as she heard any of the following words: "aching," "glistening," or "moist."

So the *Passion's Promise* audiobook played for about ninety seconds before Fortune switched to a country music station, which was their soundtrack for the remainder of the drive.

Mary-Alice stayed out of it, watching the scenery on the side of the highway. She hadn't traveled much in her life, and tried to observe as much as she could. The view consisted mostly of trees, punctuated with small towns that were little more than a restaurant/bait shop/gas station in the company of a clutch of one-story houses set on scraggly grass. As they neared the Texas border, the trees got sparser, and the land got browner.

Finally, Fortune turned off the highway to a one-lane road paved with patched-up asphalt. They bumped along on that for a while, then turned up a dirt road, which opened into a dusty parking lot.

The Beaumont Plant Nursery and Café looked like a family

restaurant, and a popular one at that; the parking lot was packed with pickup trucks. Behind the café building, rows of greenhouses reflected the lowering greenish-gray sky, which warned of an impending summer storm.

They didn't go inside the restaurant. Instead, Gertie pulled out her cell phone and talked on it as she led her party around to the back of the building, into the shade of a roof overhang. She knocked on a small, unmarked door. It swung open, and there stood the most colorful cowboy Mary-Alice had ever seen. His hat, bolo tie, and Western shirt were in shades of bright pink, electric blue, and traffic-cone orange, and his belt buckle was the size of a saucer.

"Howdy, ladies." He grinned as Gertie hugged him. Ida Belle gave him a fist-bump, and Fortune went with a conventional handshake.

"Mary-Alice, I'd like you to meet Tran Nguyen, an old friend of mine." Gertie pronounced the man's last name "Win."

"Pleased to meet you, Miss Mary-Alice." Tran's Texas drawl had only the faintest hint of a Vietnamese accent. "Now Miss Gertie, I understand you have a conundrum for me?"

"That I do, darlin'. I know how you love a good conundrum."

The two chuckled at some inside joke, and Tran waved them all inside. They walked through a messy office, across a hallway, and into a plain but well-air-conditioned break room.

"Ladies, sit down," he urged. "Please. What can I get you to drink?"

When everyone was seated at the fake-walnut-grain conference table with a Coke or a canned iced tea, Gertie got down to business. She pulled a sandwich bag out of her purse and shook the pepper-shaker gizmo onto the table.

"We found this thing in a dead man's suitcase," she said. "When Mary-Alice picked it up, it punctured her skin. Mary-Alice, show him where that thing stuck you."

Mary-Alice held out her thumb for examination.

"Now, she's perfectly okay, as you can see, but we're wondering whether there's anything we should be worried about. Poisons and the like. And we'd also like to know what this thing is, and where it comes from."

Tran was holding a pair of tiny brass tongs with rubber grips. He picked up the gray cylinder with the tongs and then, from under his cowboy hat, he flipped down a pair of brass goggles. The tongs and goggles alike were decorated with Western bright cut engraving, all scrolls and flowers and hearts.

"Interesting." He peered at the object as he turned it first one way, and then the other. "No brand name or logo. In fact, it's not quite obvious how the mechanism works. Miss Mary-Alice, might I see your thumb again?"

Mary-Alice held her thumb out once more, and he examined it through the goggles.

"No redness. Is it sore at all?"

Mary-Alice rubbed it and shook her head no.

"Y'all feelin' okay in general?"

"Should I go to the doctor?" she asked.

"I wouldn't bother. Doctor wouldn't find anything either way. Either you're gonna live or you're not."

Mary-Alice did not exactly find this reassuring.

"I can take this doohickey and test it in my lab. I'll let you know what I find. You mind leaving this with me, Miss Gertie?"

"I couldn't hope for better than that, Tran, darlin'."

"Can you have a look at this too?" Fortune placed the newspaper clipping on the table. "In case there are prints."

"What an interesting gentleman," Mary-Alice exclaimed as they climbed back into Fortune's Jeep. "However did you make his acquaintance, Gertie?"

"Tran worked for Uncle Sam during the Vietnam War," Gertie said. "He made himself very useful. So when they brought him over here, they set him up with this nice plant nursery. He's got greenhouses and labs, and every so often he does some analysis for them. He's very good at what he does. If there's anything suspicious on that little pepper-shaker-thingamajig, he'll find it. The fingerprints too."

"You didn't answer her question, Gertie," Ida Belle said from the front seat. "Don't worry, Mary-Alice. One day, over a bottle of wine, she'll tell you how she met Tran Nguyen. Although when you hear the story you may not believe it. For what it's worth, the French ambassador denied it to his dying day."

"Next stop, the McCully Inn, right?" Gertie asked brightly, eager to change the subject.

# CHAPTER 6

The McCully Inn was a low-slung brick building with a red-and-yellow banner hanging over the front entrance:

*NOW OPEN special daily, weekly, & monthly rates.*

The motel looked like it had been built in the 1950s, remodeled sometime in the 1980s, and left to its own devices after that. The tile-print vinyl flooring was curling up at the seams, and the lobby smelled like old cigarette smoke.

"You got this?" Ida Belle asked Gertie. Gertie nodded and disappeared into the bathroom. Fortune, Ida Belle, and Mary-Alice followed her, which was safer than hanging out in the lobby and risking someone asking them what they were doing there.

Gertie went into a stall and emerged after a few minutes wearing a black baggy dress, a hat with a veil, black gloves, and a giant cross necklace.

"What the heck are you supposed to be?" Ida Belle demanded. "Madonna?"

"I'm-a Michael's devoted auntie Fiorella," Gertie said, in what was apparently intended to be an Italian accent.

"I can't watch," Ida Belle covered her face.

"Oh, I'd love to watch," Mary-Alice exclaimed. "It'll be like a game of charades."

"You say charades, I say nightmare of humiliation from which there is no waking," Ida Belle said. "To-may-to, to-mah-to."

"Let's go over to the coffee shop," Fortune suggested. "If we sit by the entrance we'll have a good view."

There was a family waiting to check in. Gertie took her place and waited behind them. When it was finally her turn at the counter, she spoke briefly to the young man at the desk. He listened, nodded, and picked up the phone.

A woman came out and led Gertie over to an unoccupied section of the counter. Mary-Alice thought the woman must be a manager. She was middle-aged, with a pleasant and confident manner, and she wore a burnt-orange skirt suit with a green scarf. It was the sort of color scheme no one would wear unless Corporate said you had to.

Gertie said something to the woman, and the woman leaned forward and cupped her ear. The same thing happened again.

Then Gertie sighed, and spoke again. This time the woman nodded and started talking to her.

"Looks like she had to give up on the fake accent," Ida Belle observed. "Thank goodness."

They watched as Gertie and the manager had an animated conversation. Finally, the woman came around to the customer side of the counter and embraced Gertie, knocking her veiled hat slightly askew.

Apparently, the questioning had gone well.

The back seat of Fortune's Jeep was roomy enough for routine transport but had not been designed for costume changes. Gertie sat behind the driver's seat, pulling off her Italian Widow ensemble and occasionally jabbing Mary-Alice with an elbow or a knee.

"Now Gertie, darlin'," Mary-Alice pleaded as she held up her hands to shield herself, "it's terribly unkind of you to keep us in suspense like this. I'm sure we're all dying to know what that woman said to you."

Gertie finished changing, folded the costume up, and stuffed it into her handbag.

"Of course I'll tell you. I just wanted to get out of that hot outfit first—well, darn it!"

A muffled ringing was sounding from inside Gertie's bag. She pulled out the black dress, black hat, and black shoes, and finally retrieved her phone. Mary-Alice saw that the Caller ID was flashing BEAUMONT PLANT NURSERY and CAFÉ.

"Tran!" Gertie said breathlessly. "What did you find?"

Mary-Alice looked out the window and pretended not to be straining to hear.

"Well I'll be darned," Gertie said, and then, "now where would he have gotten ahold of a thing like that? Okay, you do that. Oh, stop it. Sweetheart, you know I'm not the marrying kind. And let's be honest, you've been in divorce court often enough to figure out that maybe you aren't either. Oh, you are a bad boy. Now really, what if the NSA is listening right now?"

Gertie giggled. "Well, maybe it is, maybe it isn't. You'll call me as soon as you find out anything else? Okay, talk to you soon, darlin'."

"Well?" Ida Belle twisted in her seat to glare at Gertie as soon as she hung up. "Are you gonna keep us in suspense for the whole ride?"

"That was Tran." Gertie gathered up the widow's weeds and refolded them primly them in her lap. "I believe he has a little crush on me."

"Thank you, Gertie, I think we all know much more about that than we need to. What did he say about the device?"

"He says he can't find any kind of manufacturer's mark on it and thinks it might have been made with a 3-D printer."

“A 3-D printer!” Mary-Alice exclaimed. “Who on earth would have a thing like that?”

“No way to know for sure,” Fortune said from the driver’s seat. “You can buy 3-D printers online these days. Gertie, did he run any tests?”

“Well, they did what he called the easy tests first, and none of them came up with anything.”

“What did they test for?” Mary-Alice asked.

“He didn’t go into specifics. But he said they’d keep looking. They can’t do everything right away cause they need to get the what-do-you-callits for the rarer poisons.”

“Reagents?” Fortune asked.

“That was it. Also, he said they probably wouldn’t be able to get any prints from the newspaper.”

“Gertie, you still haven’t told us about your conversation with the manager back at the McCully Inn.” Mary-Alice was trying with all her might to be restrained. But she was so curious that she felt like bouncing in her seat like a child, shrieking TELL ME TELL ME TELL ME!

“Well,” Gertie said, “at first I thought I might try to pretend that I was Michael Mosca’s aunt from the Old Country, but then I realized I look much too young to pull that off convincingly.”

“You mean she couldn’t understand your fake Italian accent?” Ida Belle asked.

“Please do go on, Gertie,” Mary-Alice pleaded.

Gertie glared at the back of Ida Belle’s head. “Certainly, Mary-Alice, I will, and thank you for asking so nicely. So she told me the housekeeper was the one who found Mosca at first when she went in to clean his room, but she ran screaming for help, and then, of course, everyone else went rushing in too.”

“Including the woman you spoke to?” Fortune asked. “Was she an eyewitness?”

“Yes, she was on duty that morning. She told me the man was lying on the floor next to the bed, which was all rumpled.”

"So he'd slept in it," Mary-Alice said.

"Well, he did something in it. Anyway, she said he had one hand on his chest as if he was having a heart attack, but his expression was peaceful. He'd scheduled a wake-up call for 6 am, but of course he didn't respond to it."

"Didn't they check on him when he didn't answer his wake-up call?" Mary-Alice asked.

"Most of those wake-up calls are automated now," Fortune said from up front. "If you don't pick up, I think they figure that's your problem. I don't know of any hotel that'll actually come check on you."

"Doesn't anyone want to hear the rest of my story?" Gertie asked. Everyone quieted down.

"Well now, that's better. So anyway, I asked whether the deceased had met with anyone. Now, that got her talking, because it turns out he did meet with someone and the sheriffs simply didn't want to hear it. They told her the man died of natural causes and what was the sense of dragging a good man's name through the mud. It would only embarrass his family, they told her. The sheriffs were both men, of course."

"So Michael Mosca did meet someone?" Mary-Alice asked excitedly.

"A woman, as it happens," Gertie said. "In the middle of the afternoon. In his room. Some business meeting, huh?"

"When did the woman leave?" Ida Belle asked.

"She didn't see."

"Description?" Fortune asked.

"A plastic blonde. That's how she described her. She was wearing some kind of short white dress and fishnet stockings. She said she saw Michael Mosca alive and well, heading back to his room with this woman, around four in the afternoon. The next morning, he was dead."

"Poor Gwendolyn," Mary-Alice said. "This certainly seems to confirm that her husband was having an affair."

"Like a half-used box of condoms isn't proof enough," Ida Belle scoffed.

"Any clue who this woman was?" Fortune asked.

"Just what I told you," Gertie said.

"Do you suppose it would be helpful to look at Mister Mosca's credit card history?" Mary-Alice suggested. In the police procedurals she read, there was often a clue lurking in the victim's financial records.

"It might be handy to have that," Fortune said, "and Carter has access to that information, but after we just convinced him that we're not getting involved in any kind of murder investigation, I don't see how I can ask him to pull down financial records for us."

"I was going to say, maybe Gwendolyn could get her late husband's credit card records," Mary-Alice said. "There may be bills coming in to the house that we might have a look at."

Ida Belle reached back and gave Mary-Alice a hearty slap on the knee.

"Good thinking! I guess it's not a bad thing we have someone with marital experience on our team."

"But what if Gwendolyn's the one who killed him?" Gertie asked.

"Gertie, I thought we went over this already," Ida Belle sounded exasperated. "If Gwendolyn Jackson killed her husband and got away with it, why would she come to us?"

"Well, there's what the police say, and then there's what the neighbors say," Gertie shot back. "Maybe she's doing this to deflect suspicion."

"All right, general poll, ladies," Ida Belle said. "If you'd just murdered your husband and everyone thought it was natural causes, would you do anything to call attention to it?"

Mary-Alice was seized with a sudden coughing fit.

"Sorry," she murmured. "Just a little frog in my throat."

# CHAPTER 7

Ida Belle directed Fortune to take a slight detour on the way back to buy muffulettas for dinner. By the time they reached Fortune's house, the sandwiches were at their peak of deliciousness, the olive mix having soaked into the Italian bread, and the flavors of the salami, ham, mortadella, and provolone cheese melded in meaty harmony. Gwendolyn was glad to see them and eager to learn what they'd found out. Gertie related the events of the day as they ate at Fortune's sturdy kitchen table. Ida Belle interrupted throughout as she deemed necessary.

"So do you think Mike might have been having an affair with this so-called 'plastic blonde'?" Gwendolyn asked, so casually that it was clear she cared a great deal about the answer.

"Well, now, it's possible the young lady was a business associate," Mary-Alice suggested optimistically.

"A 'business associate' who shows up wearing a short skirt and fishnet stockings to a meeting in a motel room?" Ida Belle scoffed.

"Do you know anyone who might fit the woman's description?" Fortune asked Gwendolyn.

"No," Gwendolyn sighed, "but I didn't know everyone Mike

knew. Mike was at the shop most of the time. People were in and out all day. He'd meet customers, suppliers, I never even saw most of them. So how do we find out who this woman is?"

"Professor Gwendolyn, Darlin', are you absolutely certain you want to do that?" Mary-Alice asked.

"I believe it's necessary," Gwendolyn declared. "If Mike was murdered, his lover's significant other would be the prime suspect."

"Now you believe he was murdered?" Gertie exclaimed.

"I know what you're thinking. And yes, it's possible I might be influenced by spending the day sitting inside reading murder mysteries. But if we're going to get to the bottom of this situation, I think we need to consider all the possibilities. I would never have dreamed that anyone would want to murder Mike. But I would never have dreamed he was having an affair, either. And now we have the blonde at the hotel as well as that box in his suitcase. So what do we do now?"

"Mary-Alice thinks we should have a look at your late husband's financial transactions," Ida Belle said. "That seems like the logical next step."

"With your permission, of course, Professor Gwendolyn," Mary-Alice added hastily. "One's financial records can reveal so much. Blackmail, for example. Oh dear, no offense intended to your late husband, of course."

"I suppose I'll have to go back to the city to pick up the mail in any case. Maybe there'll be some bills or bank statements that you can look at. And hopefully no more ominous newspaper clippings."

"If you really suspect murder," Fortune suggested, "I wouldn't advise going back there by yourself."

"We'll come with you," Gertie volunteered.

"It's a three-hour drive. I've already imposed on you enough. I'll go back tomorrow morning, and come back here after my night class."

"It's no imposition at all, Professor Gwendolyn," Mary-Alice pleaded. If people were going to go all the way to New Orleans to root through the late Mike Mosca's financial records, Mary-Alice did not intend to be left out.

After a solid breakfast at Francine's Diner the next morning, Mary-Alice climbed into Fortune's Jeep with Gertie and Ida Belle. They followed Gwendolyn's Prius all the way to New Orleans, and into a public parking lot downtown.

"I should have warned you," Gwendolyn said as they walked up Saint Peter Street in the soggy summer heat, "our townhouse didn't come with its own parking spot. That was one reason we could actually afford it."

"You drive two hours each way out to Mudbug Tech to teach your class?" Fortune inquired. "You must spend a lot of time driving."

"Remind me to send you my audiobook when it comes out," Gertie chimed in.

"Yeah, I'm one of those freeway fliers. Also known as 'road' scholars, ha-ha. A part-time gig here, a part-time gig there. Not exactly what I expected with a Ph.D. from Carnegie-Mellon. But tenure-track jobs are rare, you have to go where they are, and Mike can't move because of the business. Couldn't move, I should say."

"So you chose your husband over your career?" Ida Belle asked. "Doesn't seem like the best decision, in hindsight."

"You'll have to excuse Ida Belle," Gertie chimed in. "She doesn't intend to be rude. It's just that she doesn't really have a filter."

If Gwendolyn noticed the face Ida Belle made at Gertie, she kept it to herself.

"Actually, our situation is pretty common in academia. The two-body problem, it's called. It's hard to find good jobs for two people when one or both of them are academics. Honestly, it's a positive thing, if you ask me. In the old days, we didn't have any such thing as the two-body problem because it was assumed that the woman would give up all her ambitions and prioritize her husband's career. No problem."

"Yes, how times have changed," Ida Belle observed, and it was Gertie's turn to glare at Ida Belle.

"Oh, that's Mike's shop. Right over there."

The purple-green-and-gold argyle-patterned awning was slightly sun-faded, the jaunty purple lettering in the front spelling out "Jape & Jest."

A red and white For Sale sign was propped in the window.

"I've decided to sell," Gwendolyn said. "I don't know anything about running a retail store. And I'll be honest. I need the money."

# CHAPTER 8

Gwendolyn lived in the middle of a row of pastel-colored Creole townhouses in the French Quarter. The first floor of the block consisted of shops. Each door was topped with a fanlight, a half-moon-shaped window designed to admit whatever sunshine made it down to street-level. The second and third-floor balconies were decorated with potted plants and lacy iron railings.

Gwendolyn led the little party up polished wooden stairs, to a front door that opened directly into the kitchen.

"If anyone needs to use the restroom it's through there." Gwendolyn indicated a door on the far side of the kitchen. "That's the bedroom. Go in, turn right."

Gertie took the invitation and disappeared through the bedroom door.

The interior was narrow and neat, with gleaming wood floors, freshly painted white walls, and palm-leaf ceiling fans.

"It's really neat in here," Ida Belle observed.

"The cleaners were here yesterday." Gwendolyn unlatched the window and swung it open, which let the chemical smell out and a blast of hot air and street noise in. "I've been trying to convince Mike to switch over to what they call the natural-cleaning option, but it's more expensive and he says it doesn't really do the job. Wait a minute—cleaning chemicals. Is it possible to use cleaning chemicals to kill someone?

"Sure." Fortune walked over to the window, which had a view of the wall of the adjacent house. "You can use just about anything to kill someone."

"Like in Terminator 2," Ida Belle said. "Remember when Sarah Connor injected window cleaner into that guy's neck so she could break out of the loony bin?"

"That was my second-favorite scene in the movie," Fortune said. "But can you use cleaning chemicals to simulate a heart attack? That's a little harder. I don't know how you'd do that."

"Do you suppose anyone on your cleaning crew had anything against your late husband?" Mary-Alice asked.

"Not that I know of. I'm not even sure they send the same people each time," Gwendolyn said. "Would you like something to drink? I have soda. I mean Coke."

"Sure," Fortune said. "I'll take whatever's cold. Thanks."

"A Coke would be lovely, thanks ever so much," Mary-Alice said.

Gertie emerged from the bedroom, shaking her hands.

"Your towels were so nice I didn't want to wipe my wet hands on them," she explained.

"The computer's upstairs," Gwendolyn said. "Whenever you're ready. I hope I can get into his account. How embarrassing if this doesn't work."

"Don't worry," Fortune assured her. "I won't tell your students."

"Good. I can keep my cred for that much longer."

"Gertie and I can hang out down here and keep watch," Ida Belle said. "Mary-Alice, you can stay with us if you like."

"Ida Belle, you don't believe we can make it up those stairs," Gertie exclaimed, indignant. The open steps to the next floor did look more like a ladder than a proper staircase, and there was no banister.

"Gertie, I'm certain you could sprint up the side of the Great Pyramid of Giza if you put your mind to it," Ida Belle assured her. "I'm just thinking if someone's trying to harm Professor Gwendolyn, we need to be here to defend her."

"Oh. Good point." Gertie sat down at the small kitchen table and turned her chair to face the front door.

"I'd prefer to go up and help if y'all don't mind." Mary-Alice wanted to be present if any important clue showed itself.

The second floor of the townhouse was nothing more than a narrow room with a couch along one side, and a desk at the end against a brick wall. On the desk was a computer.

"We have a joint credit card, and I keep track of that," Gwendolyn explained as she made her way to the desk. "So if there's anything funky going on, it would be on Mike's business account."

Gwendolyn took a seat at the desk and jiggled the mouse to wake up the computer. Fortune pulled up the other available chair and sat down. This left Mary-Alice with the option of either sitting in a bean bag chair or standing. Mary-Alice calculated her chances of getting back up from the bean bag chair, and chose to stand.

Fortunately, the browser autofilled Michael Mosca's login information, and within a minute the three women were examining his recent purchases. Among the expected merchandise orders and utility bill payments were a few less businesslike expenses.

"Antoine's?" Gwendolyn exclaimed. "Who's he taking to Antoine's?"

"It might have been a business dinner," Mary-Alice suggested.

"How about this?" Gwendolyn pointed to the screen. "Here's

the lingerie boutique again. Okay, what kind of business deal requires fifty-dollar pantyhose?"

"What's that eleven hundred dollar charge?" Fortune asked. "What's Royal A & C?"

"It does sound fancy, whatever it is," Mary-Alice said.

"Oh *hell* no," Gwendolyn fumed. "If that man spent a thousand dollars on some kind of escort service, I'm gonna go dig him up and kill him again myself."

"Professor Gwendolyn, darling," Mary-Alice said, eager to smooth things over, "before we jump to any conclusions, maybe you might could call the number and find out what it is. It may be perfectly innocent."

Gwendolyn pressed the speaker button on the desk phone and dialed the number.

"Royal Aesthetic and Cosmetic," a voice squawked.

Gwendolyn frowned. "Wait a minute. Are you that plastic surgery center that's always advertising on the radio?"

"That's correct, ma'am. If you're a first time customer, mention our ad for ten percent off fillers. And if someone referred you, just tell us their name when you come in and you both get one hundred dollars credit toward your next procedure. Would you like to make an appointment?"

"Not at this time, thank you. But can you tell me how late you're open today?"

"Saturdays we're open until one o'clock, ma'am."

"Thank you for your help."

Gwendolyn set the phone down slowly.

"A plastic blonde!" Fortune and Mary-Alice exclaimed in unison. Gwendolyn nodded and checked her watch.

"That's a little over an hour from now. What do you say?"

# CHAPTER 9

Royal Aesthetic and Cosmetic was located in a decidedly un-regal strip mall out in Kenner, occupying a space that used to be a mattress store.

The women paused outside the tinted glass door.

"Let's just hang out in the waiting area and see what we can see," Ida Belle said. "Rendezvous at the car at thirteen hundred hours."

The women slipped in one by one, each finding an empty seat in the crowded waiting area. When it was Mary-Alice's turn, she found a recently-vacated chair close to the front desk, a perfect vantage point.

At the reception desk sat an evenly-tanned, pink-lipped woman who could certainly be described as a "plastic blonde." Mary-Alice felt a rush of excitement and was ready to find Ida Belle and report her discovery when a nurse walked up to the desk. The nurse had stiff blonde hair pulled back in a bun, a creamy beige complexion, pneumatic pink lips, Daddy Longlegs eyelashes, and although she smiled as she spoke to the receptionist, she had no expression from the eyes up. She, too, fit the description of a "plastic blonde."

In fact, with the exception of one or two artificial-looking brunettes, the entire enterprise appeared to be staffed with plastic blondes.

Mary-Alice heard a "*psst!*" She turned to see Gertie sitting next to her, looking intently at an old copy of *Vogue*.

"It's like a hall of mirrors in here," Gertie muttered at the magazine.

"What does Ida Belle say?" Mary-Alice asked.

"I'll have you know that Ida Belle is not the boss of me," Gertie said, confusingly, as Mary-Alice had long ago concluded that Ida Belle was pretty much the boss of everyone in Sinful. "Anyway, she said if I can think of some way to get information that won't land us in jail, I should go ahead and try. So here goes. You watch and see what you can see."

Mary-Alice looked around the waiting room to see that Fortune, Gwendolyn, and Ida Belle were all sitting nearby. Fortune and Ida Belle had picked up fashion magazines and were pretending to read them, and Gwendolyn was holding up a newspaper. As soon as Gertie stood up and went to the reception desk, Ida Belle came over and dropped into the seat next to Mary-Alice.

"What's Miss Gertie going to do?" Mary-Alice whispered.

"Heaven only knows," Ida Belle replied. "But we drove all the way out here, might as well let her give it a go."

"Howdy-do, my good woman," Gertie's voice rang out. "I would like to discuss the possibility of a butt lift. Might you be able to assist me in this endeavor?"

Ida Belle slumped down in her chair and lifted her magazine to cover her face.

"Certainly, ma'am," the receptionist said. "Did you have a friend refer you today?"

"Why yes indeed. I was referred by my friend Michael Mosca. Although I like to call him 'Mike.' That's my nickname for him. Oh, and he told me there was an employee here who he said was very kind and helpful. A young lady. Although her name slips my mind. She's a blonde, if that helps. He said to ask for her."

The receptionist smiled, showing perfect, blue-white teeth.

"Now don't report me to the patient-privacy police for telling you this, ma'am, but I believe you might be thinking of Jinny Kane. Mister Mosca always asks for Jinny. Oh, speak of the devil. Jinny, looks like you got yourself another referral. From Mike Mosca."

Jinny Kane looked like she could be the receptionist's twin sister. Or pod-mate, Mary-Alice mused, thinking of a late-night science fiction movie she'd seen recently on television. Jinny wore a fitted white lab coat over a short skirt. Beige fishnet stockings crisscrossed her shapely, tan legs.

"Oh, hey, nice to meet you," Jinny exclaimed. "What was your name?"

"Sarah," Gertie said. "Sarah Connor."

"Well, Ms. Connor, thanks for coming in to see us. Uh, how do you know Mister Mosca?"

"Why, from Jape & Jest. I can't get enough of that store. But do you know, now that I think of it, I haven't seen Mike for a while, and the place was closed last time I went by. Do you suppose he's okay?"

"Well, I sure hope he is," Jinny laughed. "He's due for his next appointment soon, and he's already prepaid for his ten treatments."

"He got his back hair removed, and now he's working on his chest," the receptionist piped up, having apparently forgotten her dread of the Patient Privacy Police. "And that man's about the worst re-grower I've ever seen. Wouldn't you say, Jinny? We have to crank the laser up so high you can practically see the lights dim when we zap him. Italian men, bless their hearts."

Mary-Alice could hear Gwendolyn's newspaper snap with irritation.

"Have you been in to see us before?" Jinny asked.

"Nope. I'm a plastic-surgery virgin."

"Here's some information on our most popular procedures." Ginny handed Gertie a stack of glossy brochures.

"Well look at all these nice round cheeks. How much would something like this cost me?"

"The fat injections will run you eight to eleven thousand dollars. The implants are a little cheaper and more reliable, but some people find them harder to get used to. We're closing soon, but Avery can schedule a consult for you."

"Well now, I'll think about it. That's a lot of Social Security checks we're talking about."

Gertie sauntered out of the building clutching a fistful of brochures. Then Gwendolyn folded her paper, Fortune set down the magazine she was holding, and they left together. Finally, Mary-Alice and Ida Belle stood and walked out to Gwendolyn's car.

They got in quietly. Fortune rode shotgun, and the three older ladies squeezed into the back. No one spoke until they were on the road back to New Orleans.

"Howdy-do?" Ida Belle exploded at Gertie. "For the love of—who says howdy-do?"

"Someone making sure the target kept her attention on me and won't remember any of you," Gertie shot back. "That's who."

"Hm. Fair enough," Ida Belle conceded. "I think this Jinny Kane may just be the woman who rendezvoused with Gwendolyn's husband."

"Yeah, that's her." Gwendolyn's hands were gripping the steering wheel far more tightly than necessary. "Those are the stockings. The fishnets. The kind Mike bought for me."

"Are you okay?" Fortune asked.

"No. I'm not. But I will be."

"I noticed the young woman was wearing a wedding ring," Mary-Alice said.

"I didn't even notice that." Gertie pulled out her phone and tapped the screen a few times.

"Okay. Jinny, or Virginia, Kane. Thirty-one years old. Her husband is Kevin Kane. They were married seven years ago. He's a postdoc at the University Medical Center."

"What kind of database do you have there?" Fortune twisted around from the front seat. "I don't think even the sheriff's office could come up with that."

"Facebook," Gertie said.

"Home address?" Ida Belle asked.

"Nope," Gertie said. "There are some limits."

"Well, as long as we're in New Orleans anyway," Mary-Alice said, "do you suppose there's a chance he's working today?"

"A postdoc working on a Saturday?" Gwendolyn said. "I'd bet on it."

# CHAPTER 10

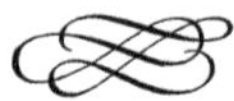

The man hunched over the laptop was slim, dark-haired, and scruffy-bearded. He would be quite handsome, Mary-Alice thought, if he cleaned up a bit. He was working near the back of a cluttered office on the sixth floor, sitting at one of the four desks that crowded the tiny space.

He looked so intent that the women were loath to interrupt him. Finally, Gwendolyn poked her head into the door.

"Excuse me. We're looking for Dr. Kevin Kane."

The man looked up.

"I'm Kevin Kane."

He didn't exactly seem delighted by the interruption.

Gwendolyn glanced back out into the hallway for encouragement, but the four women just waved at her to continue.

She cleared her throat and stepped into the doorway.

"How do you do," she said. "I'm Gwendolyn Jackson. I was wondering if you happen to know a man named Michael Mosca."

The man's jaw tightened.

"Why would I know him?"

"Uh, because..."

Gwendolyn looked out into the hallway again.

"Help me," she mouthed.

Fortune stepped into the doorway alongside Gwendolyn.

"Michael Mosca was a client at your wife's workplace," she said.

"Who are you?" Kevin Kane asked.

"I'm a friend of Doctor Jackson's."

"Okay, nice to meet you. Wait, are there any more of you out there?"

Gertie, Ida Belle, and Mary-Alice stepped into view, completely crowding the doorway.

"How do you do," Mary-Alice said. "I'm Mary-Alice Arceneaux. A pleasure to make your acquaintance, Dr. Kane."

Gertie and Ida Belle did not introduce themselves, preferring to fold their arms and scowl. This appeared not to faze their target.

"So what did you want to know?" he asked.

"Michael Mosca," Fortune repeated. "He passed away suddenly, and his widow is just trying to piece things together and make sense of it."

"Yeah, Jinny probably boinked him to death," Kevin Kane muttered under his breath.

"I'm Mike's widow," Gwendolyn said.

"Oh. Oh my gosh. I'm so sorry. That was inappropriate. I just...listen, I can't tell you much about Mike Mosca. I didn't know him. I'm sorry for your loss. Anyway, I was just leaving, so..." He started shoving papers and notebooks into a tote bag.

"You were at the Society of Math Biology conference?" Gwendolyn asked. Kevin Kane's jaw dropped.

"How did you know that?"

"It's on your bag," Gwendolyn pointed out. "In big white letters."

He checked to see *Society of Math Biology July 22-26 Montreal* printed on the side of the dark blue tote.

"Oh, right. Yes. I was there. I just got back yesterday, in fact."

"I presented there last year," Gwendolyn said.

Kevin Kane zipped his bag and looked up.

"You presented at SMB? On what?"

"Cancer modeling. I did the computational piece."

"Really? Where do you work?"

Gwendolyn shrugged. "I'm place-bound, so I've just been doing part-time gigs here and there. I mean, I'd move anywhere for a solid offer, but my husband owns—owned—a business here, and you can't exactly move a French Quarter novelty store."

"The two-body problem," Kevin Kane said. "I know it well. So who paid for your travel to SMB?"

"Self-funded. I figure it's an investment in my CV."

"Well, I hope things work out for you." Kevin Kane stood and slung the bag onto his shoulder. "I mean it. Sorry I can't help you. I don't know much about Mike Mosca except for the fact that he was scr—" he cleared his throat. "I can't really tell you anything. Sorry."

"Excuse me," Mary-Alice said, "what is that?" She pointed to an object on Kevin Kane's desk, barely visible amidst the stacks of papers and journals. It was a black cylinder that looked a bit like a pepper shaker.

"This?"

He picked it up carefully, by the sides, taking care to avoid what Mary-Alice thought of as the biting end. Gwendolyn gasped when she saw what it was. Fortune maintained an admirable poker face. Gertie and Ida Belle continued to glare menacingly.

"It's a humane injector," he said. "We're doing some prototype testing for the company that makes them."

"Does it work?" Fortune asked.

"Seems to. It's ridiculously easy to use, delivers the right dose, and the mice don't seem to show any discomfort. I mean, they're just mice, but they feel pain too. Listen, I have to catch the streetcar or I'm waiting another 27 minutes. Very nice to meet you all."

Gwendolyn handed him her business card as he passed her on the way out.

"If you remember anything about my late husband, good or bad, please don't hesitate to give me a call."

He looked at it.

"I'll do that, Dr. Jackson."

"Gwendolyn. Please."

"Gwendolyn. Yeah. Maybe we'll run into each other again."

"You gave the murder suspect your contact info?" Ida Belle demanded as they started walking toward the elevator.

"It just has my phone number and a link to my website," Gwendolyn said. "He doesn't know where I'm staying in Sinful, and he doesn't have my home address either."

"This is the second time today I've heard about the two-body problem," Fortune said.

They pulled up to the elevator and Gwendolyn pressed the "Down" button.

"Yeah, academic job openings are like shooting stars," Gwendolyn said. "You don't know where or when they'll appear, and you have to be ready or you'll miss them. That's something they don't tell you when you enter your doctoral program."

"Well, there's nothing to hold you back now," Gertie said brightly as they stepped into the elevator. "You wouldn't have any problem renting out that townhouse."

"So do y'all suppose that young man is a suspect?" Mary-Alice asked.

"He wasn't a fan of the victim," Ida Belle said. "That was pretty obvious. And he owns a state-of-the-art injector, just like the one found in the victim's suitcase. Interesting coincidence."

"But he couldn't have done it," Gwendolyn countered. "Did

you notice the conference dates? Kevin Kane was out of the country when Mike died."

The parking lot was much emptier than when they had arrived, so they found Gwendolyn's Prius quickly.

Fortune took the front passenger seat again, which was only fair because of her long legs. Mary-Alice took the uncomfortable middle seat in the back, and Ida Belle and Gertie squeezed in on either side of her.

"Professor Kane did have the bag," Mary-Alice said. "But are we certain he was really there? He could've borrowed it from someone, you see."

"Oh, I got this." Gertie buckled in and pulled out her phone. Gwendolyn rolled down the windows to let out the hot air and put the air conditioner on full blast. The sun hung low in the sky, but the heat persisted. Gertie tapped determinedly as the A/C did its best to blast the hot, soggy air out of the car.

"Kevin Kane, Ph.D.," she announced, finally. "Here he is. On the presenter's schedule. You're right, Professor Gwendolyn. Unless he hired a stunt double, he was there at the conference when your husband died."

"Is it possible he hid that injector in your husband's suitcase at an earlier time?" Mary-Alice asked. "With some kind of poison in it?"

"That reminds me," Ida Belle said. "Gertie, you heard back from Tran? He was going to test that thingamabob for more stuff, right?"

"He's still working on it," Gertie said.

"This young Dr. Kane may have a nice-looking alibi," Ida Belle said, "but he's the only person we know of so far who had a reason to want Mike Mosca dead. I'd say he's our number one suspect. Being out of town doesn't clear him, as far as I'm concerned."

"But how would he have gotten to Mike Mosca's suitcase in the first place?" Fortune asked from the front seat.

"He's a smart man," Ida Belle said. "He has access to those injectors, not to mention heaven knows what kinds of potions and poisons. He could've followed his wife to one of their rendezvous. Also, let's not forget that people can always hire people."

"Kevin Kane is a postdoc," Gwendolyn said as she rolled the windows up. "He doesn't have hitman money. Unless he's got a trust fund or something,"

Gwendolyn drove them back to the downtown lot where Fortune's Jeep was waiting, dropped them off, then followed them out of the lot.

"So what do you think?" Fortune asked once they were on the road, with Gwendolyn driving behind them. "Think we got somewhere?"

"I'm a little worried about young Jinny Kane," Mary-Alice said. "Not that she's exactly an angel, but with a jealous husband, she might be in danger."

"I think it might be worthwhile to talk to her again," Ida Belle said.

# CHAPTER 11

On Sunday, the team took a break from their inquiries. It wouldn't be right to disturb people on the Sabbath, and besides, Gertie had her no-lying-on-Sunday rule, which would have really hamstrung any investigation. So on Sunday morning, Gwendolyn joined Gertie, Ida Belle, and Fortune at the Baptist church. Mary-Alice went to the Catholic church across the street. There she sat next to Boon St. Clair in the back pew, as she did every Sunday.

When Mass let out, a group of women leaped out of their front-pew seats to speed down to Francine's Diner. Across the street, at the very same time, a detachment of Baptist ladies was doing the exact same thing. The first contingent to reach Francine's Diner would have dibs on Francine's limited supply of banana pudding.

As usual, Mary-Alice declined to participate in the weekly Banana Pudding War. Mary-Alice abhorred competition, preferring instead to amble down to the diner with her friend Boon and enjoy a tall glass of tea and whatever dessert was available. Gwendolyn, also reluctant to get involved in the hostilities, joined Mary-Alice and Boon. They sat neither with the Catholics nor the Baptists, but at a neutral table, where they enjoyed iced tea and commiserated about widowhood.

That afternoon the five women gathered at Fortune's house and made plans for Monday. Their meeting had one interruption; Gertie got a call from Tran at Beaumont Plant Nursery and Café.

"Nothing," Gertie said when she'd hung up. "No poison or anything else on the injector. No usable prints on the injector or the newspaper clipping."

"Well then," Fortune said, "Mary-Alice and I better do a good job tomorrow."

On Monday morning, Fortune and Mary-Alice drove back out to the strip mall in Kenner, for a "mother-daughter consult" at Royal Aesthetic and Cosmetic. Gwendolyn stayed back at Fortune's house with Ida Belle and Gertie.

Mary-Alice had very little experience going undercover. To be on the safe side, Fortune advised Mary-Alice to speak as little as possible. This, she found, was easy, especially once she was sitting on the exam table with a blood pressure cuff around her arm and a thermometer under her tongue.

Jinny Kane sat on a rolling stool in front of Mary-Alice, writing things on a clipboard.

"I have a question for you, Ms. Kane," Fortune stood next to Mary-Alice, making her feel very small. At six-feet-plus in her espadrilles, Fortune didn't just stand; she loomed.

"Sure," Jinny said absently, checking her clipboard as she squeezed the bulb to inflate Mary-Alice's blood pressure cuff. "But if it's anything really technical, the Doctor could probably give you a better answer than I can."

"Does your husband Kevin know about you and Mike Mosca?"

Jinny's mouth tightened, but she didn't look up from her clipboard. She kept pumping the bulb.

"Darlin'," Mary-Alice murmured, clenching her teeth to steady the thermometer, "this thing's getting awfully tight."

"What do you want?" Jinny demanded.

"Maybe just ease up the pressure a little bit, there?" Mary-Alice suggested.

"Just some information," Fortune said.

The thermometer beeped.

"I believe my temperature reading's done, darlin'," Mary-Alice muttered through her clenched teeth.

"I don't have anything to say to you," Jinny said.

Mary-Alice reluctantly pulled the thermometer from her mouth.

"My arm's falling right asleep here, darlin'," she pleaded.

"Fine," Fortune said. "We'll go downtown and talk to Kevin, then. He's probably in his office right now. Come on, Mom, let's go."

"No. Please don't tell Kevin. He'd kill me."

"Darlin, I don't mean to be tiresome," Mary-Alice said, "but I believe I can't move my fingers."

"What? Oh. Sorry." Jinny ripped off the cuff and shoved it back in the holder without reading Mary-Alice's blood pressure. It was just as well, Mary-Alice thought. There was no way that young lady would have gotten an accurate measurement, flustered as she was.

"You didn't really come here for a consult, did you?" Jinny demanded.

Mary-Alice rubbed her arm and looked at Fortune.

"You're right," Fortune said. "We're just hoping you can help us. We won't contact your husband if you don't want us to."

Jinny folded her arms and stared down at her lovely, fishnet-clad knees.

"When I married Kevin, I didn't think things would turn out like this. I mean, he has a Ph.D. He was supposed to be a college professor. Like, I could totally see him getting a full-time job at Chapman. Or at least Saddleback. But no, I had to leave Southern California and move all the way across the country, and for what? A forty-year-old husband who's making barely more than minimum wage when you figure in how many hours he works. Plus he has zero job security, and he's gonna make me move again in another year, probably for another crappy post-doc. If it wasn't for my job, we wouldn't even have health benefits."

"But then you met Mike Mosca," Fortune said.

"Mike is just a client," Jinny said quickly. "Our relationship is completely professional."

"What was the professional event that required your meeting him at the McCully Inn outside of Beaumont?" Fortune persisted.

Jinny paled under her artificial tan. "Did Kevin have someone follow me?"

"What does your husband research?"

Jinny shrugged. "Something to do with cancer cells."

"If he wanted Mike Mosca dead, would he know how to kill him in a way that made it look like a heart attack?"

Jinny scrunched her perfect nose.

"Why are you asking me about wanting Mike dead? That's so morbid!"

Fortune stared down at Jinny until Jinny looked up and made eye contact.

"Mike Mosca is dead," Fortune said.

Jinny's eyes widened (although her eyebrows didn't move) and she fanned herself with her hand.

"How?" she whispered.

"They say it's a heart attack," Fortune said.

"A heart attack? That's impossible. He wasn't that old."

"He was a middle-aged smoker."

"I don't believe you. Mike can't be dead."

"I'm terribly sorry for your loss," Mary-Alice said.

"Thank you for your help," Fortune added. "We can show ourselves out. Come along, Mom."

# CHAPTER 12

"Well, it sounds like you certainly did stir things up," Ida Belle said, as the five women dug into the dinner of spicy fried chicken that Fortune and Mary-Alice had brought back from Kenner.

"You think she really didn't know the man was dead?" Gertie asked.

"It's awfully hard to say," Mary-Alice said. "The young lady certainly seemed upset by the news, but it was very difficult to read her expression."

"Jinny indicated she was afraid of her husband," Fortune said. "I hope she's not the next one to die of quote-unquote natural causes."

"I think the idea of Kevin Kane killing anyone is a bit of a stretch," Gwendolyn said.

"Well now, it's easy to make excuses for a good-looking man," Ida Belle observed.

"Professor Gwendolyn, darlin'," Gertie added, "the man's poor wife did say she was afraid she'd be next."

"His poor wife?" Gwendolyn snorted. "I don't feel sorry for her. Anyway, should we tell them?"

"Tell us what, darlin'?" Mary-Alice asked.

"Uh-oh," Fortune added.

"While you two were out on your mission, we were doing a little detective work of our own," Gertie said.

"Don't worry," Ida Belle assured Fortune. "We didn't leave the house."

"We just went online," Gertie explained.

"So," Gwendolyn said. "I believe I mentioned my ex, Virgil Zach?"

"He's the one who showed up at her wedding without an invitation," Ida Belle said.

"And went stomping off madder than a wet hen when he realized her husband had never heard of him," Gertie added.

"I hadn't been worried about him because I knew he was in prison," Gwendolyn said.

"So we happened to be talking about him," Gertie put in. "And we decided to look him up."

"And guess who got released three months ago," Gwendolyn announced.

"So where is he now?" Fortune asked.

"There was the one little newspaper article that said he was released from prison," Gertie replied, "and that was only because it was part of a follow-up on that big mortgage scam he was involved in. But he's been smart enough to stay off social media, so even searching Facebook didn't do any good."

"So he's out, and we don't know where he is," Gwendolyn said. "And knowing him, I'm a little worried."

"I might be able to help look him up on the...on one of my databases," Fortune said. "You know, my being a librarian and all. Excuse me."

By the time Fortune reappeared in the kitchen, holding her phone to her ear, the women had cleaned up the remains of dinner and moved on to an icebox cake they'd found in Fortune's fridge. They looked up expectantly.

"Parole Officer," she mouthed, and then, "Gwendolyn, what's the name of your cleaning company?"

Gwendolyn told her the name, and Fortune repeated it.

"That cleaning company has access to the home of your client's former fiancée, Gwendolyn Jackson," Fortune said. "Yes, I'm sure. Because his fiancée is right here, and she's afraid for her safety, that's how. Yes, I'm sure you're pleased...okay, you do realize that his so-called wonderful attitude may be due to the fact that he has an opportunity to stalk and harass his former fiancée, right? Excuse me, but that doesn't sound like a model client to me. Uh huh. Well, thank you so much for your help." Fortune made quote marks with her free hand as she said this.

"Virgil's been in my house?" Gwendolyn cried.

"His parole officer claims it's probably not the same cleaning company, and if it is, it must be just a coincidence. She was going on about how hard it is to get a job with a prison record, what a wonderful attitude Virgil has. Is this guy really charming or something?"

"He can be," Gwendolyn sighed. "As I found to my sorrow."

"You said you'd had things go missing," Ida Belle said. "What kind of things?"

"Personal things. That son of a—"

"Professor Gwendolyn," Mary-Alice asked, "do you believe this Virgil might have anything to do with your husband's passing?"

"I don't know," Gwendolyn said. "He's a slithering, scamming slimeball, but it's hard to imagine that he's responsible for my husband's death. Virgil's all about deception, not confrontation. He's not the type to murder someone."

"No one's the type," Fortune said. "Until they murder someone."

"You think he might have learned to kill people when he was in prison?" Gertie asked.

Gwendolyn pressed her fork onto her plate to capture the last crumbs of her icebox cake.

"Well, that is a good point. And there are ways to kill someone without going near them—poison powder in the socks, curare on the razor..."

"So how many of Mary-Alice's mystery books have you read, anyway?" Ida Belle asked.

"Almost all of them," Gwendolyn said. "They're strangely relaxing. Thank you, Mary-Alice."

"You're quite welcome, darlin'."

"So Virgil's been in my house. Sneaking around, stealing my stuff, right under my nose. And his parole officer obviously isn't going to be any help. What do we do now?"

"First, make a list of everything that's missing from your house." Fortune plucked a magnetic notebook and pen from the fridge and set it in front of Gwendolyn. "I'll call the P.O. back and let her know I'm reporting the thefts to NOLA PD."

Fortune left a message with the parole officer. It wasn't yet four-thirty, and the office was still open, so it seemed the woman was refusing to pick up her call on purpose. Gwendolyn called the cleaning company to cancel her service, and after that, she called a locksmith.

Their work done for the time being, the women gathered in front of the television to relax with one of Ida Belle's favorite war movies. But before Ida Belle could press "Play," Gwendolyn's phone rang.

"Kevin," she exclaimed. "Hello. What a nice surprise. No, this is a perfect time."

"The husband," Ida Belle stage-whispered as if everyone in the room didn't know it.

"It's missing? Are you sure? But what do you...what?"

Gwendolyn listened for a few moments, ignoring the others' curious stares.

"What? Really? That's exactly—yes. No, I agree. Kevin, the other ladies are here. Mind if I put you on speaker?" She clicked her phone and placed it on the coffee table. "Please tell the ladies what you told me."

# CHAPTER 13

"Am I on speaker now?" Kevin Kane's voice asked from the phone on Fortune's coffee table. "Okay, I'll just say I'm not proud of what I'm about to tell you. But since you were asking about Mike Mosca…anyway. After you came to see me and told me Mike Mosca was dead—I looked it up to make sure, and yeah, I found his obituary online. So then, you know, I don't know why, but I snuck a look at my wife's phone when she was in the shower, and I found texts between the two of them. Which, okay, I already suspected. But listen: He was going to end the relationship. They were meeting at the McCully Inn for one last night together."

Gwendolyn shook her head. "Now that's just sad."

"So that woman the manager saw must have been her," Gertie said.

"Okay, but that's not why I called. Or, not the whole reason anyway. I wanted to let you know that when I was doing my lab inventory today, one of our injectors was missing. You know, the painless injector? That you asked me about when you were here?"

"Did we tell him we found one…" Gwendolyn whispered, and Fortune shook her head no.

"Now I know Jinny," Kevin continued, "and I know she has a very fragile ego. I could see her killing someone to salvage her pride."

"So you think your wife killed Mike Mosca?" Fortune asked.

"Well, I don't know, of course. But I know one of my injectors is missing, I know Mosca told Jinny he was going to dump her, and I know Jinny. She's very prideful. She wouldn't stand for being dumped."

"Well, darlin', that sounds somewhat convincing, and absolutely no offense intended, but why should we believe you?" Mary-Alice challenged. "Now then, I do apologize for my forthrightness. This is Mary-Alice Arceneaux speaking, by the way."

"No, you're right, Ms. Arceneaux. I admit it seems a little out there. Please, explain what you're thinking."

"Well now, you have ten times the motive she does, first of all. And second of all, I've met Miss Jinny Kane. That plastic surgery center has her walking around in a white coat like she's one of those doctors you see in the television commercials, but that young lady can't hardly take a person's blood pressure without practically taking an arm off. I don't believe she was hired for her medical expertise, I'll say that much."

"That's a good point, Mary-Alice," Fortune said. "Dr. Kane, you think your wife has the expertise to kill a man and make it look like a heart attack?"

"She was in the pre-nursing program for a couple of years," Kevin said. "Maybe she picked up something there. Anyway, those injectors are really easy to use. Foolproof. That's one of the big selling points."

"So you're telling us you think your wife cheated on you and then stole an injector from your lab to kill her lover?" Ida Belle asked.

"Wait, how many people am I talking to?"

"Five," the women chorused.

"Well when you put it that way, you make me sound like kind of a chump. But yes. My working hypothesis is that Mosca dumped her, and she stole one of my injectors to get back at him. And the way these injectors work, the punctures are so small, they wouldn't have found any needle marks."

"They wouldn't have found any, regardless," Ida Belle said. "They don't exactly have the team from CSI working out there."

"Suppose your wife did steal your injector," Fortune said. "What do you believe she injected the victim with?"

"Oh. I don't know. I mean, she works at a medical place. I'm sure she could find something."

"She works at Royal Aesthetic and Cosmetic," Ida Belle said. "What's she gonna do, exfoliate him to death?"

Gertie snapped her fingers. "Botulinum toxin!" she cried.

"What?" Gwendolyn asked.

"Botox," Gertie said. "They inject it into your face to keep it from looking wrinkly. It was in one of those brochures I got from the clinic. In small amounts, I suppose they've decided it's safe enough, but I bet they go through gallons of it at that place."

"Well, it does appear we have a motive, means, and opportunity," Mary-Alice said.

"The only thing that's missing is an actual murder," Fortune countered.

"According to the authorities, at least," Mary-Alice conceded.

"Should we tell him?" Gertie whispered. Everyone looked at Ida Belle.

"We found the injector in Michael Mosca's suitcase," Ida Belle announced. "That's why we asked about it."

"It stabbed me when I picked it up," Mary-Alice added.

"Are you still there?" Gwendolyn asked, after a few moments of silence.

"Yes. Do the police know?" Kevin Kane asked.

"I doubt it," Gertie said. "I gave the thing to a friend, to see if he could find any poison or anything—"

"No!" cried the phone on the coffee table. "I signed an NDA. I have to return all of the units, and I can't let any competitor see them or even know about them. They could sue me for—oh, man. Okay. Can you get it back to me? Sorry. Thank you. At least I know where it is now. This is a huge relief."

"There's no need to fret," Gertie said. "The gentleman in question is very discreet."

Ida Belle rolled her eyes.

Gwendolyn spoke up.

"I have an idea. We have all this information, but we don't have any proof, right? What if we can get a confession from Jinny Kane?"

"How are you going to do that?" Kevin Kane asked.

"Does it involve breaking the law?" Gertie asked eagerly.

"Actually, no. I don't believe it does. But Kevin, we'll need your cooperation. Now, hear me out."

Gwendolyn explained her plan.

"Why Professor Gwendolyn," Mary-Alice exclaimed, "that little scheme of yours seems to ring a bell."

"I thought it might." She grinned. "I really did read all the mystery books you brought over. I wasn't just saying it to be polite."

"I don't know that I'm comfortable with it," Kevin Kane said. "I mean, Jinny and I have had our problems, and okay, maybe she killed your husband, Gwendolyn, and I do apologize on her behalf for that, but this plan seems kind of, I don't know, risky."

"Kevin, you believe your wife murdered my husband. That's why you called me. Isn't it?"

Mary-Alice imagined Kevin Kane gulping and tugging at the collar of his plaid shirt.

"It's only speculation," he faltered. "We don't know for sure."

"This way we can be a little surer," Gwendolyn shot back. "And look. If she's not guilty, then nothing happens. No harm, no foul. Right?"

"I guess."

He didn't sound convinced. But he agreed to the plan.

# CHAPTER 14

It was decided straightaway that Fortune would be the one to execute Gwendolyn's plan. She was young and slim enough to fit in with Royal Aesthetic and Cosmetic's staff. She was also able to defend herself in hand-to-hand combat if that were to become necessary. Fake-tanned, made-up, and bewigged, she wouldn't be immediately recognizable as part of the "mother-daughter" team that had confronted Jinny Kane.

Dressed in a formfitting lab coat, short skirt, and a stethoscope that concealed a minicam, Fortune arrived at Royal Aesthetic and Cosmetic as it was opening. The clinic had a large enough staff, and high enough turnover, that a new face in the workplace would be unremarkable.

Fortune first filmed herself putting the items into place around the clinic. And then, keeping enough of a distance to stay unnoticed, she followed Jinny Kane.

The first injector Jinny saw was out in plain sight, on the front counter. Jinny did a double-take, then studiously ignored it. Fortune waited until Jinny had gone into the back with a patient, then walked by the front desk when the receptionist was busy and palmed the injector.

The injector sitting in the ladies' room, underneath the paper towel dispenser, startled Jinny enough that she shrieked. Fortune waited in a stall until Jinny left, and collected that one too.

Around mid-morning Jinny rolled open a file drawer and pulled out a patient file, only to have one of the little cylinders drop onto the floor by her foot and roll a few inches on the industrial carpet.

Still, she kept her cool.

Until she went to get her lunch from the break room refrigerator, and from her paper lunch bag pulled out one of the injectors with a yellow sticky note wrapped around it. On the paper was written the words,

I know

Jinny stood up and swept the bag off the breakroom table.

"Fine, Kevin," she screamed. "You got me. You got me. Are you happy now? Hey, guess what, you're next, you…"

Then she began to swear, which brought a crowd rushing into the break room to calm her down.

Unnoticed in the fracas, Fortune picked up the last injector as it rolled across the floor, and slipped out of the clinic.

The footage alone might not have gotten the local police to open an investigation. But together with screen shots of Jinny's text messages, the name and contact information of the motel manager, and a copy of the restraining order Kevin Kane took out on his wife, they had enough to arrest Jinny Kane for the murder of Michael Mosca.

# CHAPTER 15

Gwendolyn Jackson moved back into her New Orleans townhouse. The woman who'd murdered her husband was on trial. Her ex-fiancé had been caught with an enormous stash of her personal items in his possession and was safely back in prison. And she'd changed all the locks.

Mary-Alice was able to keep informed despite being a three-hour drive away from the action. Due to the scandalous nature of the murder, and the involvement of the celebrity lawyer, the case was constantly in the headlines. Mary-Alice knew that the newspaper left a lot of details out, and that was frustrating. She wished she could know more.

Then one evening, as she was researching the case online, Mary-Alice got an urgent phone call from Gertie.

"Gwendolyn called, and she thinks the verdict's going to come in tomorrow," Gertie said. "She wants us to be there. Can you make it?"

"Why, I'd nearly forgotten about that whole business," Mary-Alice replied. "But I suppose it would be a kindness to be there to support Professor Gwendolyn."

The Sinful crew met Gwendolyn outside the courtroom

before it opened. Gwendolyn wasn't happy. She told them that the case against Jinny Kane wasn't as airtight as they'd thought. Jinny Kane's lawyer had managed to poke all kinds of holes in the prosecution's argument.

Gwendolyn's pessimism was not misplaced. As they watched the closing arguments, they heard that the amount of Botox required to kill a man of Michael Mosca's size would be at least one hundred times the cosmetic dose. However, Jinny's colleagues testified that nothing was missing from their workplace. In addition, tests of the victim's cremated remains showed no sign of the substance. Mary-Alice hadn't even known that cremated remains could be tested for anything.

And what about the elaborate scheme that Fortune had recorded? Had all of that hard-won footage been excluded from evidence? In fact, it had been shown in court. But to Gwendolyn's dismay, what had seemed at the time like a clever way to catch a murderer looked to the jury like a cruel prank played by a scorned husband upon his emotionally-fragile wife.

The celebrity lawyer made much of the fact that Jinny never said, "I did it." She said, "you got me." And there was no way to prove that "you're next" was intended as a death threat.

So the women were disappointed, but not surprised, when the jury found Jinny Kane not guilty on all counts.

Jinny Kane threw her slender arms around the lawyer, kissed him on the cheek, and sashayed out of the courtroom clinging to his pinstripe-clad arm.

Mary-Alice and the ladies followed the crowd out into the hazy New Orleans afternoon.

"Well, show's over, I guess," Gwendolyn sighed.

"Not quite," Ida Belle pointed out. "Here comes the scorned husband now."

Kevin Kane bounded up to his wife and her lawyer. The lawyer already had his arm around his client, and at the sight of her husband, pulled her closer in a protective embrace.

"Jinny," Kevin Kane announced, out of breath. "I want a divorce."

Jinny gave him an appraising look. The hubbub quieted, and microphone-brandishing reporters converged like piranhas.

"Fine." Jinny ran her hand up and down her companion's arm. "Talk to my lawyer."

Kevin opened his mouth to reply, but she stepped forward and spoke first.

# CHAPTER 16

"How's it feel now?" Jinny's fists were clenched, and she stood nearly nose-to-nose with her estranged husband. The celebrity lawyer glanced nervously at the shoving crowd of reporters, his chin tilted up at an angle that would look good on camera. "Oh, Kevin has his Ph.D., poor little Jinny couldn't even get into the nursing program. Well, who's feeling stupid now, huh, Kevin?"

"I'm hearing a little resentment here," Kevin said carefully.

"Let me tell you something you might not know, *Doctor* Kane. When someone dies of an air embolism and you're not careful when you open the body up, all the evidence goes *poof*." (Here she waved her long-nailed hands.)

"Did you…did Mosca die of an air embolism?"

"Maybe," Jinny simpered evilly.

"What, you're not saying you injected him with an air bubble and killed him? But that's a myth, that an air bubble can kill you. Uh, isn't it?"

"*Actually,* Kevin, it's not a myth if you know what you're doing. A little air bubble in your IV line won't kill you. But someone who knows what she's doing? Yup."

"What did you use the injector for then?"

The celebrity lawyer leaned over and whispered something in her ear, but she shook her head.

"I was kind hoping they'd track it back to you."

He stared at her.

"You killed the man you were cheating on me with, and then you tried to frame me? And why are you telling me all this anyway?"

Jinny gazed adoringly at the celebrity lawyer.

"Because they can't try me again once I've been acquitted. Fifth Amendment, right, sweetie?"

Gwendolyn couldn't contain herself any longer. She strode over and interrupted them.

"Excuse me. First of all, Mrs. Kane, a defendant convicted of a crime isn't immune from a civil lawsuit for damages from the victim of the crime. Which in this case would be me. But as long as you're running your mouth, let me ask you something."

"Mrs. Kane, we really need to go," murmured the lawyer.

"Hang on," Gwendolyn commanded. "The voicemail. From my husband to me, sent after his death. Did you have anything to do with that?"

Jinny looked Gwendolyn up and down.

"So this was my competition? Oh, honey, you've aged since that wedding photo, haven't you? Girl, you must have some hidden talents. *Well* hidden."

"The voicemail," Gwendolyn repeated evenly. "I got a voicemail from my husband after he died."

"Oh, are you talking about the one that said, *Hey baby, I'll be seeing you tomorrow. Can't wait.*"

Gwendolyn blinked as if she'd been slapped.

"Yes."

"Well, I hope you aren't saving it or anything. Cause it was sent to me, not to you. Notice how Mike would always call you baby and darling and sweetheart, and never use your name? That was so he wouldn't get us mixed up. Anyway, all I had to do was forward the message back to his phone, and then from his phone to yours."

"Why would you do that?"

Jinny shrugged.

"Why should I be the only one who's hurting? Oh, and the newspaper article in the mail slot? That was me too. I knew the 'unidentified man' was Mike. I mean, duh, of course I did."

This time she allowed her companion to urge her away. But they had only taken a few steps when a woman pushed through the crowd and stepped in front of them. She looked very much like Jinny, but about two decades older.

"Shana!" the celebrity lawyer cried, snatching his arm away from Jinny Kane. "Sweetheart, you're back! So soon! How was Switzerland?"

Loud popping noises split the air. Jinny Kane and the celebrity lawyer crumpled to the ground in tandem. The woman called Shana watched them fall, then, with the reporters' cameras rolling, stretched her arm downward and shot them each again to be sure. She tucked her gun into her red Hermes bag, turned smartly, and sauntered off, her Pilates-toned backside working her red snakeskin miniskirt. The crowd of reporters surged after her, a few staying behind to snap photos of the lifeless Jinny Kane and her equally deceased attorney.

"Let's get out of here," Ida Belle said, and they all agreed that was a good idea.

# CHAPTER 17

They had to push two tables together at Francine's Diner that night. Gertie, Ida Belle, Fortune, and Mary-Alice were there, and that was enough for one whole table. Gwendolyn had come back to Sinful with them and had invited Kevin Kane. Deputy Sheriff Carter LeBlanc was invited too, as he had been so helpful in advising them, and thoughtful enough to stay out of their investigation. And Mary-Alice had asked her good friend Boon St. Clair, whom she sat next to at Mass every Sunday, and that made eight. The ladies filled Carter and Boon in on the details of the investigation, while Kevin Kane beamed at Gwendolyn and occasionally filled in bits and pieces of his own.

"Carter," Fortune said, "you're taking this surprisingly well."

"I'm not happy that you put yourselves in danger," Carter said, with a significant look at Fortune, who was sitting next to him, "but it wasn't on my turf, so what could I say? By the way, how'd you manage to sneak around that medical center and plant all those devices?"

"You put on a lab coat, grab a clipboard, and walk around like you're doing something important, no one stops you," Fortune said.

"So Professor Gwendolyn," Gertie said, "what are you going to do? Are you going to stay in New Orleans?"

Gwendolyn and Kevin exchanged a glance.

"I'm definitely going through with the sale of the store," she said. "But I am fond of my townhouse. And I'm starting to like New Orleans. So I think I'll just stay for now and see what happens."

"Well, you don't have the two-body problem anymore," Ida Belle said.

"It's not the worst problem to have." Kevin Kane glanced at Gwendolyn and blushed bright red.

"True," Gwendolyn said. "As long as you're not talking about actual bodies. Hey, has everyone else decided what you're going to order?"

# BLACK WIDOW VALLEY

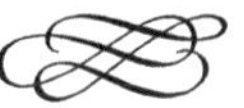

Stock art: Pixabay, Freepik, Vecteezy

# CHAPTER 1

Mary-Alice Arceneaux was relaxing on her back porch with a glass of iced tea and a brand-new murder mystery. A cool breeze from the bayou caressed her cheek, and every so often a fishing party drifted by in a flat-bottomed pirogue. Her new mosquito repellent was working, and she thought she couldn't imagine a more perfect afternoon.

And then she heard a knock on the door.

She got up to answer it, a little annoyed at being interrupted, but curious who her visitor might turn out to be.

"Sheriff Lee," she exclaimed, genuinely surprised to see him at her door. "To what do I owe this great pleasure? Please, come in and let me get you a glass of tea."

Mary-Alice did not know the precise age of Robert E. Lee, the semi-retired sheriff of Sinful, Louisiana. But he was certainly older than Mary-Alice, and Mary-Alice herself was on the sweet side of seventy.

"Why thank you kindly, Miss Mary-Alice." Lee removed his campaign hat and followed her into the kitchen. "There's a matter of some urgency I wish to discuss with you, if I may."

Mary-Alice fixed Sheriff Lee a glass of iced tea and a plate of icebox cake, then joined him at the kitchen table.

"Now Miss Mary-Alice, I am reluctant to involve you in this affair, but I have been most urgently asked to approach you. I shall be brief. Do you happen to be acquainted with a lady named Althea Kilmer?"

"No," Mary-Alice said, wonderingly.

"You may know her as Althea Burroughs."

"Althea? Why, yes. We were in school together, and the best of friends. But I don't believe Althea and I have spoken in years. No, decades."

Even all these years later, the mention of Althea Burroughs provoked a pang of envy. Althea had been pretty and vivacious, with bouncing blonde curls and fetching dimples. Upon leaving school, Althea had married a kind and wealthy man, honeymooned in Europe, and had moved into a grand mansion somewhere up north.

Mary-Alice had married Joe Arceneaux, who was neither wealthy nor kind, and spent her entire life in the bayous.

There had been no quarrel or falling-out; the two friends had simply drifted apart.

"Dear Althea!" Mary-Alice exclaimed. "Is she doing well?"

"Well, now, I didn't mean to get your hopes up, Miss Mary-Alice. Her husband passed several years ago, and she followed him soon after. Only her three children remain."

"Oh dear," Mary-Alice fretted. "When we left school we swore we would always stay in touch and visit each other every year. And of course we didn't, and now it's too late. But Sheriff, where are her children now?"

"Up in New York."

"New York," Mary-Alice gasped. "I knew Althea had gone up north, but I never imagined she was in New York!"

"Now, this is not New York City, mind. The place in question is what they call upstate. Miss Mary-Alice, have you ever heard of a place called Black Valley?"

"Why no, I haven't."

"And you may count yourself fortunate as far as I'm concerned." Lee picked up a napkin and dabbed tea from his white moustache. "Miserable place. They call it Black Widow Valley, for reasons I'll explain shortly. But it's where your friend's husband's people are from, and it's where her children live to this day."

"I see," Mary-Alice said. "And Sheriff Lee, did you come by simply to tell me of my friend's passing?"

"Well, now, don't rush me, Miss Mary-Alice. It seems this remote area has been the scene of something quite peculiar. During the last five years, four young men have disappeared there, and no one knows how or why."

"Oh, dear. How terrible for the families of those poor young men."

"It surely is. They've been awfully eager to get to the bottom of this. Well, it seems someone got the idea to do some research into all the residents of Black Valley, and they dug up this connection back to you."

"Hoping I might have been in touch with Dear Althea, and could give you some clue," Mary-Alice said sadly. "But instead, you're the one who told me of her passing. I am dreadfully sorry, Sheriff Lee. I can't provide any assistance in this matter."

Sheriff Lee chuckled.

"The fact is, you can be of great assistance. This case has not been solved, Miss Mary-Alice, and as you know, the police can't run roughshod into folks' houses looking for things without a warrant and such. Not even in New York."

"So what is it they're asking, exactly?"

"I'm asking you to arrange a stay with your friends' children. It should be no trouble at all for them. They live in a mansion with servants and big limousines and all that kind of thing, or so I hear. It should be no trouble at all for you."

"I'm sorry, Sheriff, are you asking me to spy on my friend's children?"

"Not at all, Miss Mary-Alice. I'm simply asking you to make a social visit, and use your normal powers of observation. And in doing so you may help to right a great wrong. Now you'll want to write for an invitation right away. I've brought you the names of the children, and the mailing address."

"Why Sheriff, I haven't said I'd do it."

"So you haven't. Well, I do understand. I suppose it was a lot to ask."

Sheriff Lee made as if to leave.

"Wait a moment, Sheriff. I didn't say I wouldn't do it. Here, let me refill your tea."

# CHAPTER 2

The next morning, Mary-Alice met her friends Ida Belle, Gertie, and Fortune for breakfast at Francine's Diner and told them all about Sheriff Lee's visit.

"So you'll do it?" Ida Belle asked, sounding both deeply interested and a little envious. Ida Belle was the founder of the Sinful Ladies' Society, and accustomed to being involved in everything important that happened in town.

"I believe I will do it, Ida Belle. I've already mailed a note to them, inviting myself over for a stay. I suppose I'm rather committed."

"What did Lee tell you about the case?" Gertie asked excitedly.

"Well, I'll tell you," Mary-Alice replied, with a furtive glance around the restaurant. "But Sheriff Lee did ask me to be discreet. Now, up there in this little town called Black Valley, up in New York State, it seems four young men have gone missing. The first was a young college man, traveling on his summer vacation. One day they found his backpack in the woods, but they never found him. Well, people sort of forgot about it eventually, but then a couple drove through on vacation, and one afternoon the husband disappeared."

"What was the wife doing?" Fortune asked. "Those things are usually the spouse, aren't they?"

Fortune was the youngest and the most worldly of Mary-Alice's friends in Sinful. She was also the only Yankee, and consequently quite blunt and outspoken.

"I believe they never found the husband, nor any evidence the wife had anything to do with it. And then there was another young man, come to visit his aunt and uncle. He walked out of the front door and never came back. They said it was as if the road had swallowed him and closed again."

"If that happened here, I think everyone would just assume it was gators," Gertie said.

"They don't have gators in New York," Ida Belle retorted.

"That's why I said if it happened here, Ida Belle," Gertie shot back. "Now, what do the police think?"

"They did call in the police from across the river, but they were never able to find anything. And Black Valley's started to get a bit of a reputation. A couple of families moved away, and Sheriff Lee tells me more would if they could, and the house prices are going down and down. Well, now people are coming to town looking to buy a place for cheap. And then wouldn't you know, one of the visitors, another young man, was walking around the town, and he disappeared too. Well, he came from a well-off family and his parents raised a fuss, and they got the police in again, and still they found nothing."

"Did the young men have anything in common?" Gertie asked.

"I believe all but the first stayed at the town's hotel, but Black Valley only has one hotel, so that doesn't really tell us anything."

"Well those young men didn't simply disappear," Ida Belle protested. "They should start checking under people's rose-bushes and basements and things. What are they waiting for?"

"Well now, I more or less asked Sheriff Lee the same thing, and he said you'd need a warrant, and have a judge sign it and all. You can't just go into folks' houses and start tearing things up. It seems they're awfully strict about that kind of thing up north."

"Theoretically, they're strict about that kind of thing everywhere in the United States," Fortune interjected. "Because of the Fourth Amendment to the U.S. Constitution."

"Well now, how are you involved, Mary-Alice?" Gertie asked.

"The police looked into who in the town had connections elsewhere. My late classmate Althea Burroughs lived in Black Valley, and her children are there still. From there, they found me. Sheriff Lee told me that a civilian—like me, you see—wouldn't put people on their guard the way a known LEO would. That's Law Enforcement Officer."

"Mary-Alice," Fortune said, "This seems like it could be dangerous."

"Well Miss Fortune, I admit I viewed it that way myself at first, but when you think about it, I would simply be a lady visiting the children of an old friend. The police aren't getting anywhere. Black Valley is a little like Sinful, it seems, where folks don't like to tell their business to any policeman who happens by. In any event, I do owe poor Althea's children a visit. And if I happen to see anything in the normal course of things, why, it's no trouble at all for me to pass my observations along to Sheriff Lee."

"Did he say you had to go alone?" Ida Belle asked shamelessly.

"Ida Belle!" Gertie remonstrated. "Don't you dare think about leaving town. You need to stay here and help me bottle the cough syrup before the church bazaar. We can't run out like last time."

"I surely wish you could come with me so I could take

advantage of your advice," Mary-Alice said. "Y'all have a lot more experience with this kind of thing than I do."

"We can keep in touch by phone," Ida Belle said.

"Or even video chat," Gertie added. "It is the twenty-first century, after all."

# CHAPTER 3

Mary-Alice received a handwritten reply to her within days, indicating any friend of mother's was certainly welcome, if she could be satisfied with the humble accommodations on offer. It was signed, "Lucetta," whom Mary-Alice knew to be Althea's youngest daughter. She remembered how Sheriff Lee had described the multi-room house in which Althea's children lived, and while modesty was always becoming, describing an honest-to-goodness mansion as "humble" might be overdoing it a bit.

Sheriff Lee arranged transport for Mary-Alice, which involved a long flight with a couple of plane changes from Lake Charles to a small airport in upstate New York, and after that an hour's drive into the northern woods to Black Valley.

Mary-Alice had obediently shut off her cell phone as soon as she stepped on the plane, and didn't have a chance to turn it on again until she was in the unmarked car that was to take her to the Kilmer mansion. She left a message for Gertie, asking her to tell everyone she'd arrived safely in New York State. And then she noticed a text message on her phone.

Transient known as Silly Rufus missing, last seen Saxton Lane. Please cancel trip. Too dangerous. --Lee

"Excuse me, sir," Mary-Alice asked the young officer who was driving her.

"What is the name of the street that the Kilmers live on?"

"Saxton Lane, Ma'am."

"I see. Thank you."

Well, she was here now. Was she going to tell the driver to turn around and take her back to the airport?

No, she would see this through. She had already wangled an invitation, and it would be rude to back out now. And Althea always loved luxury and pretty things; how happy she must have been to live in a grand mansion!

The summer twilight lasted a long time this far north, Mary-Alice realized. And the quality of the light was different; in the bayous the air was humid and gray-green, forever threatening a thunderstorm; here, the darkening sky was delicate violet, while the forest grew lush and dark along the highway. Mary Alice recalled reading The Legend of Sleepy Hollow when she was a girl, and found it easy to imagine Washington Irving's Headless Horseman galloping down the road.

"Almost there, ma'am," said the plainclothes officer who was driving her.

"Oh dear, I'd better reply to Sheriff Lee."

I'm already here, she typed. Too late to turn back. Will keep you posted.

She pressed "send," and an error message popped up on her phone.

"Excuse me," she asked her driver, "is there a problem with phone reception here?"

"I couldn't say, ma'am. I'm not from around here."

They were now on the town's main road, such as it was. A few small shops, and an elegant little hotel. It was late evening, and the shops were closed and still in the summer twilight.

Sheriff Lee wasn't going to get an answer from her. And how was she going to keep her friends notified?

They turned up a narrow road, then turned right again, into a narrow lane choked by tangled woods.

"Your destination, ma'am," the officer said, pulling up in front of what looked to Mary-Alice like the set of a horror movie.

Had it not been for a single light in the window, Mary-Alice would have thought the hulking mansion was abandoned. A tangle of vines covered the front of the house and the forlorn front porch, and even in the dark Mary-Alice could see the house was overdue for a repainting.

Mary-Alice picked her way down the overgrown path. In the dark, the night time animal sounds were magnified, and Mary-Alice could swear she heard the malicious hiss of a cat.

She found the front door and knocked. Perhaps the house was abandoned; no one came to the door.

She turned around to tell the trooper she'd had second thoughts, but he was already gone. No matter; she'd call Gertie, who could get in touch with Sheriff Lee, who would call the driver and get him to turn around.

But there was still no signal on her phone.

Mary-Alice knocked again and waited in the dark.

Finally, the door opened to reveal a pale young woman of about forty years of age.

Mary-Alice stared. She had been trying to remember her friend Althea, but the passage of decades had faded her memory. Now the years fell away before her eyes, and her classmate stood before her. The young woman wore a blue print dress that flattered her blue eyes. Her wavy blonde hair was worn shoulder-length and parted on the side, just like Althea's.

"Mrs. Arceneaux?" asked the vision from Mary-Alice's past. The effect was strange; she looked so much like Althea, but she talked like a Yankee.

"Why, you must be Althea's daughter," Mary-Alice exclaimed. "You're the very picture of her."

"Yes, I'm Lucetta," she acknowledged. "We are so glad for your visit. Won't you come in?"

Lucetta led Mary-Alice into a dark hallway and into a side sitting-room, making apologies for the shabby condition of the house.

"Please make yourself comfortable, Mrs. Arceneaux." she invited

Mary-Alice to take a seat on a wood-framed Empire sofa upholstered in faded green velvet. "My sister will be here soon. My brother is not at home."

Lucetta seemed distracted and not all too glad to have company. Mary-Alice did not like to impose as a rule, but in this case, she would have to. There were crimes to solve.

"Goodness, Miss Lucetta," Mary-Alice said as she made herself as comfortable as she could on the stiff couch. "I must say, I didn't expect Althea to have chosen to settle in such a quiet little town. Not that I've anything against quiet little towns, as I live in one myself."

"Well, it suits me," Lucetta said, "Of course Black Valley is not as peaceful as it first appears. Or haven't you heard?"

Lucetta spoke with the kind of archaic, mid-Atlantic inflection that one only heard in black-and-white movies.

"Well," Mary-Alice replied carefully, "I have heard your lovely town referred to as Black Widow Valley. Although my information might be wrong. Do correct me if that's simply a rumor."

"Oh, it's not just a rumor." Lucetta's blue eyes widened. "Young men—in the prime of life—have disappeared here. Some right here on Saxton Lane."

"How interesting." Mary-Alice considered calling for a ride straight back to the airport. And she might have, if her phone had a signal. Did this haunted mansion even have a telephone, she wondered?

"Mrs. Arceneaux, I understand if you're not comfortable staying here in the house. We can book you at the hotel in town. It's no trouble at all, really."

Before Mary-Alice could answer, another woman appeared in the doorway, abruptly breaking the time-travel illusion. The new arrival's raven hair was styled in the latest fashion, and unlike the pallid Lucetta, she sported an even tan. Her aggressive floral fragrance carried a whiff of cigarette smoke.

"MRS. ARCENEAUX, this is my sister Janice," Lucetta said as she rose and smoothed her dress. "Janice, this is Mary-Alice Arceneaux. You remember, Mother's childhood friend."

Lucetta then leaped up and scurried away, as if she couldn't wait to be out of the room.

# CHAPTER 4

Janice watched her sister leave, then threw open a window looking out onto the front yard, sat down on the overstuffed chair her sister had vacated, pulled a pack of Newports, and stuck one in her mouth.

"Welcome to Grey Gardens," she said through clenched teeth as she fumbled with a hot pink lighter. "You don't mind if I smoke."

Even if Janice had asked Mary-Alice's permission to smoke —which she had not—Mary-Alice hardly thought it her place to object. She was at least grateful for the open window, although the breeze appeared to blow the smoke back into the room almost as quickly as Janice blew it out.

"Listen, Mrs. A," Janice said, "It's real nice of you to come visit, and I know Mom would have appreciated it. But as you can see, our house is a wreck. You don't have to be polite and deny it. Look, we got a cute little hotel downtown. I'll call to make a reservation, and when Pinhead comes back with the car, I'll have him drive you down."

"Pinhead?" Mary-Alice asked.

Janice laughed, dropped her smoldering cigarette butt into the rose vase, and started on a fresh cigarette.

"My brother Logan. He's an idiot. We'll get you set up down there, and tomorrow we can have you up for breakfast. I'd offer to take you out somewhere, but as you probably figured out if you saw our downtown, everything's closed. There's days I could kill for some decent Chinese. I guess that's what I get for moving back upstate."

Mary-Alice was by now aflame with curiosity, as she was certain the Kilmer sisters were hiding something. She wouldn't have left the creepy old Kilmer house for anything.

"Oh, Janice dear," Mary-Alice assured her, "I certainly don't wish to be any kind of trouble. But I was so looking forward to staying in the house dear Althea inhabited. It would be such a privilege to be allowed to stay in any room, however simple."

Mary-Alice was not accustomed to being pushy. But she reminded herself that this was not a social call; Sheriff Lee and others had pulled strings and spent money to get her here; she wouldn't back out now. Not only that, the Kilmer house was enormous, and Mary-Alice estimated they could have accommodated dozens of overnight guests without a problem.

Janice looked skeptical.

"We're in a valley here." She sucked her tan cheeks in as she took a pull of her cigarette and then exhaled a cloud of smoke. "No internet, no cell, no data. At least the hotel has cable."

"I brought along plenty of reading," Mary-Alice retorted. "I just got an e-reader for my birthday. I can carry hundreds of books around right here in my handbag."

Janice parried; "We don't have any room ready for guests right now. You'd have to hang around until we can get something set up. It's already late, and you must be tired."

"The time is no problem at all," Mary-Alice countered sweetly, "and I'm sure I'm grateful for your humoring an old woman's whim."

Janice studied Mary-Alice through the haze and appeared to decide she could be trusted—or at least, was no threat. She finished smoking her second cigarette, dropped the butt into the water with a sizzling sound, and then dumped the entire contents of the vase out the window. She shook out the last drops of water and placed the empty vase back on its doily.

"Okay, no problem," Janice said. "I'll get Hannah to make you up a room. You can hang out here till she's done. You want some iced tea?"

"I'd love an iced tea," Mary-Alice said hopefully.

"Sure. Let me go see what's in the kitchen."

Mary-Alice sat by herself in the dim sitting room. Dust motes floated in the amber glow of a velvet-shaded lamp.

Janice returned with what looked like two glasses of iced tea, only Janice's tea was paler and had a whiff of ethanol, exactly as if it had been mixed with vodka.

"Your room's not gonna be ready for a while," Janice said as she plumped down onto the chair. "Sure I can't get you a place at the hotel? Our treat, of course."

"Well I'm sure I didn't come all the way up here just to stay at a hotel," Mary-Alice said with a sweet smile. "I do so regret losing touch with Althea before she passed. It's such a gift to become acquainted with her children."

"You wanna know about me?" Janice drained her vodka-tea and pulled out another cigarette. "Lived in the city for twenty years, until one night that ungrateful son of a—long story short, recently divorced, two grown kids, came back here lick my wounds and help keep this heap from collapsing."

"I only knew your mother as a young girl," Mary-Alice said. "And we were such good friends. I would have loved to have known what she was like, what she grew up to be."

Janice took a thoughtful pull on her cigarette.

"She was a perfect Southern lady, which was kind of a novelty in upstate New York, you can imagine, but everyone loved her. She always looked great, she'd never let anyone see her unless she had her face on, never a hair out of place. Until she got sick. "

"I do wish I had been better at staying in touch," Mary-Alice lamented.

Janice shook her head.

"Better you remember her as young and pretty. It's what she would've wanted."

JANICE STOOD AND LEFT, taking the empty glasses with her.

Mary-Alice waited a few minutes, and when no one else came in, she decided she would find a washroom. She wandered down the dark hallway until she found one. It smelled of damp and mildew, and the iron pedestal sink was chipped, but the room was functional. She freshened up, and using her cell phone as a flashlight (it was good for something!) ventured further down the hallway.

The house had been grand at one time, but it was badly in need of maintenance. The carpet was shabby, the wooden paneling had dark patches, and little mounds of sawdust next to the baseboards announced the presence of termites.

Mary-Alice found herself thinking of every haunted-house movie she'd ever seen, and although she know that it was highly unlikely that she'd be sucked into the walls, she decided to return to the forlorn sitting-room. She pulled out her electronic reader and immersed herself in a murder mystery, which she found was an excellent way to both pass the time and stimulate the mind.

At length a sturdy silhouette filled the doorway. Mary-Alice looked up to see a woman in a faded green dress and a thread-bare frilled apron. She might have been forty, or sixty; her hair was a compromise between mousy brown and iron gray.

"Dinner's ready, missus," the woman muttered, and turned to

leave. Mary-Alice quickly gathered her handbag and followed, as she had no idea where the dining room was.

Mary-Alice was ushered down the bare hall into a dining-room whose only light came from a glass chandelier hung with dusty strands of dangling glass beads. Lucetta was already seated. The other chairs were empty.

"Well, hello, Lucetta darlin'." Mary-Alice tried her best to sound cheerful, but felt she could not overcome the oppressive atmosphere of the dining room. "Where's Janice got to now?"

"Something's come up," Lucetta said vaguely.

"And your brother?" Mary-Alice persisted, remembering Sheriff Lee's briefing on the family.

"Oh, he will be home presently." Lucetta stared into the distance. "Logan is never very punctual. We'll start dinner without him. It's already late, and Hannah doesn't like to stay up."

"Hannah?"

"She showed you in to dinner."

"Oh, yes. Of course."

The prodigal Logan sauntered into the room just as Hannah was setting out the evening meal. Lucetta fixed him with a disapproving stare.

"Logan, this is Mrs. Arceneaux. Mother's childhood friend, who has come to visit and is staying here with us."

Logan goggled at her briefly, then said,

"Hey."

"How do you do," she replied politely. "It's ever so nice to meet you."

Both Janice and Lucetta were attractive young ladies. But Logan, with his thick neck and small features, looked like a thumb.

Logan plunked down in a chair and began to shovel food onto his plate.

"Logan," Lucetta scolded, "can you leave some food for our guest?"

"Oh, no, please, I have eaten my fill," Mary-Alice assured her. "I couldn't possibly have another bite."

This was true. Mary-Alice was perfectly happy to leave the squishy dinner rolls with margarine, canned green beans, and boiled sausage to Logan.

She wondered why, with the house in need of repairs and the food budget obviously tight, the family had decided to hire Hannah.

She couldn't ask that, of course, but she could try to get them talking about themselves.

"What a lovely, secluded setting you have here," Mary-Alice said cheerily. "Do you have any neighbors?"

"Sure we do," Logan declared. "You should've seen 'em when you drove in, depending on which way you came."

"It was already getting dark when I arrived." Mary-Alice tried not to sound annoyed at Logan's rudeness.

"We mostly keep ourselves to ourselves up here," Lucetta said. "I suppose our closest neighbor is Old Mother Sophie."

"She's crazy," said Logan placidly through a mouthful of sausage. "You can't even talk to her. Mr. Peck's cool. He's got all these fruit trees, and man, he knows what he's doing. These peaches—"

"You promised me that you would never again ask Mr. Peck for any of his fruit," Lucetta remonstrated.

"I didn't ask! I was just walking by, we started shooting the breeze, and he offered. What's the big deal?"

"I don't know how you can bear to talk to that man after what he did."

"Look, Peck's a good guy. Business is business, personal is personal. You can't take business stuff personally."

"Are you in business?" Mary-Alice asked, hoping to defuse the tension between the siblings.

"He's between projects," Lucetta remarked acidly. "As he has been for some time."

"That's not true, Lucetta. I guess you forgot about the pigeons."

Lucetta fixed him with a glare.

"I have not," she said, "forgotten about the pigeons."

"Goodness," Mary-Alice exclaimed, "It is getting late, isn't it? It's ever so kind of you to take me in, and I was wondering if I might—"

"No, no, Mrs. Arceneaux, please," Lucetta pleaded. "Hannah hasn't brought out coffee and dessert yet."

Mary-Alice smiled bravely.

"Well, I'm sure that sounds lovely."

# CHAPTER 5

Logan and Lucetta excused themselves after dinner, leaving Mary-Alice alone in the dismal dining room. Just as she was considering whether to get up and snoop, or try to find someone who would show her to her room, Hannah entered the dining room.

"Oh, Hannah, darlin," Mary-Alice said, "I wonder if you could show me where I'll be staying tonight."

"Room's not ready yet, Ma'am." Hannah made no attempt to clear the table quietly; the plates and saucers clattered as she stacked them. "Miss Kilmer sends her apologies, and says she understands if you'd like Logan to drive you down to the hotel in town. She's already called ahead and gotten a room for you."

"Well, that's ever so kind, I'm sure," Mary-Alice parried, "but I rather did have my heart set on staying the night here."

"Means you have to wait a while," Hannah replied. "There's no room ready."

"Why, I'd like nothing better than to wait," Mary-Alice declared. She squared her dainty shoulders and followed the larger woman back to the gloomy sitting room. Althea's children had known of her arrival, and there must be dozens of rooms in this old house. What were they hiding?

Mary-Alice sat and read for a while. Then she noticed an old upright piano in the corner. She was wandered over and idly pressed two black keys at once. One of the keys didn't make a sound at all.

Lucetta came rushing into the room and seized Mary-Alice's arm.

"Don't do that!" she cried.

"Why, I'm terribly sorry," Mary-Alice replied with a look of utter innocence. "I didn't think I'd be disturbing anyone, in this great big house. I suppose I assumed that the four of you were still awake. I promise I'll be quiet as a mouse from now on."

"The four of who?" Lucetta demanded.

"Why, you, your sister, your brother, and Hannah. Unless there's someone I haven't had the pleasure of meeting yet."

Lucetta stared at Mary-Alice.

"No, it is just the four of us," she said, slowly. "You're correct, Mrs. Arceneaux. It's simply that every sound goes through me tonight. I'm afraid I'm not in a position to be a good hostess."

"Are you not well?" Mary-Alice asked quickly, before Lucetta could "invite" her once again to leave the house and stay at the hotel.

"I am never very well," Lucetta replied piously, and in that moment Mary-Alice was reminded Althea's various and often dramatic attempts to get herself excused from Physical Education class. Lucetta was undoubtedly Althea's daughter.

"Might I use your telephone?" Mary-Alice asked. "There doesn't seem to be a signal here and I'd like to let my friends back home know I arrived safely."

"Telephone?" Lucetta repeated, as if Mary-Alice had asked her to fetch a spaceship or a printing-press. "Oh. The telephone's disconnected. It's been that way for a while now."

Lucetta drifted from the room, leaving Mary-Alice alone with her e-reader.

Promptly at eleven o'clock Janice came in, looking harassed.

"Okay, Mrs. Arceneaux, your room's all set. Ready to go up?"

Janice took Mary-Alice's overnight bag and led her out of the sitting-room, down the dark hallway to the base of a broad. A strip of lighter wood ran up the center of the steps, indicating that it was covered by a carpet runner at some point.

"You know," Janice said, "If you'd rather go down to the hotel, I already called in a reservation and my credit card, and of course you'd be our guest. You know what? I have your bag, why don't I drive you down right now? We can come pick you up for breakfast."

"I do apologize for the imposition," Mary-Alice said sweetly, "but it's such a privilege and a pleasure to stay in the house of my dear friend. I thank you for graciously indulging the whim of an elderly woman."

"It's no imposition at all, Mrs. Arceneaux." Janice nearly managed to sound sincere.

As she followed Janice up the creaking steps, Mary-Alice summoned her courage to ask a question that had been on her mind.

"Why is it that I rarely have the pleasure of seeing you all together? Do you have other guests in the house that need to be attended to?"

"Other guests? Yeah, right." Janice laughed stiffly, and Mary-Alice noticed that she tightened her grip on the handle of Mary-Alice's suitcase. "People aren't exactly lining up to stay with us, Ms. Arceneaux."

Mary-Alice heard an outburst of voices from somewhere in the house. Janice didn't acknowledge it, so Mary-Alice ignored it too. The sound was quickly smothered by a slamming door.

Were they male, or female voices? Two voices, or three? Or perhaps more than that? It had happened so fast, Mary-Alice couldn't be certain. And Janice had appeared to hear nothing at all, which made Mary-Alice wonder whether she had imagined it.

Janice was leading Mary-Alice down a narrow hallway, past door after door, to what appeared to be the most distant point of the most forsaken wing of the Kilmer house. Here, the flooring was simple pine, and the walls were plain white.

"My goodness, I seem to have the entire hallway to myself," Mary-Alice exclaimed as Janice opened the door and switched on the overhead light, which appeared to a forty-watt bulb in a simple dome of milk glass.

"Yeah, you're at the end of the wing." Janice might have been avoiding eye contact, or perhaps she was looking for the right place to set down Mary-Alice's suitcase. "The windows actually open in this room, which believe me is a blessing when you don't have a/c. Got its own bathroom. Nice and quiet up here."

"Yes, it does seem quite serene." Mary-Alice shot a nervous glance at the silhouetted tree branches scraping the window.

After Janice left, Mary-Alice went to lock the door, and realized she couldn't; the knob was the old-fashioned kind that required a key. She showered quickly, surmising (correctly) that the supply of hot water would be limited. As she dressed for bed, she noted with some irritation that one of her earrings was missing. She must have dropped it somewhere, although it was anyone's guess where. She packed its twin—a shimmering, sea-blue opal—in her bag so she wouldn't lose it too.

With some effort, Mary-Alice was able to push the narrow bed against the door to prevent its being opened from the outside. Then she sat down in a chair to think.

Sheriff Lee had set up her travel, so he knew where she was, at least. But she hadn't been able to contact him, or anyone else.

She pulled out her phone, but once again, there was no signal. She tried dialing Gertie Hebert's number anyway, but it didn't go through.

She typed in a text, but when that didn't send either, she deleted it.

Mary-Alice normally liked to read herself to sleep with a murder mystery, but she didn't feel like it tonight. She scooted the bed firmly against the door, climbed under the covers, and promptly fell asleep.

# CHAPTER 6

Mary-Alice was awakened at dawn by a rustling, flapping and whistling outside her window. She went to the window and rapped the glass to scare the pigeons off the windowsill. They fluttered over to the near branches, where they strutted insolently.

Mary-Alice made sure that her bed was still firmly wedged against the door, and fell back asleep. It seemed she had only been dozing a minute when a knock on the door roused her. It was full daylight outside.

"Who's there?" she called.

"It's Hannah, ma'am. Breakfast will be ready soon."

"Thanks ever so much, darlin'. I'll be down in two shakes."

Mary-Alice got ready quickly, and started back down toward the staircase. Once again, she was struck by how narrow the hallway was. She had certainly been lodged in the servants' quarters.

She was just starting down the stairs when she heard voices.

"How are we gonna keep her out of the house till it's over?" said a voice that sounded like Logan's.

"Lucetta has a plan," said someone else--Janice?—before a door closed and she could hear no more.

Mary-Alice was determined to thwart the plan, whatever it was. Mary-Alice had never been able to abide anyone keeping secrets from her. She arranged her features into a pleasant smile, and continued down the stairs.

Mary-Alice came down to the dining room to find the table set for breakfast and a platter of scrambled eggs and gray sausage patties cooling in the center of the table. No one was around, so she took a seat in the same chair she'd occupied the previous evening. Within a few minutes, Logan showed up. Mary-Alice said good-morning. He grunted acknowledgement, which was the extent of the breakfast conversation. The other two place settings sat untouched.

When Hannah came in to clear the dishes, Logan didn't take any notice of her. Mary-Alice made a point of thanking her for a lovely breakfast.

Hannah merely grunted acknowledgement.

Logan dabbed his mouth and placed the used napkin on his plate just as Hannah lifted it off the table.

"Mrs. Arceneaux," Logan said as he dabbed his mouth, "you want a tour of the grounds?"

Mary-Alice had anticipated another attempt to get her off the property, and so was pleasantly surprised at Logan's offer.

"Why, that would be delightful," she exclaimed.

"The kids around here call this the Haunted House," Logan said as they came out to the front yard.

"Well, it is a bit overgrown," Mary-Alice said. "Do you by any chance have an interest in gardening? It's a wonderfully rewarding pastime, and a bit of trimming and weeding here and there would do wonders."

"Yeah, some people love that stuff. Like Mister Peck, he's really into it...oh, hey, speak of the devil. Here he comes now."

"Is this the neighbor you were talking about?" Mary-Alice asked. "The man who grows the nice peaches?"

They were being approached by a man only slightly younger than Mary-Alice. He was tall and lean, with chiseled features and thick hair that had faded gracefully from blonde to white.

"Good morning," he called out cheerily, and when he came closer, he looked expectantly at Mary-Alice and then at Logan.

"Hey, Mr. Peck." Logan jutted his chin at Mary-Alice. "This is Mrs. Arceneaux. She was a friend of mom's. Mrs. Arceneaux, this is Mr. Peck."

"Well, Mrs. Arceneaux, what a stroke of luck." Mr. Peck flashed a relieved smile at Mary-Alice. "This envelope came addressed to you, and was left at my house by mistake. I live there, just below. Is this your first visit to Black Valley?"

"Why, yes it is." Mary-Alice was relieved to be talking to someone with such nice manners. "But I've already learned so much about your lovely town from Mr. Kilmer. For example, I understand you grow the finest produce around."

Mr. Peck beamed and puffed up a little.

"Well, I don't like to brag, but I've been working for years on getting just the right combination of…oh, here comes Lucetta. Well, I apologize that I must take your leave, Mrs. Arceneaux. I fear Miss Lucetta and I do not see eye to eye on a certain matter."

Lucetta came rushing up.

"Why Mr. Peck, what a surprise," she said, breathless. "To what do we owe the honor?"

"I was just leaving," he said, without rancor. "I was rather unexpectedly entrusted with a letter for your agreeable guest here, and I have merely come to deliver it." Mr. Peck nodded and returned the way he had come.

Lucetta's arrival gave Logan an excuse to leave and attend to his pigeons, so Mary-Alice walked back to the house with Lucetta.

"My dear," Mary-Alice said, "I can't help but notice that you seem terribly worried about something. Now, is there anything I can do to help?"

Mary-Alice suspected that she could lift Lucetta's burden by leaving the Kilmer House, but that was one thing she was not willing to do.

"No. Everything's fine."

"In that case, I believe I'll retire to my room and—"

"Please don't go up there yet! We haven't tidied it yet for you."

Mary-Alice was never angry (such an unladylike emotion!) but she certainly felt annoyed. Not only had she been banished to a cramped room at the far end of what appeared to be the servants' hall, but now, according to Lucetta, even that was off-limits.

"Please allow us this courtesy," Lucetta pleaded. "You were my mother's friend, and we have so few guests. Now make yourself comfortable in the sitting room. I'll get you some iced tea."

So it was back to the dusty sitting-room.

Lucetta brought Mary-Alice a glass of iced tea, set it on a yellowed doily on the side table next to the armchair, murmured something about having to attend to something, and left.

When Mary-Alice was certain Lucetta had gone, she reached into her bag and brought out the letter.

It had a local postmark, but when Mary-Alice opened it, she saw it was from Sheriff Lee.

*My Dear Mrs. Arceneaux:*

*Your friends in Sinful have been trying to contact you. I have reassured them as to your probable safety. I have been informed that Black Valley is notorious for its unreliable mobile telephone signal, and that Saxton Lane in particular is in a "dead zone" (I apologize for the unfortunate colloquialism). It is my belief and my hope that although you are not reachable, you have not yet come to harm. Ida Belle in particular has gone to great pains to impress upon me the importance of your safe return and the penalties—as yet unnamed, yet all the more fearsome for all that—that I will suffer should any injury befall you.*

*Had I not the great good fortune to be as well-acquainted with your character as I am, I might recommend you depart posthaste and return home immediately. However, knowing your determination I suspect you will see this through no matter what, and I fear any appeal to your personal safety would serve only to strengthen your resolve. I only pray that you keep these instructions in mind:*

*1. Do not trust anybody.*

*2. Do not proceed into the woods, either alone or with a companion.*

*3. Having advised you to trust nobody. I should have excepted Mr. Obadiah Peck, as it was he who contacted the authorities in the first place, leading to my involvement in the case and yours. However he is not aware that you are in Black Valley for any but personal reasons, and has made no vow of silence, so please do not reveal to him your true purpose if you can avoid it. You know how quickly news can spread.*

*4. If you do find yourself at an impasse, go at once to the hotel in town where you will ask for Room Three.*

*Respectfully,*

*Sheriff Robert E. Lee*

Mary-Alice was heartened to learn that she had not been forgotten. She decided to see whether she could find a working telephone before Lucetta or her siblings could come back and thwart her. Mary-Alice went through the empty dining room, through the far door to the kitchen. It was spacious and should have been cheery, with its high ceiling and its red-painted wooden floor. But the overgrown bushes along the side of the house blocked most of the sunlight. A single ceiling light glowed yellow in the gloom. Hannah was at the sink with her back to Mary-Alice, scrubbing pots.

"Excuse me," Mary-Alice said, "do you have a—"

Mary-Alice found herself suddenly off-balance, and only by grabbing the counter did she avoid falling on her face. She looked down to see what had tripped her. An iron ring, about six inches across, was fastened to the floor.

Hannah turned around, wiping her hands on a towel.

"Watch out for the cellar door, ma'am."

"Yes, I see that. Thank you. What an unusual place for a cellar door, I must say."

"Winter's too cold for an outside door," Hannah said. "You can freeze to death outside if you're not careful."

"Well, isn't that clever. I suppose I never had need of that back in Louisiana. Now, Hannah, darlin', might I use that telephone right there to let my friends back home know I arrived safely? I know they must be awfully worried about me by now."

Hannah shrugged and turned back to the soapy sink.

"It's disconnected."

"May I try it anyway?"

"Suit yourself, ma'am."

Mary-Alice picked up the receiver, but just as Hannah had said, it was dead.

"Well, thank you all the same, Hannah," Mary-Alice said as she hung up. Maybe it would be worth going into town if only to find a working phone.

As Mary-Alice headed back to the sitting-room, she nearly collided with Janice. Janice quickly placed the tray she was carrying on a side table and stepped in front of it, but not before Mary-Alice saw the covered dish.

*Whose breakfast had that been?*

"Mrs. Arceneaux," Janice said, sounding out of breath. "Your room's all ready for you now. We can move you to one of the larger rooms if you like, but I'm not certain we can do it today."

"Oh, I'm quite comfortable with my existing room, thanks ever so much. Do you happen to have a working telephone in the house, by any chance? I promised to call my friends in Sinful when I was safely arrived and it completely slipped my mind."

Janice's face lit up.

"No, not here in the house, but we can take you into town. One of the stores might let you use their phone."

"Well, I certainly don't want to be a bother."

Mary-Alice felt outmatched; she had sworn that she would not be tricked into leaving the Kilmer house, and now she was going willingly.

"Logan's heading down, and he'd be happy to give you a lift. Heck of a lot more interesting than hanging around this old dump all day."

The siblings' eagerness to get her out of the house made Mary-Alice not want to leave under any circumstances. On the other hand, she did want someone to know where she was. And she could scout out the hotel, in case she had to resort to calling on Room Three, whatever that might mean.

"Why, how very kind of you." Mary-Alice put on her sweetest smile. "Yes, I'd love to see a little more of Black Valley."

# CHAPTER 7

The family car turned out to be a repurposed hearse, painted a dark metal-flake gray. Mary-Alice correctly perceived that Logan was not about to go out of his way to open the door for a seventy-year-old lady, so when he slowed the car down she let herself in.

"Why, what an unusual automobile," Mary-Alice remarked as she buckled the seat belt.

"I got a good deal on it," Logan said. "Not real pretty, but it's good for hauling the pigeon stuff."

Mary-Alice discreetly pulled a handkerchief out of her purse and held it to her nose.

"And this is your family's only car?" she asked from behind the handkerchief.

"It is now, after my Beemer got totaled. Stupid insurance company."

"Those insurance companies can be tricky to deal with," Mary-Alice said sympathetically. "Are they stalling on your payment?"

"Idiots refused to insure me in the first place." As if on cue, the engine stalled. Logan cranked the key and pumped the gas, and finally the hearse bucked to life.

But as soon as he rounded the corner, he was brought up short by the hunched figure of a woman standing in the middle of the road. She faced away from the car, and it wasn't until Logan braked, inches from her, that she turned around.

Despite the pleasant temperature, the old woman was bundled up with scarves and sporting a lavender knit cap. She fixed them with a malevolent glare. Mary-Alice cranked down the window and leaned out.

"Didn't you hear us, dear?" The woman was standing so close that Mary-Alice could smell the fruity aroma of tobacco from her pipe.

"It's Mother Sophie," Logan muttered. "She's deaf as a rock. Used to be good friends with Mom. You wouldn't know it now."

Logan leaned on the horn, which had no effect except to make Mary-Alice clap her hands over her ears.

"Well, then that's not likely to work, is it, dear?" Mary-Alice let herself out of the car and stood in front of Mother Sophie.

"Hello," Mary-Alice signed at the woman. Mary-Alice was glad she had taken a night class in American Sign Language at Mudbug Technical Institute, and hoped she would be able to decode whatever Mother Sophie signed back at her.

But the old woman only continued to glare at her as Logan drummed impatiently on the steering wheel.

At least the woman was looking at her. Waiting. Waiting for her to do what? Did the woman want something?

Mary-Alice considered offering her money, but feared that might be taken as an insult. Then she noticed that they were stopped in front of a well-kept cottage with a neat garden.

"Pardon me," Mary-Alice said, moving her lips clearly, but not exaggerating. "I would love a bunch of that lovely bee balm you have growing there."

Then she drew a twenty-dollar bill from her purse and held it up.

"I will pay you, of course."

Mother Sophie narrowed her eyes at Mary-Alice and puffed her pipe. Then she went over to her garden, broke off several of the blood-red blooms, and returned with a nicely-arranged little bouquet.

As Mother Sophie plucked the bill from Mary-Alice's hand, she spoke for the first time:

"Seventy; twenty-eight; and now ten."

"That was a twenty, darlin'," Mary-Alice said. "Twenty."

"Seventy, twenty-eight, ten," Mother Sophie repeated. "Won't John be surprised!"

And then she hurried back into her cottage and slammed the door behind her. Logan started driving again as Mary-Alice buckled the lap belt.

"How old is Mother Sophie?" Mary-Alice asked. "She seems remarkably spry."

"In her eighties, I guess."

"She has a lovely garden. That must be what keeps her so fit. And who is John?"

"John was her son. About fifty years ago he went out hiking with his buddies. There was some accident, the kid died, but she still thinks he's coming back."

Logan took one hand off the steering wheel to make circles around his ear.

As they drew into sight of the tiny downtown, Logan said,

"Uh-oh. Do you hear that knocking sound?"

"Knocking sound? I must say, I don't."

"From the engine," Logan said cheerfully. "Guess I'm going to have to call for a tow."

"Well that is unfortunate," Mary-Alice pulled her phone from her purse. "I don't seem to have any cell phone signal here either."

“Nope, no point having a cell phone in Black Valley. I’ll make the call from Knickerbocker’s.”

Logan stopped the hearse in front of a squat cinderblock building with a satellite dish perched on the edge of the roof.

"How long do you suppose the repair will take?" Mary-Alice asked.

"Two or three hours," Logan replied promptly. "They’ll have to send a tow truck. Hey, but look, there's all kinds of shops here, and I know you ladies love shopping. Why don’t you come back and meet me here in three hours?”

So whatever was going on in the Kilmer house would be over in three hours.

"Three hours in your quaint little downtown sounds absolutely heavenly." Mary-Alice glanced around the cluster of shops that constituted Black Valley’s Man Street. In addition to Knickerbocker’s Bar, she noted a knitting shop, a check-cashing establishment, an off-brand convenience store, a run-down diner, and a beauty shop.

“Is there by any chance a hotel downtown?” Mary-Alice asked.

"Oh, sure." Logan pointed to the end of the street where a two-story Victorian stood. “Make sure to tell the Van Burens that Logan Kilmer sent you."

# CHAPTER 8

The lobby of the Black Valley Hotel was dim and cozy. A motley collection of chairs clustered around an unlit stone fireplace, and the reception counter and walls were paneled in dark wood. The hotel appeared to be entirely devoid of people.

Mary-Alice gently pressed the bell on the counter, and a plump woman with a pile of gray-blonde hair rushed out from the back.

Mary-Alice introduced herself and inquired about getting a ride back up to the Kilmer mansion.

"Not right now," the woman said. "Mr. Van Buren's got the car. Now, Mrs. Arceneaux, I believe we have a reservation for you. Let me check."

"I understand Miss Janice Kilmer called one in for me," Mary-Alice said, "but I don't believe I'll be using it, as they've graciously invited me to stay with them at the house."

Mrs. Van Buren stopped paging through the papers on the counter and looked up at Mary-Alice with surprise.

"You're staying at the Kilmer mansion? Overnight?"

"Why, yes. I stayed last night. Mister Logan drove me down from there a few minutes ago."

"Mrs. Arceneaux, I'm sure I can flag down a ride for you if you don't mind waiting a bit. In the meantime, can I invite you to join me for a cup of coffee? Do you have time?"

Without transportation, Mary-Alice had nothing but time. And Mrs. Van Buren appeared to be a sociable woman stuck in a lonely job. A chat might be informative as well as pleasant.

So Mary-Alice joined Mrs. Van Buren by the unlit fireplace and feigned delight at the instant coffee served with powdered creamer and packaged off-brand cookies.

Mrs. Van Buren asked Mary-Alice offhandedly what had brought her to Black Valley. Mary-Alice explained, quite truthfully, that she was a childhood friend of Althea Kilmer, had only recently heard of her passing, and had come to visit Althea's children.

"This is such a lovely town," Mary-Alice continued, "and I've no doubt she loved it here."

"Such a shame about…everything," Mrs. Van Buren said. "You know, back in the day, Althea was a real beauty. A Southern belle. Lucetta looks so much like her."

"It did give me rather a start when I met Lucetta," Mary-Alice confided. "It was like seeing dear Althea again. Why, her dress even looked like one I recall Althea wearing!"

Mrs. Van Buren set down her stained coffee cup and leaned across the little table.

"She's been more and more like this since her mother died," Mrs. Van Buren whispered. "The blonde hair, the dresses, the whole bit. I mean, I can't blame her. She misses her mother and wants her back. Kind of an unusual way to go about it, though, if you ask me."

"Why, whatever do you mean by 'the blonde hair?'"

"Lucetta's a natural brunette, like her sister. Oh, don't worry, I'm sure she's harmless. I don't think she'll go Psycho on you when you're in the shower or anything. At least I hope not."

Mary-Alice did her best to laugh along with Mrs. Van Buren,

but made a mental note to make sure the bed was well-braced against the door again tonight.

"Have the children always lived at home?" Mary-Alice asked.

"No, they've come back over the years. Lucetta got some kind of poetry prize when she was in school, and thought she'd make her living from writing. That didn't exactly work out. Logan went to college to study business and ended up getting involved in some pyramid scheme. When it all came crashing down, he had to drop out and come crawling home. That's when the Judge died. Blew a gasket when he found out Logan had lost his college fund, is what I hear."

"The Judge?" Mary-Alice asked.

"Judge Kilmer. Their father. Althea's husband. Anyway, I don't think Logan's learned a thing from his experience. He's still trying one harebrained get-rich-quick scam after another. I think he's raising pigeons now."

"Oh, yes. I believe I heard them this morning. What about Janice?"

"Went to work in the city, ended up marrying some hedge fund guy, divorced, just moved back here a little while ago."

"And neither Logan nor Lucetta ever married?"

The phone at the front desk rang.

"You wait right here, Mrs. Arceneaux," Mrs. Van Buren urged as she got up. "I won't be a moment."

Mrs. Van Buren returned quickly, bringing the carafe of burned coffee. She refilled both their cups without asking.

"Looks like we'll have someone checking in this afternoon," she announced happily. "Anyway, you were asking about the Kilmer twins marrying?"

"Logan and Lucetta are twins?" Mary-Alice asked.

"Uh-huh. I know, Logan seems so much less mature, doesn't he?"

"Bless his heart," Mary-Alice agreed.

"I don't know about Logan's personal life. If you ask me,

anyone with an ounce of sense would steer clear of him. Lucetta, now, she's always had men interested in her. I think she might be seeing someone now. But it's hush-hush for some reason. You've met her, you know what I'm talking about. She likes to go around acting mysterious."

"I'm surprised Logan has decided to make his home in Black Valley," Mary-Alice said. "He seems like someone with more big-city ambitions. I don't get the feeling he likes it much here."

"Yeah, I know what you mean. The thing is, they each own a one-third share of the house. That's a story right there. I think Logan and Janice would be happy to be rid of the place, even if they had to pay someone to take it off their hands. But Lucetta would never agree, and of course Miss Poet of the Year doesn't have the money to buy them out. And anyway, good luck selling a house on Saxton Lane, not after ... I mean, you must know about the disappearances?"

"I have heard the stories," Mary-Alice said casually, as if that were not the precise reason she was in Black Valley to begin with. "But it seems to be only young men who are disappearing, and as I am clearly neither, I do believe I'm quite safe."

Mary-Alice had intended this last remark to come across as lighthearted, but Mrs. Van Buren was serious.

"That's so brave of you, Mrs. Arceneaux. If you can stay in the Kilmer mansion and come out unharmed, that would do a lot to reassure people that there isn't anything, you know. Not me, of course. I'm sure the Kilmers are all perfectly lovely people. But some people around here, well, you can imagine how rumors spread in a small town."

"I do have some idea. That reminds me, the Kilmers don't have telephone service. May I use your phone?"

"Is it long-distance?"

"Oh, I'm perfectly happy to pay you back for the call. I simply want to let my friends in Sinful know I arrived safely."

"No, no, it's okay. You can use the phone in my office. Go

through that door and turn right. Just keep it short, if you don't mind."

Gertie didn't pick up the phone, so Mary-Alice left a short message saying she'd arrived safely. It was a shame she wasn't able to talk to Gertie in person. Mary-Alice wanted to get back up to the Kilmer Mansion to discover why they were so eager to get her out of the house, and Gertie always had clever ideas.

As she returned to the lobby, she saw that Mrs. Van Buren had been joined by Mr. Peck.

# CHAPTER 9

Mr. Peck was happy to offer Mary-Alice a ride back up to the Kilmer mansion. And Mary-Alice was not exactly disappointed to have the opportunity to ride with Mr. Peck. Although he was not yet seventy, his manners were so courtly that they struck even Mary-Alice as charmingly old-fashioned. He helped Mary-Alice up into the seat of his truck and made certain she'd buckled her seatbelt before he went around to the driver's side. "It looks like I picked a good time to stop in at the hotel," Mr. Peck said as pulled out onto Main Street.

"Do you have business with the Van Burens?" Mary-Alice asked. "From what I hear, they would be fortunate to get some of your produce for their guests. Young Logan is quite impressed with your crop of peaches."

"I happened to visit because I have a business associate coming in this afternoon," he replied. "I wanted to be certain his accommodations were ready. The Van Burens are not customers of mine. But I am pleased to hear that Logan enjoyed the peaches."

Mary-Alice correctly sensed that Mr. Peck would welcome the opportunity to discuss his farming. Before long he was chatting earnestly about sugar content, firmness, fragility, and other minutiae of fruit-growing. He had been a military contractor, Mary-Alice learned, and he used what he'd learned about water pumps and irrigation systems and the like, and applied it to his own orchards. Mary-Alice glanced at her watch, and was pleased to note that she would be making her appearance at the Kilmer mansion a full two hours before she was expected.

They turned onto Saxton Lane, which became narrower and gloomier as they drove on.

"Who lives in that little house back there?"

Mary-Alice indicated a low cottage set back among the maples and gum trees that proliferated along Saxton Lane.

"Why, that's Deacon Spear," Mr. Peck replied. "He's one of our new neighbors."

"Oh, I was under the impression that folks weren't moving in to Black Valley. How long has he lived here?"

Mr. Peck considered this question.

"I'd say around ten, fifteen years. He claims to be a writer."

Mr. Peck's tone was faintly disapproving.

"Like Lucetta," Mary-Alice said. "I understand she's a poet."

"Of course, I'm no judge of literature. But Miss Kilmer did win a poetry prize some years ago. It was a proud moment for Black Valley. Deacon Spear, now, well, I don't know."

Mr. Peck continued to make his careful way down the potholed, one-lane road. Abruptly, the wild forest gave way to manicured orchards. Mary-Alice noted blade-like leaves, and clusters of green globes tinged with gold.

"Well now, isn't this lovely," Mary-Alice exclaimed as they drove on. "These must be your peaches, if I'm not mistaken"

"Yes they are," Mr. Peck proclaimed. "You're quite observant, Mrs. Arceneaux. From here on is my land. And I tend to all these trees myself."

"With no help at all?" Mary-Alice asked.

"I've mechanized a good deal of the work," Mr. Peck

remarked placidly. "Watering and composting and such. And simply walking around the property is a good way for a man to keep fit. These fruits that you see are not ripe yet, but I have another variety, a white peach, that's just coming to its peak. I allowed young Mr. Kilmer to sample the fruit recently and I believe he was rightly impressed. I'll bring you one when it's ready, and you can experience it for yourself."

"Why, that's ever so thoughtful of you, Mr. Peck. I'd be delighted. So it seems you enjoy living here on Saxton Lane."

"Wouldn't live anywhere else," he replied with satisfaction.

"You don't seem to be much frightened by the disappearances."

"Mrs. Arceneaux, the missing men were all young and vigorous. I am not so vain as to imagine that I would be in any personal danger. Most of the residents of Saxton Lane are concerned, of course. In fact, they urged me to contact law enforcement about these disappearances."

"How interesting. Well, your neighbors must think very highly of you to have elected you as their spokesman, Mr. Peck."

He chuckled. "I happen to be taking my turn as the president of our neighborhood watch."

"You said that most of the residents were concerned about the disappearances," Mary-Alice said. "Not all?"

"Well, there's poor Mother Sophie, of course."

"Oh, yes, I've met Mother Sophie," Mary-Alice said.

"Beautiful garden she has, though. I must say that for her. And Deacon Spear keeps to himself, hasn't come to any of the neighborhood meetings at all. People can be disappointing, Mrs. Arceneaux. I suppose that's why I enjoy spending time with my trees. Why, I sound like a grouchy old man, now. I suppose I am. Ah, and here we come to my house."

As they rounded the corner, Mary-Alice gasped with delight. The cottage was small and neat, freshly-painted, and much enhanced by the riot of roses around the front entrance and the velvety green lawn. A beam of sunlight had broken through the upstate gloom and illuminated the pale-yellow building.

"This is absolutely lovely," Mary-Alice exclaimed. "I don't imagine you maintain the house yourself as you do your orchards?"

"I do indeed," he said proudly. "And there are worse ways for a man to spend his days than to keep his house ship-shape and his land prosperous. Now, are you in a particular hurry to get back to the Kilmer house? We might stop for a cup of tea."

Mary-Alice was tempted, but it was against her upbringing to enter a bachelor's house unchaperoned. Perhaps that was how they did things up north, but to Mary-Alice, the idea was simply too wanton to consider.

"Perhaps another time," she demurred. "It's ever so kind of you to offer, Mr. Peck."

"Well, onward to the Kilmer place then. You are a brave woman to stay there, Mrs. Arceneaux. I'm not a superstitious man, but I do worry about those children. I don't think it's a healthy house. It has a bad history."

"Why, Mr. Peck, they may seem like children to you and me, but those children, as you call them, are forty if they're a day."

"Well, that's true enough," Mr. Peck chuckled.

They reached the heart of the forest and Mary-Alice saw the chimney-tops of the Kilmer house rising above the trees. Mr. Peck looked serious now.

"Mrs. Arceneaux, I beg your pardon for my presumption, but I must say, I don't like to leave you here. Are you sure you want to go back inside? You saw for yourself how pleasant the Van Burens' hotel is. I can drive you back down into town right this minute if you like. In fact, if you have any bags I can fetch them from the house."

Mary-Alice herself, faced with the sight of the Kilmer mansion, was not feeling eager to go back inside. Especially in contrast to Mr. Peck's pleasant cottage, it seemed grim and forbidding. But she reminded herself that Althea's children had schemed to get her out of the house, which meant that something interesting and important was undoubtedly going on inside.

"Are you certain you want me to drop you off here?" Mr. Peck asked again. "It's simply that—well, this can't be good for any of them to live shut up inside the place like that, and especially young Logan...I apologize if I sound hopelessly old-fashioned, Mrs. Arceneaux, but I believe a young man needs to spend time outdoors."

"Logan does have his pigeons," Mary-Alice said.

"Yes, that he certainly does. They're rather fond of cherries, as I found to my cost earlier this summer. I'm happy to say they're leaving my peaches alone, for the most part. Well, here we are."

Mr. Peck parked, hopped down from the driver's seat, and came around to let Mary-Alice out. Then she heard him say,

"Well, Logan, I see you've gotten your car fixed. I've brought back your guest for you. She was ready to spend her entire afternoon in downtown Black Valley."

Mary-Alice was surprised to see Logan, and from the look on his face, he was equally surprised to see her.

"It's a wonderful thing you got the car fixed so quickly," Mary-Alice agreed.

"I was about to come down and pick you up," he retorted, a little defensively.

"I'm certain you were," Mary-Alice said sweetly. "But Mr. Peck beat you to it. Everyone has been so kind, I must say."

Logan grunted in a most un-charming way, turned his back to Mary-Alice and Mr. Peck, and headed back into the house, leaving Mary-Alice to follow.

# CHAPTER 10

Mary-Alice noticed another car parked nearby, a sensible silver economy car of recent build.

"Do you have another visitor?" she called after Logan's retreating back.

"Someone to see Lucetta," he said, without slowing down or turning around. Mary-Alice sped up and pulled alongside him.

"She's not expecting you," he said rudely, and then stopped in front of Mary-Alice, blocking her. "So you can't interrupt her. You understand?"

"Why Mr. Kilmer," Mary-Alice said. I am a guest in your home, and ever so grateful for your hospitality. Why should I interrupt your sister or give her or you a moment of pain?"

"Humph," he snorted, and stepped aside, leaving Mary-Alice to continue on her way toward the house. Mary-Alice, a little unnerved, didn't look back to see whether he was following her.

She noticed that Mr. Peck stayed by his truck, watching until Mary-Alice was inside the house.

As soon as she opened the door, she saw Lucetta and her visitor, a man of about Lucetta's age, standing close to her and clasping her hands.

"It's not going to be much longer," Lucetta was pleading. "Maybe a week, if that. But before then I can't—"

They both paused and turned to look at Mary-Alice.

"Good afternoon," Mary-Alice said, breezily. "Please don't let me intrude. I'm just on my way up to my room."

She sped away, to hear the young man say,

"Lucetta, I want to be with you, but if you keep putting me off..."

Mary-Alice hesitated, but they'd lowered their voices and she couldn't hear any more. She continued back up to her room, wondering whether she wouldn't have learned more by staying in town.

Although she did get a chance to ride with the handsome and hardworking Mr. Peck, so her time hadn't been entirely wasted.

Mary-Alice puttered restlessly in her room, feeling like a bluebottle fly caught in a jar. Lucetta had told her young man to give her a week. What, Mary-Alice wondered, was going to happen in a week?

And what, for that matter, was going to happen to the young man?

Mary-Alice felt unequipped for what she might have stumbled into. She didn't want to believe that her friend's children were capable of evil, but their caginess, their unwillingness to have her stay the night, the remoteness of her room from the central activities of the house, the fact that the most recent disappearance took place right on their street...they were hiding something, and Mary-Alice did not like to imagine what it was.

Mary-Alice could try to get to a phone and have the police search the house. But hadn't Sheriff Lee himself told her that they'd tried something like that before, only to have the judge had refuse to sign a search warrant? And really, where was the proof? Strange bits of overheard conversation, and what else?

Besides, she didn't want to subject the Kilmer children to the embarrassment of having their house torn apart. They had already lost their parents and most of their fortune.

Mary-Alice needed time to think, and she didn't like being cooped up in her room, especially not on a lovely, sunny afternoon. Not wishing to be more of a burden on the sisters than necessary, she sprayed herself with mosquito repellent, went downstairs, and found Hannah in the kitchen. She asked if she might sit on the front porch and read.

"Of course, Ma'am," Hannah said flatly.

"But I haven't had a tour of this marvelous house," Mary-Alice continued. "I certainly would be much obliged if one of the sisters could show me around when they get a chance. It truly is a lovely building."

"I'll let them know, Ma'am," was the emotionless reply.

"Do you happen to have any iced tea?" Mary-Alice persisted.

Hannah rummaged in the refrigerator, brought out a dark pitcher of tea, poured out a glass, and handed it to Mary-Alice.

Mary-Alice sat down in one of the outdoor chairs and found it surprisingly comfortable, considering it was made of wooden slats. She sipped her tea and read.

The time went by quickly; her mystery novel was absorbing, her mosquito repellent was working, and not a single car drove by.

Mary-Alice was surprised when Lucetta came out and sat in the other chair. She closed the cover of her e-reader and turned her attention to her young hostess.

"My mother loved tea," Lucetta said, looking at Mary-Alice's empty glass. "She taught us how to make it properly. Three Luzianne tea bags to one cup of sugar. Lipton will do in a pinch."

For the first time since she arrived, Mary-Alice detected a trace of a smile as Lucetta spoke. She seemed to have gotten over her confrontation with her young man.

"You do remind me of your mother," Mary-Alice said.

Lucetta patted her blonde hair self-consciously.

"I've heard that before," she said.

Althea had never been melancholy like Lucetta, though. Of course, Mary-Alice hadn't known Althea at age forty.

"Do you know," Mary-Alice said, "this is one of the most interesting houses it has ever been my good fortune to enter. Would you mind my having a little look around? I understand you haven't prepared every room for company, but I'm so interested to know where dear Althea spent her days."

Lucetta's smile vanished. "I'm afraid today wouldn't work. To be perfectly honest, there's not much to see. But I'm sure I can give you the full tour before you leave."

"Oh, I do hope so," Mary-Alice enthused. "It would be ever so interesting. Such an old place, there might even be an old ghost or two. In fact, I believe there must be ghosts. I certainly don't feel I'm the only guest here."

Mary-Alice took care to say this in a lighthearted way, but Lucetta jumped and nearly knocked over the table.

"Ghosts," she laughed in a strained way. "Why, how ridiculous. I don't believe in haunted houses, Mrs. Arceneaux."

"Well, now, that's a little disappointing." Mary-Alice put on a wistful smile. "I truly would like to meet a ghost here before I leave. Why, I was wondering where in this wonderful old place I'd be most likely to find a restless spirit. I must say, I do wonder what's behind those double doors at the end of that first floor hallway."

"That would be the great drawing-room," Lucetta said stiffly, "and it is not off-limits. You may explore it as soon as I can locate the key. But please do not be disappointed if you fail to find any ghosts."

"Oh, it's so frustrating when you lose your keys, isn't it?" Mary-Alice asked sympathetically. If her memory served, she had a pretty good idea where those keys were, and she suspected Lucetta knew exactly where they were, too.

"I'm sure they'll turn up," Lucetta said. "But those rooms have been shut up for a long time, and I don't believe any of them is properly furnished. We can barely keep up the part of the house we live in, as you have no doubt observed already. Now if you'll excuse me, I have some things to attend to. Dinner will be at seven o'clock. If you'd like something before then, please help yourself to more tea and biscuits from the icebox."

# CHAPTER 11

Mary-Alice watched Lucetta hurry back into the house. When she was sure the young woman was gone, she brought her glass back into the kitchen and placed it in the sink. She did not know what Hannah's cleaning methods were, and knew better than to presume upon that intimidating woman's routine. On the way out of the kitchen, Mary-Alice reached up to a hook by the doorway, from which hung a ring of age-stained keys.

Mary-Alice ducked into the hallway, then put on her reading glasses. The keys were old, judging from the darkened metal and the worn, rounded cuts. Each one bore a small, yellowed label on which a name was written in rusty ink. "Blue Chamber," "Library," "Flower Parlor," "Shell Cabinet," "Dark Parlor"—all quite mysterious and intriguing.

But it was upon a key marked "A" she first fixed her attention. It was the largest and rustiest key, so Mary-Alice assumed the room it unlocked would be the most interesting.

Listening carefully for approaching footsteps, she tried the "A" key in each door, without success, until she reached the double door at the end. The key moved easily in the lock, and the doors swung inward with a squeal of the hinges.

So this was the room that Lucetta had called the great drawing-room.

The stench of mold and thick coating of dust made it was obvious no one had been here recently. Mary-Alice couldn't decide whether to breathe through her nose or her mouth. The windows had inner wooden shutters, which were quite effective at keeping out the light. Rather than open the shutters (and risk being seen from outside) Mary-Alice found an old-fashioned light button. Pressing it illuminated two dim wall sconces, while half a dozen more remained dark. She wondered whether the electrical wiring in this part of the house was the knob-and-tube kind, which she recalled her contractor friend Boon St. Clair telling her was a fire hazard.

But despite the age and former grandeur of the great drawing room, there was little to see. Two decrepit fireplaces, a stained parquet floor, and no furniture.

Mary-Alice pulled the double doors of Room A shut behind her locked them back up, and brushed a cobweb from her cheek.

Mary-Alice went to the next doorway and started trying the keys one after another. The key that finally fit was labeled Dark Parlor. The room had dark ebony furniture and a wooden floor painted black. *That was rather on-the-nose,* Mary-Alice thought as she locked the door of the Dark Parlor.

The next door yielded to the key labeled Flower Parlor. The room had subdued rose-on-gray wallpaper that was peeling at the seams. The wooden floor was swept, and there were cheap but new shades in the windows. The overstuffed floral chintz furniture struck Mary-Alice as very much Althea's style, and she wondered whether her friend had picked it out herself.

An oak bookshelf--not an antique as the sitting-room furniture was, but of recent build, and cheap—held a few books. There was a slim pink paperback titled *Fragments*. It appeared to be a volume of poetry, the modern kind where words were placed on the page seemingly at random, and nothing rhymed. Mary-Alice flipped to the copyright page, which indicated the book had been published twenty years earlier, by an imprint Mary-Alice had never heard of. The author was Lucetta (no last name). She closed the book and gently replaced it on the shelf.

Mary-Alice was about to pick up the next book, but paused when she saw the title:

*Mortuary Science: A Sourcebook.*

Next to that was a small, innocuous-looking paperback titled *Final Exit,* which appeared to be all about ways to end one's life.

Mary-Alice backed away from the bookshelf with a shudder and took another look around the room. Despite its cheery floral furniture, it seemed less welcoming than it had moments earlier. She noted a closet that protruded out into the room, built in such a way that it looked like an add-on. She went over to it, carefully stepping around a large discoloration in the middle of the floor (which Mary-Alice hoped it was the result of a spilled drink or an incontinent house cat).

Mary-Alice opened the closet and found it led to a small spiral staircase going up to the floor above. She entered the closet and tiptoed up toward a rectangular outline of light. When she was in reach of the trap door, she carefully reached up and pushed it. It opened.

And then she heard the rumble of Logan's voice. She quickly eased the door down, backed down the stairs and pulled the closet door shut. She wanted to get out of that room as quickly as possible, but before she did that, she unlatched the window (it swung open easily), pulled out her peach nail polish, and made a small mark on the windowsill outside. From this, she might locate the room above later.

She shut the window, and with a last uneasy glance at the bookshelf, left the room and locked the door behind her. So much for the Flower Parlor.

Mary-Alice did not wish to push her luck, and for the moment, her normally insatiable curiosity was quiescent. She returned to the kitchen, quietly replaced the ring of keys on the hook, and retreated to her room to ponder her discoveries and dress for dinner.

# CHAPTER 12

Logan and Janice were at dinner that evening; no place had been set for Lucetta. Janice asked Mary-Alice how she'd spent the day. Mary-Alice perceived that answering this question was full of possible minefields, so she gave the most truthful, yet superficial, account she could come up with.

"It's a shame Logan brought you back so soon," Janice remarked; it seemed more for Logan's benefit than for Mary-Alice's. "Downtown Black Valley has a lot of charm, if you look for it."

"Wasn't me, Janice," Logan protested. "Peck brought her home. Look, I couldn't stay down there all day. I had to get back to the pigeons."

"Logan was not at all derelict in his duties," Mary-Alice insisted. "It's simply that Mr. Peck happened by the hotel, and I accepted a ride from him."

"It's nice of you to say so, Mrs. Arceneaux," Janice replied, fixing Logan with a disapproving stare. "But if Logan had been a more attentive host, we all could've avoided an awkward scene."

"I am terribly sorry," Mary-Alice said, although she wasn't, really. She had learned that something important was going to happen within a week. That might be an important clue.

On the other hand, she may have simply witnessed Lucetta trying to put off an unwanted suitor.

That night, Mary-Alice pushed her bed against the door as she had the previous night, but instead of getting into bed and falling asleep, she decided so sit up and listen. Gradually she dozed in her chair, and was jolted awake shortly after midnight by a sense that someone was outside her door.

She heard a key turn in the lock, followed by the rapid withdrawal of feet down the corridor. She leaped up, scrambled across the bed, and tried to turn the knob—it was locked. She rattled the knob, hoping that she might shake the key onto the floor, when she heard from somewhere in the house a cry so anguished that she stopped struggling with the doorknob and listened.

But there was only silence.

She checked her phone, but as before, there was no signal. She tried dialing 911, thinking that telephone networks made an exception for emergency calls. If someone were to answer, she would tell them that there was a murder in progress, and deal with any fallout afterward.

But even the emergency call did not go through.

Mary-Alice unlatched the window and opened it. If she needed to escape, she could. It would involve climbing down a tree, but at least she wasn't completely trapped.

She lay down on the bed to think. The next thing she knew, she was being awakened with a rap on the door and Hannah calling out:

"Eight o'clock, ma'am. Breakfast is ready."

"Well, I'd love to come down and join y'all for breakfast," Mary-Alice said as she pushed the bed away from the door. "But it seems that I've been locked—"

Mary-Alice pulled the door open effortlessly, and she found herself with her nose practically in Hannah's bosom.

"Hannah, darlin'" Mary-Alice said, stepping back to a more polite distance, "I may have dreamed this, but I recall hearing a disturbance last night. Are the girls and Logan all right?"

Hannah shrugged.

"I believe everyone is fine, Ma'am. I'm sure they'd thank you for your concern. You can join us for breakfast whenever you're ready."

Mary-Alice watched Hannah plod off down the hall, and wondered if she had dreamed the whole thing.

She was surprised to find all three of the Kilmer children at the breakfast table.

"Hannah tells us you had a nightmare," Lucetta said as Mary-Alice took her seat.

"This house will do it," Logan observed mildly. "I grew up here and even I think it's creepy."

"Oh, please don't say that," Mary-Alice protested. "Your house is absolutely lovely."

"Well, you haven't yet seen all of it, Mrs. Arceneaux," Lucetta said.

That was true, although after her unauthorized tour of the previous day, Mary-Alice thought she'd seen quite enough for the time being.

"Well I imagine Althea must have loved this place," Mary-Alice said. "I can so easily picture her here."

Lucetta burst into tears and rushed from the table.

Janice and Mary-Alice stared after her. Logan continued stuffing scrambled eggs and sausage into his mouth.

"It'll take her a while," Janice murmured sympathetically. "Logan, can you show Mrs. Arceneaux around after breakfast? I'm sorry I can't join you. I have some errands I need to run."

Logan made a sort of snuffling noise of assent, never breaking his stride as he shoveled food into his mouth.

"It looks like such a beautiful morning, I can take myself out for a walk, if y'all don't mind," Mary-Alice said. "I don't want to be an imposition."

Without Logan watching her, Mary-Alice thought she might wander around until she found a spot with cell phone reception. She might even go over to see Mr. Peck and ask if she could get a ride back into town, so she could return to the hotel and contact whoever was in Room Three.

"It's no imposition at all," Janice said. "Logan's probably dying to show you his pigeons. Right, Logan?"

Logan's pigeon loft sat at the edge of the Kilmer property, where the vast back lawn met the edge of the forest.

"It's a long walk," Logan complained. "But my sisters said I couldn't bring it any closer to the house than this. They said it's noisy and smelly."

Logan seemed annoyed that his sisters had pointed out what to Mary-Alice was an obvious fact. He either had an impaired sense of smell, Mary-Alice thought, or an inflamed sense of entitlement.

"Did you build this?" Mary-Alice asked. "It looks like a little cabin for the birds. It's very well-crafted."

"Yeah, I built it. I mean I paid some guy in town to do it. I was only gonna give him half cause he took so long, but then Janice found out and freaked out and paid the rest of it. Now she thinks I should pay her back. No offense, Mrs. Arceneaux, but girls just don't understand how business works."

"And why pigeons?" Mary-Alice asked, eager to move the conversation to less contentious ground. "What do these pigeons do?"

"Well, these might look like regular old city pigeons," Logan said, puffing his chest out and looking not unlike a pigeon himself. "But I'm breeding racing pigeons. The Chinese will pay a fortune for these things. You know, horse racing isn't legal in China, but pigeon racing is."

"How interesting! And how do the pigeons get from here to China?"

"I'm still working out the details. That's the other thing Janice and Lucetta don't understand. You're never going to see a return on your investment right away. Have you heard of patient capital?"

Logan went on to talk about his long-term plans, and Mary-Alice listened politely as she surreptitiously dug her phone out of her bag to see if there was any signal in this remote spot.

"Oh, sorry," Logan said with heavy sarcasm as he noticed what Mary-Alice was doing, "am I boring you?"

"Certainly not," Mary-Alice retorted. "I was hoping to take a picture of your lovely loft."

She then lifted her phone and snapped several photos of the wooden coop.

Mollified, Logan let Mary-Alice take a few pictures, then insisted on getting in the shot himself. Mary-Alice dutifully played along, then apologized for "forcing" Logan to spend so much time explaining the pigeon loft to her. She asked whether she might have a guided tour of the house—the exterior only, as it was such a lovely day she wouldn't dream of spending it inside.

Logan didn't have much to say about the ragged landscaping; it clearly did not interest him. So it was up to Mary-Alice to natter on about growing seasons and shade cloths and cold snaps as they crunched along the gravel path next to the ground-floor windows.

Finally, she saw it: the glittering dot of peach nail polish she'd put on the windowsill of the Flower Parlor the day before.

Carefully, she stepped back and stole a glance at the window above.

It was the third window from the rear corner, which was consistent with the placement of the first-floor room. But what she saw there startled her so that she blurted out,

"My goodness, why is there a knot of black crepe tying the shutters together?"

Logan—oddly, for him—was tongue-tied.

"Um, I couldn't say, Mrs. Arceneaux," he came up with, finally. "Maybe someone's trying to keep the shutters closed."

"I see," Mary-Alice answered. "Of course. Logan, I am ever so grateful to you for showing me around. I know you must be terribly busy, and I don't wish to keep you for a moment longer. I believe I'd like to take a walk down Saxton Lane, and I do understand if you cannot accompany me."

Logan, naturally, took the opportunity to make himself scarce, leaving Mary-Alice to consider what she'd seen so far.

Of course, Mary-Alice was not satisfied with Logan's answer about the black crepe on the shutters. What was black crepe—an old-fashioned symbol of death—doing there? What was in the room above the Flower Parlor, at the top of that hidden staircase?

Mary-Alice decided that Lucetta must be the one behind the display of crepe. She clearly had a taste for the archaic. Janice was too practical for such a display, and Logan too oblivious and self-centered. And perhaps the display of mourning held the key to Lucetta's emotional collapse at the breakfast table.

Mary-Alice strolled down to the front gate, wondering whether she should go for a stroll after all. Sheriff Lee had warned her not to go anywhere alone, but the day was bright and warm, and Saxton Lane looked positively inviting. Perhaps a stroll in the fresh air would restore her sense of proportion. Maybe it was simply a dream that someone had locked her in her room the night before. And the scream of anguish, too, was simply her imagination.

Mary-Alice was surprised to see Mr. Peck walk up to the gate.

"Good morning, Mrs. Arceneaux. It's a great relief to me to

see you in such good spirits this morning. How did you pass the night?"

"I slept well, thank you," Mary-Alice replied. "My hosts have been terribly gracious. Why, only this morning, Logan took me out to see his pigeon loft. I had no idea that pigeon-racing was so popular around the world."

"Well, I'm glad to see you've survived another night," he said, dubiously. "I must be honest with you, Mrs. Arceneaux. It's no coincidence that my morning constitutional took me by the Kilmer House this morning. I came by to assure myself that you are safe and in good health."

"That's ever so thoughtful of you Mr. Peck."

"Mrs. Arceneaux, I do not wish to disturb you further, but if a walk down Saxton Lane sounds agreeable to you, I would be honored to have your company."

So Mary-Alice had her morning walk after all, and in pleasant company. As she let herself back into the house, Lucetta was suddenly in front of her. Her hair and makeup were carefully done, and she looked more like her late mother than ever.

"What did Mr. Peck want here?" Lucetta demanded.

"Why, he was simply out for a walk," Mary-Alice replied, more or less truthfully. She did not see any reason to add, "He wanted to make sure I was safe after spending the night locked in my room in your creepy scream-filled house." Instead she said, "He saw that I was enjoying the morning air as well, and invited me to join him."

"Simply out for a stroll," Lucetta repeated. "That man doesn't do anything without an ulterior motive. And the fact that he's sneaking around and spying, today in particular..."

"Well I'd hardly call it spying," Mary-Alice objected.

"What a pleasure it must be, Mrs. Arceneaux, to go through life armed with such blinding naiveté. Excuse me please."

Lucetta pushed past Mary-Alice and went a short way down

the road to Mother Sophie's, where the old woman was outside tending to her herb garden.

Mary-Alice stood and watched Lucetta remonstrate with the old woman, follow her into her cottage, and come out again in a state of sullen displeasure. She came storming back to Mary-Alice, her mood even worse than before.

"Mrs. Arceneaux," Lucetta said when she reached the gate. "I wonder if you might do me a favor. Mother Sophie is in one of her stubborn fits today, and won't give me a hearing. She may not be so deaf to you, as you are much closer to her in age than I. Will you go with me and speak to her? It would be a great help to me, and I can assure you, the old lady is harmless."

Mary-Alice was stunned by Lucetta's rudeness, but composed herself and followed the young woman over to Mother Sophie's cottage.

Mother Sophie's abode was surprisingly neat, and a contrast to the old woman's chaotic appearance. The walls were white-washed plaster, and the floor and fireplace were brick. In this tidy room, Mother Sophie sat before the unlit fireplace with her back to the door, swaddled as before in a threadbare down jacket, at least three scarves, and her shapeless lavender hat.

"Please ask her," Lucetta pleaded, "if she will come to the house before sunset. Janice has some housework for her to do. She will pay generously. Here, show her this."

Mary-Alice took the hundred-dollar bill that Lucetta had handed her and took the chair next to Mother Sophie's. The older woman turned her face away.

"Seventy," Mother Sophie muttered.

"One hundred," Mary-Alice held out the bill that Lucetta had handed her. "This is yours if you will do some work at the Kilmer house to-night."

Slowly she shook her head and then pulled her hat down over her ears.

"Go away," the old woman muttered. "Go away!"

Mary-Alice turned back to Lucetta.

"What kind of work is it?" Mary-Alice asked.

“Cleaning. More than Hannah can handle. It’s difficult to get a proper cleaning service all the way out here, and we believe in spending our money in the community when we can.”

“I see,” Mary-Alice said, although she could see no reason why three able-bodied, middle-aged adults couldn’t clean up after themselves. Mary-Alice could not deny that Althea’s children were spoiled. And as much as Mary-Alice hated to admit it, Althea herself had been rather spoiled in her day. Perhaps it was not entirely accidental that they had drifted apart.

Mary-Alice folded the rejected hundred-dollar bill and stood up.

“Miss Lucetta would genuinely appreciate your help,” she said to the old woman’s back.

“Just be there tonight,” Lucetta snapped, and then added, more gently, “please, Mother Sophie. If you have any memories at all, you must know…please.”

Mother Sophie’s gnarled hand shot out and snatched the bill from Mary-Alice.

“Before sunset,” Lucetta repeated. "Don’t forget.”

# CHAPTER 13

Mary-Alice went up to her room to dress for dinner that evening, and was surprised to find a tray on her dresser with a sticky note that read: "There will be no formal dinner tonight. I pray that you will excuse our lapse of hospitality and that this meal will be to your satisfaction."

Mary-Alice lifted the cover to find a plate of cold cuts, a loaf of sliced French bread, a ramekin of butter, and a small plate of sugar cookies. She unscrewed the Thermos and sniffed; it was full of good, strong iced tea.

She was tempted, but something told her not to consume anything from the tray. Maybe she was being silly, she told herself, but better that than take a risk. Whoever had locked her in her room (assuming she hadn't dreamed it) would have no compunctions about slipping her a sedative. She made a meal of an emergency protein bar she had tucked away in her overnight bag. Then she took her handbag and her cell phone—useless, except for its flashlight function—and slipped into the room next door.

This room was similar to the one Mary-Alice had been quartered in, except the door could be locked from the inside. There was no bed, only a single rocking chair. From the window she could see was the road, and behind that a belt of forest illumined by a gibbous moon.

She sat in the rocking chair and read to stay awake. It was several hours before Mary-Alice heard anything, but there it was; footsteps coming down the hallway, the turning of a key in the lock next door-her room!—and steps retreating.

Mary-Alice waited, then ventured back out into the hallway. She tried the door of her room, but as she suspected, it had been locked.

So far, so good; they thought she was locked in her room. Mary-Alice felt a pang of hunger, but was glad she hadn't consumed anything from the dinner tray.

She crept down the narrow hallway until she was just short of the landing. She flattened herself against the wall and listened.

From the adjoining hallway, Mary-Alice heard footsteps approaching. Then she saw them: The two sisters, their brother Logan, the maid Hannah, and Mother Sophie were carrying a long wooden box, just as if they were pallbearers. The procession halted at the top of the stairs, and Mary-Alice heard a murmur as the party appeared to discuss the best way to transport their burden to the floor below.

Mary-Alice held her breath until she saw them proceed downstairs. When they were out of sight, she darted back down the other hallway, retracing their steps, to find one door ajar—the room that stood above the Flower Parlor. The one that had the black crepe tied to the window.

A glance up and down the hallway assured Mary-Alice that she was alone and unobserved. She slipped into the room and waited for her eyes to adjust.

The room had a sickly-sweet smell. In the center was a device that looked like a hospital bed. It had been stripped; only the white plastic-covered mattress remained on the chrome frame. A simple side table held an open Bible and a pink disposable bedpan, the latter containing a soapy sponge and a balled-up paper towel.

Mary-Alice had not brought her reading glasses, and couldn't read the Bible's small print in the moonlight. She plucked a bright-red hair from her head (fortunately she'd had her roots redone before her trip) and laid it in the gutter between the open pages.

Mary-Alice scanned the floor for the trap door she'd found the previous day. She found the outline of the door next to the wall. A drawer pull, screwed into the floor, served as a handle. Mary-Alice pulled the door up, and there were the spiral stairs, concealed inside the closet of the Flower Parlor below.

She eased herself onto the stairs. The metal swayed disconcertingly, but the staircase held. She made her way to the floor below and cracked the door open.

The Flower Parlor was empty and dark.

Mary-Alice heard a scraping sound and a hubbub of voices. She slipped out into the hallway and followed the sound to the kitchen.

She peeked in just in time to see Logan and Hannah easing the trap door shut. The long wooden box they had been carrying earlier was nowhere to be seen. Everyone looked grim, and Lucetta's face was streaked with tears.

Mary-Alice quickly withdrew. She skipped the secret stairway and ran right up the main staircase. Her room was still locked, so she let herself into the adjoining room, pulled the door shut behind her, locked it, and planted herself in the chair.

She dozed off eventually, and woke to see that the sky had lightened to pearl gray. She tiptoed out to the hallway and tried the door of her room.

It was unlocked now, and she was able to let herself in.

# CHAPTER 14

Mary-Alice dressed and descended to the dining room, only to find it empty. So she went outside, making sure the front door was unlocked so that she could let herself back in. She had brought her phone, and was prepared to take a picture of the knot of black fabric in the upstairs window.

It was gone.

NOW WOULD BE a good time to go into town, call the police, and contact whoever was in Room No. 3 at the hotel.

But she needed someone to drive her. She hurried down the road in the direction of Mr. Peck's place and knocked on the door of his neat cottage, but there was no answer. With a sigh, she turned back toward the Kilmer mansion.

When she came back inside, the three siblings were in the dining room, drinking coffee.

"Well, good morning," Mary-Alice said cheerily, trying to sound as if she hadn't witnessed them dumping a body the night before after one of them tried to lock her in her room.

"Oh, Mrs. Arceneaux," Lucetta sipped her coffee and smiled. "Did you sleep well?"

"Like the dead…" Mary-Alice started, and then gulped. "I slept quite soundly, thank you for asking."

"I'll be glad to fix you some breakfast." Janice stood and pushed her chair back.

Where was Hannah? Mary-Alice wondered.

"Oh, I'm not hungry in the least," Mary-Alice said, truthfully. "I do wonder if I might catch a ride into town, though."

"Logan can drive you down," Janice said. "He has to go in for a job interview anyway. Right, Logan?"

The ride down to the village was quiet and sullen. Mary-Alice was glad she couldn't read Logan's thoughts.

"I'd love to have a look at that little knitting shop," Mary-Alice suggested as they neared the downtown.

"They've been closed for almost a year," Logan said.

"Oh. In that case, perhaps the hotel. I'd love to see that Mrs. Van Buren again. She's terribly nice."

"Whatever," Logan grumbled, and pulled up short in front of the hotel. "I'll be back in an hour."

Mary-Alice found the hotel desk unoccupied. Instead of ringing for Mrs. Van Buren, she headed straight back to the guest rooms, and quickly found Room 3.

She knocked on the door and waited. She was about to give up, when the door creaked open. She was not sure what she had expected to see, but it certainly wasn't this.

"Sheriff Lee!"

# CHAPTER 15

Sheriff Lee invited Mary-Alice to come in. Mary-Alice hesitated, but saw that the room was a suite, with the sleeping area separate. At least she wouldn't be alone with Sheriff Lee in a room that contained a bed.

The desk was piled with files and papers. A half-empty bottle of Early Times served as a paperweight.

"Sheriff Lee," Mary-Alice said excitedly, "I believe I know what's behind these young men disappearing. And as much as I hate to say it, but I believe my friend Althea's children are behind this foul plot. You see—"

"Now, hold your horses there, Miss Mary-Alice," Lee eased himself into a chair, and indicated to Mary-Alice that she should do the same. "You should know that we've found something pretty definitive. And it's outside the Kilmer house, not inside. It seems our culprit is Mother Sophie."

Mary-Alice was taken aback at his confidence.

"Are you certain?" she faltered. She would be relieved to know that the Kilmer children were off the hook, but after what she had witnessed...

"Some new evidence has come to light," Sheriff Lee said. "Would you like to hear what we've found?"

"IT SEEMS that Mother Sophie's cabin contains evidence that implicates her in these crimes. Believe me, I was as surprised as you look now. Would you like to know the details?"

"Sheriff, I am in a state of the liveliest curiosity. Of course I want to hear the details."

"Well, you know how she repeats these numbers to herself, and they seem to mean something to her. I thought it might be some kind of code. So I had the men searched the bricks inside the house—seventy up, twenty eight across, and so forth. We found nothing. But then I had the idea to look at the garden. Have you seen Mother Sophie's garden?"

"Why, yes I have, Sheriff. She appears to take great pride in it."

"Well, we thought that maybe the numbers had something to do with the plants. And you'll never guess, Miss Mary-Alice. When we reached the twenty-eighth clump of pennyroyal counting from her front gate, we dug underneath it and found this."

Lee pulled open the desk drawer and produced a plastic evidence bag. It contained a silver ring with a yin/yang symbol in onyx and mother-of-pearl.

"This ring has been identified as belonging to the backpacker who was one of the victims in whose fate we are interested."

"Oh dear," Mary-Alice exclaimed. "Was there anything else?"

"Yes. Underneath the seventieth plant was a single diamond cuff link. It had been the property of the real estate speculator who had disappeared shortly after he was seen walking in the direction of Saxton Lane."

"But Sheriff Lee, are you saying that this elderly woman is

responsible for these murders? That she, on her own, is powerful enough to murder these healthy young men, and clever enough to hide their bodies? And what, do you suppose, is her motive?"

"There you have me, Miss Mary-Alice. We have not been able as yet to unearth any bodies. Have you?"

"Not exactly." Mary-Alice ignored Lee's defensive tone. "But I believe I can show you where you might unearth one."

"Then you were not locked up in your room last night?"

Mary-Alice gazed at the sheriff, wondering how much she should tell him.

"I was not," she said. "Although I must say that's a fascinating question for you to ask me. May I ask where you were?"

"It was no human being whom you saw buried last night, Miss Mary-Alice. Did you know that Mister Logan, before he invested in pigeons, had sunk a good deal of the family fortune into raising ostriches?"

"Ostriches!" Mary-Alice exclaimed.

"He expected that ostrich eggs would be much in demand, as a single egg can make an omelet large enough to satisfy a party of twelve. Unfortunately, the costs of production were higher than he had anticipated, and the demand for the product far lower. Moreover, there were some issues with permitting and the like, so when the last survivor of Mister Logan's ill-fated investment at last went to meet her maker, the family decided to dispose of her discreetly."

"Ostriches!" Mary-Alice exclaimed. "Where on earth was he keeping ostriches?"

"It was a little enclosure out on the forested part of their property. You wouldn't have run across it unless you knew where to look."

"Sheriff Lee," Mary-Alice pleaded, "with all due respect, the secrecy, the sadness—this could only be a human being who was laid away in this manner."

"Miss Mary-Alice, it is quite possible to mourn the loss of a non-human companion. And extremely likely that a family would lament the loss of a substantial investment."

Mary-Alice pondered this. And then she said,

"But what about the open Bible in the room above the flower parlor? And Lucetta was absolutely distraught. I can't believe that display of grief was about an ostrich. And, Sheriff, what about the knot of black crepe?"

"What knot of black crepe would this be?"

"Well, the other day...Sheriff, how is it that you know so much about what happened in that house last night? Did Mother Sophie tell you? How on earth were you successful in getting her to talk to you?"

"I have not succeeded in getting Mother Sophie to talk any better than you have. However."

Lee lifted a towel from the back of the chair, threw it over his head, and, rocking himself to and fro muttered grimly:

"Seventy! Twenty-eight! Ten! No more! I can count no more! Go."

"Sheriff Lee, you posed as Mother Sophie?"

"To many folks, one older person looks much the same as another," he observed serenely. "It was I whom you interviewed in Mother Sophie's cottage, and to whom you offered one hundred dollars for helping out with an unpleasant household task. And it was I who helped bury what to you may have appeared to be a human being."

# CHAPTER 16

So it was Sheriff Lee whom Mary-Alice had seen. Bundled up with shawls, stooped over, and with his face contorted with the emotion of a conversation only he could hear, he had convinced both Lucetta and Mary-Alice that he was Mother Sophie.

"But then where was Mother Sophie this whole time?" Mary-Alice asked.

"It wasn't hard to convince Mother Sophie to change places with me." Lee poured himself a glass of bourbon and offered one to Mary-Alice. She declined.

"I promised her I'd tend to her garden and watch out for the return of her son John," he continued. "She spent the night and much of this morning here at the hotel as my guest. In a different room, of course. She's now safely home, and I don't believe she has any idea we've been digging in her garden."

"And how did you know something was happening that night at the Kilmer House?"

"Well now, it seems young Logan told Mr. Peck that something was up, and Mr. Peck in turn informed me. Quite a talker, our young Logan."

"So it was you that Mr. Peck was meeting here. And what did you find, Sheriff?"

"It seems that Lucetta has hired Mother Sophie for odd jobs before. It's also clear to me that the young lady doesn't take much notice of Mother Sophie. Not only did she accept me as a substitute for her neighbor, but she talked openly to Hannah about me. 'There is no use trying to explain anything to her. Show her when the time comes what there is to do and trust that she will forget it before she leaves the house.' Just as clear as you please, and I heard every word of it."

"And how did you know that I had been locked in my room?"

"Simple enough," Lee chuckled. "I overheard the older sister say,

'I locked her in, Lucetta. But I'm not sure it was necessary.'"

"So how did you come to be a pallbearer?" Mary-Alice persisted.

"Hannah brought me up when they were already moving the box. It was she who told me what was inside."

"Well, Sheriff Lee, I must congratulate you on a well-executed deception."

"Thank you, Miss Mary-Alice. Now, what's all this about crepe?"

Mary-Alice told him all that she had seen, and what it might mean. Certainly some of her suspicions seemed far-fetched. But then, more far-fetched than the secret midnight burial...of an ostrich?

"Now, hanging crepe is an old-fashioned custom," Mary-Alice said. "I'm sure many younger people have never heard of it. But Lucetta is an old-fashioned young lady. And it was she who seemed the most emotional at the ceremony, or whatever you'd care to call it. I think it was Lucetta who took pity on the poor young man they murdered."

"You've certainly given me something to think about," Lee

mused. "I do recall that Miss Lucetta seemed terribly torn up about what I thought was merely an overgrown turkey."

"And she warned her young man away," Mary-Alice added.

"What young man was this?"

Mary-Alice told Sheriff Lee about the scene between Lucetta and her disappointed suitor.

"So she told him to wait about a week," Lee said. "Enough time to dispose of the body. Well, now, whose body could it have been?"

"Why, Silly Rufus, of course," Mary-Alice said. "The most recent young man to go missing."

Sheriff Lee shook his head.

"That young man was described as weighing around two hundred and fifty pounds. The box weighed barely a hundred, including the wood it was made from."

"It's someone new, then," Mary-Alice said. "Even a child, perhaps! Has any young child been reported missing?"

"Miss Mary-Alice, at any time there are over twenty thousand missing children in the state of New York. But then how do you explain the evidence found at Mother Sophie's?"

"As much as it pains me to say this, Sheriff Lee, if the Kilmers are accustomed to hiring Mother Sophie to do odd jobs for them, it's quite possible they paid her in trinkets, rather than money, thinking she wouldn't know the difference. And what better way to get evidence out of the house?"

Sheriff Lee nodded.

"I believe it's time for me to pay a visit to the Kilmer house. Very frustrating that I still am not able to get a warrant to search the premises, although I've already gotten permission to dig up Mother Sophie's entire lot."

"What about what you witnessed?" Mary-Alice asked. "The burial? Surely that would be enough to convince any judge."

Sheriff Lee chuckled.

"My masquerading as Mother Sophie was an independent

and entirely unauthorized action on my part. I believe it would do far more harm than good to let anyone know about it. In fact, Miss Mary-Alice, I hope I may rely upon your discretion in this matter."

"You certainly may," Mary-Alice said firmly.

"Now, when I come to the house today, I think it's best if you are sure you're occupied elsewhere. I don't want to pretend I don't know you, nor do I wish to bring up any uncomfortable questions about the remarkable coincidence of two folks from the bayous showing up in Black Valley at the same time."

Mary-Alice was disappointed that she'd have to miss out on Sheriff Lee's questioning, but thrilled to be in his confidence.

"I can certainly make myself scarce," Mary-Alice declared. "But if there's anything else you'd like me to look into, I'm happy to help. You only have to say the word, Sheriff."

Mary-Alice left Room 3, and as she passed the counter, was hailed by Mrs. Van Buren. She stopped and accepted a cup of Mrs. Van Buren's instant coffee, grateful that this would give her an alibi in case anyone wondered why she had spent so much time inside the hotel. As usual, Mary-Alice listened more than she spoke, a habit that made others think her a brilliant conversationalist, and in addition allowed her to collect all kinds of interesting information. Today, Mrs. Van Buren tried out various theories on Mary-Alice about the recent disappearances. Mrs. Van Buren herself did not believe that it was necessary for the police to "make such a big deal" about the disappearances, and was careful to add that she was not expressing this opinion out of self-interest, although the latest surge of law-enforcement activity certainly wasn't helping to attract tourists, that was for sure.

"This has been the worst summer I can remember," Mrs. Van Buren fumed. "I was so happy we had a guest yesterday, and it turned out to be some sheriff who's probably going to dig the whole town up looking for bodies, and pay government rate to boot. Honestly, Mrs. Arceneaux, I can't imagine that our little community is harboring a serial killer. I believe they'll find that there's a perfectly reasonable explanation behind these disappearances."

"And what might that be?" Mary-Alice asked, genuinely interested.

"Well, it's not the Kilmer kids, and I don't care what everyone else thinks about it. I mean, no one suspects Janice, but those twins! Lucetta's ghoulish, and Logan seems like he sold his soul somewhere along the way, and got the bad end of the deal as he always does. I mean, no wonder people think they're up to no good. But now you're staying with them, right in their house, and if there was anything creepy going on in there, why, you'd have noticed something strange, right?"

"I suppose you're talking about hidden passages, secret midnight burials, things like that," Mary-Alice said with a forced smile.

"Exactly," Mrs. Van Buren laughed. "Now, if it isn't the Kilmer children, then I think the next most-likely thing is animals."

"Animals?" Mary-Alice repeated.

"Yes. We have black bears, coyotes, and bobcats here. You're not from around here, Mrs. Arceneaux, so I can hardly blame you for having no idea what it's like to live among dangerous wild creatures."

"We have alligators in the bayous," Mary-Alice pointed out.

"Yes, but alligators have been unfairly portrayed as killing machines. The fact is, they won't bother you unless you bother them."

"Is that so?"

"I just saw a documentary about alligators."

"Well, around ten years ago a gator ate my husband while he was taking a nap outdoors," Mary-Alice said. "But I believe that was an unusual case."

# CHAPTER 17

Logan arrived on schedule to take Mary-Alice from the hotel back to the house, where he promptly left her to her own devices. This was fine with Mary-Alice. Sheriff Lee had instructed her not to interfere with his visit to the house, but he had said nothing about continuing to investigate on her own.

Mary-Alice had her reading glasses, and the advantage of daylight. It was time to go back to the room above the Flower Parlor.

A trace of the sickly-sweet odor lingered, but the hospital bed was gone. Mary-Alice found the Bible in the night table drawer.

She put on her reading glasses, found the gleam of red hair that now served as a bookmark, and opened the pages to 1 Corinthians 15.

*For the trumpet shall sound, and the dead shall be raised incorruptible, and we shall be changed.*

"A funeral reading." Mary-Alice closed the Bible gently, replaced it in the drawer, and hurried back to her room.

Mary-Alice had made her peace with being stuck in her room until Sheriff Lee could finish his inquiries. She was surprised, then, to have her reading interrupted by a knock on the door. She was even more surprised to see Janice standing there.

"Mrs. Arceneaux," Janice said, "Would you mind coming downstairs? We have some visitors and Lucetta's being a little bit of a basket case about it. I think you'd be a calming influence on her."

"Me?" Mary-Alice exclaimed. "I don't understand."

"It's Mr. Peck," Janice sighed.

"Mr. Peck is here?"

"He's coming down the walkway right now. The sight of him sets Lucetta off."

"She doesn't seem to care for him, I notice."

"It's a long story, Mrs. Arceneaux."

As Mary-Alice collected her handbag and started to pull the door shut, Janice added,

"He has someone with him. An older gentleman."

So Mr. Peck was with Sheriff Lee. Who had specifically instructed her to stay out of his inquiry.

"Ah. Are you quite sure you want me to come down?"

"Please, Mrs. Arceneaux. If you wouldn't mind. Lucetta hasn't been doing well lately. She misses our mom, I mean we all do, but she seems to think of you as sort of a connection to her. I hope you don't think that's weird or anything."

"Not at all." Mary-Alice followed her down the broad, creaking stairs. "I still miss my mother, at my age."

"Aw, I'm sorry to hear that," Janice said. "When did she pass?"

"Oh, she's still alive. But she moved to Hawaii. It's terribly far."

Janice reached the door ahead of Mary-Alice, and opened it to Mr. Peck and Sheriff Lee.

"Miss Kilmer, a thousand pardons," Mr. Peck said. "I've come to introduce Sheriff Robert E. Lee, who has been called to help with the investigation of the tragic disappearances in our town."

"Good afternoon, ladies." Sheriff Lee did not acknowledge Mary-Alice, nor did she acknowledge him. "I am here to assist with the investigation of the disappearances that have made this town notorious. To that end, I will need to make an official search of these premises as I already have those of Mother Sophie and of Deacon Spear."

"And my house will be investigated as well," Mr. Peck added eagerly.

"Sheriff Lee." Janice sounded unimpressed. "You got a warrant?"

Sheriff Lee pulled out a piece of paper and showed it to Janice. So he had managed to get his warrant after all.

"There's no reason not to cooperate, Miss Kilmer," Mr. Peck pleaded. "None of us has anything to hide."

"Fine," said Janice. "Mr. Peck is right. We have nothing to hide from law enforcement. You might as well come in, Sheriff."

Sheriff Lee gave a signal, and seemingly from nowhere, uniformed police officers streamed onto the property and fanned out around the mansion. Even Mr. Peck seemed surprised at their sudden appearance.

"Let's start with the cellar, shall we?" Sheriff Lee announced as he strode through the front door. Mr. Peck, realizing he was no longer needed, took his leave as two uniformed troopers followed Sheriff Lee inside.

Janice followed the men to the kitchen, and Mary-Alice followed Janice. Lucetta was already there, standing with her back to the refrigerator and hugging herself. At the sight of Sheriff Lee and his entourage, her eyes widened, and Mary-Alice was afraid she would once again burst into tears. But she did not.

"Do they have to go into the cellar?" Lucetta asked weakly.

"I'm afraid so, Miss Kilmer," Sheriff Lee replied kindly. "But never fear, we are interested only in the disappearances that have occurred in your fair town."

"I want to go too," Lucetta declared abruptly. "Into the cellar."

"Lucetta..." Janice shook her head at her younger sister.

"Help yourself," Lee said jovially as his two men lifted the cellar opening. "Long as you stay back and don't get in the way."

"Fine," Janice sighed. "I'll come too. Mary-Alice, you don't have to come down there if you don't want to."

"No, it would be my pleasure," Mary-Alice said quickly. She would have perished of curiosity had she been left out.

As one of the troopers held up the section of kitchen floor that served as a cellar door, the rest of them descended the steps. A low-wattage light bulb illuminated the space. The floor was dirt, and the ceiling was dusty wood festooned with cobwebs. Along the walls Mary-Alice saw stacks of canned food, mildewed books, and cardboard boxes bound with packing tape.

Sheriff Lee shone his flashlight around the packed-earth floor. Despite the season, the cellar was chilly and damp. Mary-Alice wished she had brought a sweater.

Lee abruptly signaled the man closest to him.

"Dig here," he commanded. The man produced a shovel, braced his foot on the blade, and started to dig.

Janice heaved a sigh and shook her head.

Lucetta ran forward and flung herself onto the ground.

"Stop it," she sobbed. "Stop it! This is a grave."

"Is that so?" Sheriff Lee signaled for the man to stop digging. "And whose grave might this be?"

Janice stepped forward."

"Our mother's," she said.

# CHAPTER 18

"Your mother's grave?" Mr. Lee looked from Lucetta to Janice with skepticism. "I was informed that your mother died seven or more years ago, and this grave has been dug quite recently."

"She has been dead for many years," Lucetta whispered. "But it was only the night before last that she closed her eyes for the last time."

"She was suffering from advanced dementia," Janice explained. "We said our goodbyes long ago."

"This is highly irregular," Sheriff Lee said. "You understand that we must investigate."

Lucetta picked herself up from the ground and dusted dirt crumbs from her dress. Once again, her face was streaked with tears.

"Come on, Lucetta." Janice placed her arm around her sister's shoulders and gently guided her back toward the steps. "You don't need to see this."

The other police officer came forward and joined the first one in digging. Mary-Alice stood next to Sheriff Lee.

"If this is Althea Kilmer," Sheriff Lee said to Mary Alice, "you'd be able to tell me."

Mary-Alice did her best to keep her composure as the horror of what Sheriff Lee was asking of her sank in.

"Well, it's been a long time," Mary-Alice said. "But I'll do my best."

"This is not going to be pleasant, Miss Mary-Alice."

"I understand."

Finally, the men hauled up the wooden box. They pried open the lid, then stood back.

"Take your time," Sheriff Lee instructed Mary-Alice.

Mary-Alice took a few breaths, and then gazed at the woman in the coffin as Sheriff Lee shined a light on her face.

"It is Althea Kilmer," she said, finally. "Of course Althea isn't there any more, if you get my meaning. What are you going to do?"

"Well, I suppose it'll have to be part of our report," Sheriff Lee said. "But for now, let's put things back as we found them."

"Are you sure, sir?" One of the policemen asked.

"Yes, for the time being," Sheriff Lee said. "Don't worry. We've got plenty of digging to do yet, boys."

Mary-Alice went to seek out Lucetta and Janice. As the shock of coming face to face with Althea Kilmer subsided, she found that she was full of questions, and not a little indignant. Her childhood friend had been alive, in the house where she was staying, and Althea's very existence had been kept secret from her.

Mary-Alice found Janice and Lucetta side by side on the faded velvet couch in the sitting room. Lucetta's face shone with tears, and even Janice's eyes were red-rimmed.

Mary-Alice came in and sat quietly on a chair.

"I suppose you want an explanation." Janice took her arm from around her sister's shoulder.

"I certainly don't want to make this time any more difficult than it needs to be," Mary-Alice said. "But I must say, this is all rather...surprising. I'm not sure I know what to make of it."

Mary-Alice would have liked to say goodbye to her friend, even if Althea could not recognize her. But there was no point in telling Lucetta and Janice this. It was too late to do anything about it now."

"Look, I'm sorry, Mrs. Arceneaux," Janice said. "You weren't supposed to see any of this. No one was. The thing is, we had a good reason for doing what we did."

"Well, I'm sure you did." Mary-Alice could not for the life of her imagine what that reason might be.

Janice glanced at her sister, who was staring glumly at her folded hands.

"Mrs. Arceneaux," Janice said, "Our mother, as charming and sweet as she could be, was not quite herself toward the end. And I'm afraid she made a bad decision. She succumbed to temptation and used someone else's credit. Of course, when it came out we wanted to pay the money back, but this was after Logan had lost everything in that pyramid scheme, our father was gone, and the victim was not exactly forgiving."

"He's no victim," Lucetta blurted out. "He's a viper! He wanted to see our mother in prison!"

"So she left the country," Mary-Alice said, softly. "Which made her a fugitive."

"And then she fell ill," Janice said. "Her decline was quick. We decided to announce her death—it was more of an exaggeration than an outright lie, when you think about it—and bring her home. Hannah was her hospice nurse."

"I wondered why you employed a maid when you were having financial troubles," Mary-Alice said.

"We had to have some explanation for her being here, so we paid her a little extra," Janice explained.

"To act as the cook and the maid, with a generous severance bonus when it was all over," Lucetta added.

"Where is Hannah now?" Mary-Alice asked.

"Gone," Lucetta said bitterly. "She didn't stay a moment

longer than she absolutely needed to."

"Lucetta, she wanted to be with her own family," Janice said gently. "You can't blame her for that. Mrs. Arceneaux, you won't tell anyone, will you?"

"Why, of course not," Mary-Alice said. "But do you think such measures were absolutely necessary? Surely if you intended to repay, and your mother was ill, there would be some mercy—"

"Not in this case," Lucetta said coldly. "When he heard she'd left the country, he swore that if she ever set foot in Black Valley again, he'd call the police on her. We've lived in fear of discovery for years, Mrs. Arceneaux. But at least we were with her when she passed on. And she was at home, not in prison."

"I suppose I'm beginning to understand," Mary-Alice said. "So I imagine my note to you, announcing my visit was not a cause of celebration, precisely."

"Now you understand why we placed you in the far guest room," Janice said.

"And locked me in?" Mary-Alice asked. "Heavens, I hate to think what might have happened had there been a fire."

Lucetta clapped her hand to her mouth.

"Mrs. Arceneaux, I'm so sorry. It didn't even occur to me. I see now that we should have taken you into our confidence."

"Yes," Mary-Alice agreed, "I believe it would have been better to do so."

"Of course Logan's been no help at all," Janice said bitterly. "We could've paid off the debt years ago if it weren't for his harebrained business plans. Who eats ostrich eggs?"

"Perhaps the pigeons will pay off," Mary-Alice suggested.

"Are you suggesting that one of Logan's harebrained schemes might succeed?" Lucetta said acidly. "Why Mrs. Arceneaux, how kind of you to provide some comic relief for us in this sorrowful moment."

"Yeah, we're not holding our breath," Janice added.

# CHAPTER 19

Mary-Alice thought she might sleep well that night. She did not, partly because the mystery of the disappearing young men was no closer to being solved, and partly because her childhood friend, who had until only recently been alive in this very house, was buried in a box in the cellar.

But despite an uneasy night, she woke up at her usual early time the next morning. She still thought it highly unlikely that the addled Mother Sophie could be the mastermind behind the disappearance of several healthy young men. But the victims' effects had been found buried in her garden, and Sheriff Lee was not inclined to ignore that evidence.

She decided a stroll would help her to clear her mind. And although Sheriff Lee might not approve, she would go out alone.

Mary-Alice was passing by Mr. Peck's house when she saw him out in his orchard. She waved at him, and he hurried out to the road.

"Mrs. Arceneaux, what a delightful surprise. Nothing came of the investigations made by Mr. Lee yesterday, I assume?"

Mary-Alice perceived that he was fishing for information.

She could hardly blame him, as she would have done the same in his place.

"It was a singularly unproductive investigation," Mary-Alice said. "But on a happier topic, I noticed you were checking your trees. Is there any news?"

Mr. Peck looked thoughtful.

"I have a particular white peach that I've reserved for you, Mrs. Arceneaux. When it's ready I'll bring it up straightaway. I guarantee, you've never tasted a finer piece of fruit.

"Why, that's awfully kind of you, Mr. Peck. I'm sure I can't wait."

"I only hope the birds show more mercy to my peaches than they did to my cherries."

As Mary-Alice continued on her morning walk, she turned her mind to the disappearances. Perhaps Mrs. Van Buren's theory was correct, and the unfortunate travelers had been eaten by bears and bobcats. That theory seemed at least as likely as anything else she could think of. Mother Sophie had the victims' property buried in her garden, but she could have found that ring and cuff link—or someone could have given them to her.

And the men seemed to have nothing in common, except for the fact that they had all passed through Black Valley. What possible motive would account for someone murdering all of them?

After a good hour of strolling and thinking, Mary-Alice's knees were starting to ache, and she was no closer to a solution. When she arrived back at the Kilmer house, Lucetta greeted her from the front porch.

"I am glad to see you looking so bright this morning," Lucetta declared. "I saw you chatting with our neighbor, Mr. Peck. I would not like to think you told him about the events of yesterday."

"Certainly not," Mary-Alice replied. "I told him that nothing of interest had taken place, and with regard to Sheriff Lee's investigation, that's the truth. I did not believe it was my place to share your personal information."

"Thank you," Lucetta said. "No one must know about Mother. Mr. Peck especially."

And before Mary-Alice could ask why Mr. Peck especially should not know, Lucetta had disappeared into the house.

Mary-Alice followed her inside, and found her in the kitchen with Logan and Janice.

"Lucetta dear," she said, "it's hard not to notice that you don't much care for your neighbor Mr. Peck. I know it's not my place to ask, and I do apologize for my inquisitiveness, but if you were to inform me on this matter I'd be most grateful."

Lucetta and Janice exchanged a look.

"Mr. Peck is our mother's persecutor," Lucetta said.

"The identity theft business," Janice added. "Peck was the one whose credit card info Mom took."

"Mr. Peck?" Mary-Alice exclaimed. "Mr. Peck is the one who threatened to call the police if your mother set foot in the country?"

"Peck's a straight arrow," Janice sighed. "You know, rules are rules."

"That's why he's such a good farmer," Logan interjected. "He's super particular about his trees. This kind of fertilizer, this much water, this much sunlight, blah blah blah, but then he gets this awesome fruit out if it."

"If you don't mind my asking," Mary-Alice said, "how did Althea managed to defraud Mr. Peck in the first place?"

The Althea that Mary-Alice had known could not in any way be described as a financial mastermind.

"You know those credit card applications they send you in the mail?" Janice said. "Well, one that was addressed to Mr. Peck ended up in our mailbox, and I guess Mom found it and filled it out."

"But he seems to bear you no ill will," Mary-Alice said.

"That's because it wasn't us who ripped him off," Logan chimed in. "Lucetta, he just wanted his money back and his credit fixed. You can't blame him for that. And you have to admit, when he thought Mom was dead, he backed off."

The growl of an engine interrupted their conversation.

"They're digging up Mother Sophie's!" Logan exclaimed, and rushed out of the kitchen.

Mary-Alice and the two sisters followed him out. Sheriff Lee and several of the townspeople were standing around Mother Sophie's cottage. Some had spades and picks. A red-faced woman in a Day-Glo orange vest was reversing a mini backhoe onto Mother Sophie's property. Mother Sophie stood on the porch, muttering to herself and shaking her head.

Mary-Alice turned sadly and went back to the house. She knew Mother Sophie would be devastated at the sight of her garden being torn up, and she did not want to witness the old woman's anguish. She retreated to her room and out of habit, plugged in her phone. She remembered that she had taken some photos on her morning walk, and decided to go through them. They were all of green trees and blue sky, but Mary-Alice thought they were nice, and in any event they were a different kind of trees and sky than the ones she saw every day back home in Louisiana. She deleted the photos that were out of focus and spent some time admiring the ones that had turned out well.

Then she reached a photo of Logan's pigeon loft. She was about to delete it when something in the picture caught her eye.

She jumped up and ran downstairs to catch Sheriff Lee.

# CHAPTER 20

So quickly had Sheriff Lee and his officers torn up Mother Sophie's garden that they were already finishing up when Mary-Alice approached them. The yard looked like a giant rototiller had run over it. A lone pigeon strutted on the freshly-turned earth.

"Sheriff Lee," Mary-Alice cried. "Might I have a word?"

Sheriff Lee gave some instructions to a trooper and broke off to talk to Mary-Alice.

"Sheriff Lee, look at this. Come under the eaves; the sun's glare is terrible out here. Oh. By the way. Did you find anything else on Mother Sophie's property?"

"Well, now, Miss Mary-Alice, I'm not at liberty—"

"If you'd found something, everyone would be talking about it by now. There wasn't anything, was there?"

Sheriff Lee cleared his throat.

"Now Miss Mary-Alice, did you have something you wished to discuss with me?"

"Yes, I do."

She showed him the picture on the phone.

"Well now, this looks to be young Mr. Logan's pigeon loft."

"It is," Mary-Alice confirmed. "Now, I'm going to enlarge the picture. What do you see?"

"Why, it's a pigeon." Sheriff Lee squinted at Mary-Alice's phone. "And it appears to be holding something in its beak. Something blue. What is it?"

"I believe it's my missing earring," Mary-Alice said. "Logan's pigeons seem to have a taste for shiny things. And they are all over the neighborhood, including Mother Sophie's cottage. Which, I believe, might explain a few—"

At that moment Mr. Peck strode up, holding something wrapped in a clean muslin cloth.

"Oh my." He gazed sadly at the turned-up earth. "Poor Mother Sophie. I understand it couldn't be helped, Sheriff. Still, it's heartbreaking. Mrs. Arceneaux, I told you I would share one of my white peaches with you, but instead, I come to offer you my most profound apologies."

He unwrapped the cloth to reveal a lovely, ripe peach. Then he turned it over to reveal the other side. It had been pecked to mincemeat.

"Well I do thank you for thinking of me," Mary-Alice said. "It looks like a lovely piece of fruit. And I am sorry the birds got to it before me."

"Logan's pigeons," Mr. Peck said, dispiritedly. "I don't believe he feeds them as he ought, so they go foraging all over town. It's a terrible disappointment, Mrs. Arceneaux. But I shouldn't feel too sorry for myself. You should see how they're all over Deacon Spear's barn."

"Is that so," Mary-Alice said sweetly, but looking pointedly at Sheriff Lee. "Pigeons everywhere, you say. Doing as they please, and likely stealing things and depositing them all over the place."

"Well, now." Sheriff Lee removed his hat and ran his fingers through his white hair. "I surely do wish I had known about all this earlier, Miss Mary-Alice. This rather broadens the field, I'd say."

Sheriff Lee strode off toward the house, leaving Mary-Alice standing with Mr. Peck.

"So I believe I've discovered the source of Lucetta's bad feelings toward you, Mr. Peck."

"I cannot speak for Miss Kilmer, Mrs. Arceneaux."

"That's admirable, Mr. Peck. I can only assume that your silence on this topic is due to your reluctance to speak ill of the late Althea Kilmer."

He let out a relieved sigh.

"So you know."

"Yes, I do. My old friend Althea succumbed to temptation and defrauded you. It broke my heart to hear it, but it did clear up some questions I had."

"Mrs. Arceneaux, I was only trying to get recompense for my losses. I'm a fair man. And you can see that I don't blame the Kilmer children for the actions of their mother."

"Do you know, I don't believe that peach is entirely ruined," Mary-Alice said. "I can take it back to the house and cut off the bad part."

"I wouldn't expect you to do that." Mr. Peck smiled as he wrapped the peach back up. "I only brought this as evidence of my good intentions. Never fear. There's another set to be at its peak in two to three days. I hope you'll still be here in town, Mrs. Arceneaux?"

# CHAPTER 21

That evening at around nine o'clock, Mary-Alice noticed that she was hungry, and went downstairs to the kitchen to forage for a snack.

She found Janice there, drinking white wine from a tumbler, and squinting at what Mary-Alice recognized as a cash flow statement.

Janice removed her reading glasses and looked up as Mary-Alice entered.

"Oh, hey, Mrs. Arceneaux. Sorry, I guess we don't have a meal schedule now that Hannah's gone. Although I gotta say, not paying her's gonna save the trust a bundle. Help yourself to whatever we have."

Mary-Alice found a nectarine in the produce drawer, rinsed it off, and sat down at the table with Janice.

"Gracious," she exclaimed as she took a bite. "This is delicious."

"Yeah, that's one of Peck's."

"Well, isn't that nice of him to share. Where are Lucetta and Logan?" Mary-Alice asked.

"Probably already in bed," Janice said. "We're exciting like that. Oh, no, wait. Logan said he was going over to Mr. Peck's tonight."

"This late?" Mary-Alice asked.

Janice shrugged. "I think Peck said he had some new white peaches come in and he wanted Logan to come over and try them."

"Well I'm sure they're delicious, if they're anything like this nectarine." Mary-Alice finished the fruit, dabbed her mouth, wrapped the stone in her napkin, and threw it away.

"Wait a minute," Mary-Alice said. "Are you sure he said white peaches?"

"I think?" Janice was already absorbed in her financial paperwork again.

"Because Mr. Peck told me he had one that was ready, but it had been ruined. May I use your phone for a moment?"

"It's not connected. You might be able to call 9-1-1."

"That'll do."

Janice stared at Mary-Alice as she spoke with the dispatcher.

"Do you think Logan's in trouble?" Janice asked when she had hung up.

"I believe he may be," Mary-Alice said.

Mary-Alice and Janice ran down the dark road toward Mr. Peck's orchard.

A man appeared from behind a hedge, and Mary-Alice realized it was Sheriff Lee.

He held his finger to his lips, and as he approached, he whispered,

"They're back there, in the trees. Please stay back."

There was still a silvery trace of dusk, and Mary-Alice could make out the figures of Mr. Peck and Logan. She felt suddenly foolish; here she'd called in the cavalry, and for what? Two men having a conversation in an orchard. About peaches.

Janice was looking at her with a mixture of impatience and amusement.

"I'm so sorry," Mary-Alice whispered. "I was certain there was something amiss. This is all my fault. I suppose I should apologize to Sheriff Lee, and then we can—"

Suddenly Janice was gripping Mary-Alice's arm.

"Mary-Alice," she hissed. "Where is he?"

Mary-Alice looked out to the orchard to see Mr. Peck in silhouette, strolling back toward his house. Logan was nowhere to be seen.

"Sheriff Lee!" Mary-Alice cried out. Obadiah Peck stopped, looked around, and then continued his deliberate pace.

"Sheriff Lee!" Mary-Alice shouted again. "Logan's gone!"

Janice ran toward where she'd last seen her brother. Now Mr. Peck started to run too, which was the wrong thing to do. A pack of New York State Troopers appeared from the shadows and dogpiled him.

Mary-Alice and Janice searched the patchy grass underneath the trees. At length Mary-Alice felt something hard and metallic. It looked like a latch. She and Janice poked, prodded, and jostled it until they heard a "click," and a disc of turf the size of a manhole lifted in slow motion.

Mary-Alice shone her cell phone flashlight down into the hole to see Logan Kilmer slumped motionless at the bottom.

# CHAPTER 22

Gertie was waiting at Lake Charles Airport to pick up Mary-Alice and Sheriff Lee that evening. Although it was past ten when they got back into Sinful, they found Francine's Diner open and a whole crew of people waiting at a large table for them. Ida Belle, Fortune, Sheriff Carter LeBlanc, Carter's uncle Walter, and Mary-Alice's friend Boone St. Clair were sitting around a large table in the center of the dining room. Francine herself waited on them and listened eagerly as Mary-Alice and Sheriff Lee took turns relating their adventures in upstate New York.

Sheriff Lee gave everyone the background and history, and Mary-Alice described what it was like to stay in the Kilmer house. Then Sheriff Lee and Mary-Alice took turns relating the key events.

Sheriff Lee had been present at Mr. Peck's interview, so he was able cast some light on motive, which was the thing that had been puzzling Mary-Alice.

Mr. Obadiah Peck, Sheriff Lee explained, believed himself to be a fair man. It was why he had pursued the case against Althea Kilmer, but had dropped it when he believed she had died. So fair-minded was he, that when he caught young men trespassing on his property, helping themselves to his fruit, he exacted only what he considered proper recompense. And for Logan, who had allowed his pigeons to decimate and befoul Mr. Peck's crops, the penalty was the same. The fact that he had known Logan since the latter was a small boy did not make any difference to the scrupulously fair-minded Mr. Peck.

"The restitution does not accrue to me alone," Mr. Peck had explained. "When I return the nutrients to the earth, the entire ecosystem benefits. The balance is restored."

To Mr. Peck, this seemed entirely sensible and fair. And, as he quite reasonably pointed out, his trees had flourished thanks to his fertilization scheme, proving that Nature clearly took his side in the matter.

"I believe the Kilmer family owes Miss Mary-Alice a great deal," Sheriff Lee declared. "Her timely telephone call saved Logan's life. It was a matter of some urgency, you understand. Mr. Peck's compost pit was airtight. To minimize odors, he informed us."

"It was only because of the peaches," Mary-Alice said. "Mr. Peck had told me there weren't any ripe ones. It didn't make sense for him to tell Logan there were. That's when I knew something was wrong."

Mary-Alice got to bed late that night—well past nine o'clock. As she drifted off to sleep, she realized she was a lucky woman. She did not envy poor Althea Kilmer. And when she thought about it, she really had no reason to envy anyone.

# THE NO-TELL MOTEL

This story is based on a series created by Jana DeLeon. The author of this story has the contractual rights to create stories using the Miss Fortune world. Any unauthorized use of the Miss Fortune world for story creation is a violation of copyright law.



Stock art: Pixabay, Freepik, Vecteezy

# CHAPTER 1

Inside the navy-blue Victorian house two blocks off Main Street, four women sat around a sturdy kitchen table.

As you watched them chatting and sipping sweet tea, you might assume you were observing a church committee or a quilting circle.

You would be wrong.

The young blonde pouring tea was living under the identity of Fortune "Sandy-Sue" Morrow, children's librarian and retired beauty queen. Fortune was in fact in the employ of the CIA, who had placed her under cover until they could catch the arms dealer who'd put a price on her head.

The white-haired ladies cheerfully bickering with each other were longtime Sinful residents Gertie and Ida Belle. They were retired now, pillars of the community who filled their time leading the Sinful Ladies' Society. Half a century ago they had spent time in Vietnam, Gertie as a secretary, Ida Belle as a nurse's aide. They had used their positions as cover for counter-intelligence work, a fact not widely known.

Like Gertie and Ida Belle, Mary-Alice Arceneaux was on the sweet side of seventy. Unlike them, she had not gone gracefully gray. Instead, she colored her hair a vivid red that did not imitate Nature as much as surpass it.

Mary-Alice had only recently moved to Sinful. She was not aware of Fortune's CIA career, nor of Ida Belle and Gertie's spy background. She only knew she enjoyed the company of her new friends. She found them far more interesting than her old crowd back in Mudbug, and a sight more agreeable than her sole relative in town, her cranky cousin Celia.

The women were discussing what they might do with fifty thousand dollars apiece. What had spurred this conversation was a story on the local news about a two hundred thousand dollar reward for a pair of escaped convicts.

"It's one thing to poke around and get to the bottom of a local murder," Ida Belle was saying. "But I wouldn't mess with that. They say Ma Woodham killed two guards on the way out."

"You don't have to be so practical all the time, Ida Belle," Gertie chided. "Sure, I'm not gonna run out and try to catch them, but there's no reason I can't daydream about the reward. With that kind of payout, I could get an airboat like Fortune's. Then no one could stop me from driving it whenever I wanted."

"Well sure," Ida Belle came back, "as long as we're blue-skying, maybe I'll get another motorcycle. You know those big fat fancy Harleys they sell to middle-aged doctors? I mean, I'm not getting any younger. I deserve a little luxury in my old age."

"What about you, Mary-Alice?" Gertie asked.

"Oh, well, I've been so blessed I can't think of a single thing. Well, maybe I'd use a little bit to redo my dining room. I'm not so terribly fond of that shag carpet. With the humidity coming off the bayou, it's always a little damp, you see. And then I suppose I'd use the rest of it to help out folks who needed it more than I did."

"Aw, come on, Mary-Alice," Ida Belle complained. "What are you trying to do, make the rest of us feel guilty about how we spend our money? You don't have to be such a goody-two-shoes all the time."

"I'm with the goody-two-shoes faction on this," Fortune said. "I'm pretty happy with my life right now. I feel like I have everything I need."

"Of course you do," Gertie retorted. "You inherited all Marge's stuff plus you have an awesome airboat."

"Not that it wouldn't feel great to catch two fugitives," Fortune conceded. "But that's kind of a big job for Fortune Morrow, P.I."

"Why Fortune, are you going to quit your librarian job after all, and stay in Sinful when the school year begins?" Mary-Alice clasped her tiny hands with joy. "I mean to say, it's wonderful news. I know we'd all miss you terribly if you had to leave."

Fortune took a thoughtful sip of sweet tea.

"I do want to stay in Sinful. I'm starting to think I've done what good I can in my 'librarian' capacity. But it's not like there are a lot of jobs here that can use my particular skills. Private investigator seems to be the obvious choice."

"What does Carter think?" Gertie asked.

"Why should she let Carter decide what she's going to do with her life?" Ida Belle demanded. "I don't see him asking Fortune what he should do about his career."

"Why, working as a private investigator sounds perfect," Mary-Alice exclaimed. "A private investigator and a deputy sheriff. Why darlin', y'all could solve crimes together like Nick and Nora Charles!"

"That's exactly what Carter doesn't want," Fortune sighed. "He hates the idea of my being in danger, and you know how he feels about our getting involved in his investigations. I keep telling him being a P.I. is safe and boring. Mostly doing tedious stuff like background checks."

A knock on the door interrupted the conversation, and Fortune stood up.

"Were you expecting your young man?" Mary-Alice asked.

"No, but he has a way of knowing when we've been talking about him, doesn't he? Good thing I didn't give him my key."

"You were going to give him your key?" Ida Belle demanded as Fortune sailed out in the direction of the living room.

"Should we leave?" Mary-Alice asked the others.

"Leave? Of course not." Ida Belle stood up. "If Carter wants us to go, he'll let us know. Come on, let's go see what's going on."

# CHAPTER 2

The women emerged from the kitchen to find Fortune seated on the couch, talking to someone who most definitely was not Carter LeBlanc.

The young woman appeared to be in her late twenties, and unconcerned with matters of hair and makeup. She wore jeans and a clean t-shirt in an unflattering shade of yellow. Her straight brown hair was pulled back in a serviceable ponytail.

"Oh, hello. I don't know if you remember me." The young lady stood and offered a firm handshake to Ida Belle, Gertie, and Mary-Alice in turn. "I'm Ainslee MacEntire. I work at the McCully Inn, over in Lemon Tree."

"Why, I believe I do remember you," Gertie exclaimed.

"Yeah. The situation with that guy from New Orleans. With the wife. You did such a good job on that case I was hoping you could help me out."

"Well, you made a smart decision to call the Sinful Ladies' Detective Agency," Gertie declared.

"How did you find us?" Fortune asked.

"I remembered you said you were from Sinful. I called the

sheriff's department here and talked to someone named Myrtle. She knew all about you guys."

"Myrtle gave you our information over the phone?" Ida Belle exclaimed. "I think I'll have to have a chat with her."

"Oh, no, nothing like that," Ainslee assured Fortune. "She said the women I'm looking for might be here, or you might not, but if I really was serious, I'd get myself over to the General Store and talk to someone named Walter, and he'd decide whether he thought it was safe to give me your information. So I drove out here, found the General Store, talked to Walter, and I guess I made the cut, 'cause here I am."

Mary-Alice sensed from the woman's clipped speech and direct manner that she was a Yankee; aside from that, however, she seemed nice enough. And if Walter liked her, that was certainly a point in her favor.

"So how can we help you?" Fortune asked.

Ainslee fidgeted and checked her watch.

"Sorry, it took longer than I thought to drive out here, and I have to be back in time to pick up my daughter. Okay, so I'm the head housekeeper at the McCully Inn. One of our employees, who was living on-premises, disappeared from her room last night."

"Did you call the police?" Gertie asked.

"Yes, I did, right away. But it seemed like they didn't want to do anything about it. They asked me if she had dementia or Alzheimer's disease, or was she on life-saving medication, and when I told them no, she's like, twenty-two years old, they kinda tuned out. But I know she didn't leave on her own. She would've told me. And all her stuff's still there in the room."

"What does your manager say about it?" Gertie asked.

"Mr. McCully?" Ainslee shook her head. "He doesn't know, and I hope I don't have to bring him into it. He inherited the McCully Inn when his father passed away, so he's still learning the business, and dealing with his loss…I don't want to burden him. And to be honest, I kind of feel responsible. I was supposed to be the one looking out for her."

"So you lost one of your employees, and you want to get her back before the boss finds out," Ida Belle said.

Ainslee examined her folded hands.

"I guess you could put it that way. Her clothes and jewelry are still there. Her window was open. And a chair was on its side like it had been kicked over. I'm really worried about her. Do you think you can come out today?"

"We haven't said we'll take your case," Fortune pointed out.

"Please? I can't pay a whole lot, but I have a little bit saved up. Her name's Solange Smith. She was...is... twenty-two or twenty-three, I think. Black hair. Petite."

"Did you bring a copy of her driver's license?" Gertie asked.

Ainslee cleared her throat.

"I don't have anything like that. It wasn't a formal employment relationship. I was kind of helping her out. I'm sorry. I know I should have better information for you. I'm worried sick about her. Please?"

All eyes turned to Fortune.

"We can go out and have a look around," Fortune said. "And then we can decide whether to take the case."

Ainslee exhaled with relief and stood up.

"Oh, thank you so much. Okay, I have to go get my daughter, but you know where the McCully Inn is, right? Just ask for me at the front desk whenever you get there. Ainslee MacEntire."

"Why, that poor young girl," Mary-Alice exclaimed as soon as Ainslee had closed the door behind her. "What do you suppose the chances are of finding her?"

"Now Mary-Alice," Ida Belle said in a warning tone, "it's not public knowledge that Fortune's looking at becoming a private eye. So don't go telling your cousin Celia. You know she's hated us since elementary school, and she practically lives to make trouble for Fortune. We don't need her digging up some old law about no private detecting during days that end with a "y" or anything like that."

"Please, Mary-Alice," Fortune pleaded. "Celia can't find out. She'll ruin everything."

Mary-Alice thought quickly. She was not particularly close to her cousin by marriage, and even if she were, she wouldn't dream of betraying her new friends. On the other hand, she didn't want to risk getting left out of all the excitement.

"I wouldn't dream of troubling Celia," Mary-Alice said with a sweet smile. "And I do so appreciate your inviting me to participate. I would never betray your trust!"

And so it was that Mary-Alice gently extorted her way into the investigation.

# CHAPTER 3

Fortune, Ida Belle, and Mary-Alice were packed and on the road within the hour. Gertie stayed behind to oversee the brewing and bottling of the current batch of Sinful Ladies' Cough Syrup, which everyone agreed was a high priority. The popular cold remedy was the Sinful Ladies' Society's main source of income. Alcoholic beverages were forbidden in Sinful, but medicine was not; the distinctive pink bottles could be found on the shelves of the General Store, at the church bazaars, and in the handbags and lunch pails of the local citizenry.

Mary-Alice was not entirely comfortable embarking on this adventure without Gertie. Of all her new Sinful friends, Mary-Alice felt most comfortable with Gertie Hebert. Gertie was a free spirit with a gift for putting people at ease. She had a knack for disguises, too; Mary-Alice had seen how Gertie could transform herself into a fashion plate, a barfly, or an Italian widow (although the latter costume would have been more convincing had Gertie known even a few words of Italian).

Mary-Alice did not feel quite so comfortable around Ida Belle. Ida Belle was not at all what you'd call "ladylike." She could be gruff, and she was prone to start shooting things when she got excited. Young Fortune Morrow was terribly intense, especially for a children's librarian. She used military lingo, and acted serious all the time (except when she was with her young man, Sinful's deputy sheriff). Then again, Fortune was a Yankee, bless her heart, so she had an excuse for being peculiar.

The McCully Inn looked very much like they left it. It was a brick building, with a one-story main structure and a two-story wing out back. It stood to the side of a wide, flat highway, between a Waffle House and a tire store.

As Fortune nosed the Jeep into one of the few vacant parking spots, one of the second-story doors opened. A silver-haired man popped his head out, looked around, and then strolled out to the parking lot, straightening his suit jacket. About thirty seconds later, a muscular young man in snug jeans and a tank top exited the same door, ambled over to a truck, hopped in, and drove off.

"Why, that gentleman in the suit looked awfully familiar," Mary-Alice said.

"You've probably seen him on TV," Ida Belle said. "With his wife and two lovely daughters."

"Oh, he's the one running for re-election," Mary-Alice said. "My heavens, his poor wife."

"Probably one of those guys who thinks your marriage vows don't apply once you cross state lines," Fortune said. "I've met a few of those. Anyway, Ainslee said she'd meet us around the back, by the stairs."

They found Ainslee talking to a middle-aged man in coveralls. When she saw the ladies, she tried to wind up the conversation and send the man on his way, but he seemed determined not to leave until he could greet the newcomers.

"Afternoon, ladies!" He flashed them a grin. "You have a wonderful time at the McCully Inn, now."

"That's Manny," Ainslee explained when he'd gone in through the service entrance. "Our handyman. He's a good guy, but boy, does he love to talk. We just spent half an hour talking about light switch covers... anyway. Thank you so much for coming out."

Ainslee held open the service door so Mary-Alice, Ida Belle, and Fortune could go through ahead of her. The hallway was bare white, with an unpainted concrete floor and glaring fluorescent lights overhead.

"Sorry to bring you back this way, but I was afraid if you came in through the front, you might—oh, Mr. McCully!

"Miss Ainslee," the man replied, faintly startled. He was perhaps thirty, of medium height, with brown hair, hazel eyes, and unremarkable features. "Ladies. I hope you'll find everything at the McCully Inn to your satisfaction."

He continued on his way without as much as a look back.

"Did he think we were hotel guests?" Mary-Alice asked. "He didn't seem to think twice about the fact that we were coming in through the service entrance."

"You could have told him we'd just run away from the circus, and he wouldn't have batted an eye," Ida Belle exclaimed. "I don't believe he heard a word you said. That space case is your manager?"

"Oh, please don't call him that," Ainslee pleaded. "Poor Mr. McCully. He's doing his best. Old McBully passed away less than a year ago and left the whole thing over to his son."

"McBully?" Fortune asked. "Who's that?"

Ainslee grimaced.

"Did I say that out loud? That might've been what some of the staff called him behind his back. The old man was a total control freak. Lionel Junior—Mr. McCully—is still learning, but I like working for him way better. At least he listens, and he gives me room to run things. One of the things I've been trying to do is make this place more family-friendly. Honestly, I'm proud of what I do, but I'm not crazy about the fact that I'm running a no-tell motel. It's not a good example for Bethany, and I'm not comfortable with it either. Anyway..."

Ainslee eyed Ida Belle and Mary-Alice.

"Here's the stairway. Is everyone okay with taking the stairs, or should we go around to the elevator?"

"We can take the stairs," Ida Belle declared, and then whispered to Fortune, "you should charge her extra for that."

Ainslee led them up the concrete stairs and down a narrow hallway to the room at the end.

"This room looks like it has a good view of the entire hallway," Fortune remarked.

"That's not why I put her here. I just thought she'd like being tucked away, no one walking past her door." Ainslee produced a key and unlocked the door easily. "Anyway, I don't think Solange left of her own accord. Take a look and see what you think."

At first glance, the room looked like a normal, lived-in hotel room, with one unmade queen-sized bed. A half-empty bottle of Jack Daniels sat on the bar, and the sliding mirrored closet door was open.

But a chair had been knocked over, and the vertical blinds clacked in the breeze of the open balcony window.

Fortune pushed the blinds aside and stepped out onto the balcony.

"Look at this," she called back. "You can just walk out onto the roof."

Behind Fortune, past the balcony railing, Mary-Alice saw an expanse of new tar paper.

"We're replacing the shingles," Ainslee said. "I think that's how they took her. Not through the front. Someone would've noticed if they'd taken her out the front."

"May I?" Fortune asked.

"Sure?" Ainslee wasn't sure what Fortune was asking until

Fortune lightly vaulted over the railing onto the new roof and sprinted out of sight.

Ainslee stared after her.

"Wow. Is she a gymnast?"

"A librarian," Mary-Alice said, at the same time Ida Belle blurted out, "Pageant queen."

"Pageant queen," Mary-Alice corrected herself, just as Ida Belle said, "librarian."

"Whatever. I think we can all agree she's very spry." Ida Belle went over and slid the glass door shut.

"Don't you have to be old to be 'spry'?" Ainslee asked.

"The young lady does have a point, Miss Ida Belle," Mary-Alice agreed. "No one ever describes a young person as 'spry'. I've always heard it used in sentences like, 'my, Mrs. Johnson is awfully spry for ninety-five, isn't she?'"

"Right?" Ainslee put in. "That's exactly what I'm talking about."

Ida Belle threw up her hands.

"Well, Fortune's young and spry. She's a freak of nature. Now let's take a look around and see what we have. Ainslee, have you tidied up this room at all or rearranged the contents in any way?"

Ainslee shook her head.

"Good."

Ida Belle pulled a handful of purple nitrile gloves from her handbag. She handed one pair to Mary-Alice and one pair to Ainslee.

"Mary-Alice, you go through the drawers. I'll look in the wardrobe and under the bed. Miss Ainslee, you can observe us to make sure we're being careful and thorough. Put the gloves on just in case you're tempted to touch anything."

"I'll just sit over here." Ainslee sat on the bed and watched as Ida Belle and Mary-Alice searched the room. Mary-Alice opened the dresser drawers to find them full of folded jeans and t-shirts. Except for the top drawer, which held a few scattered pieces of jewelry.

"Whatever might this be?" Mary-Alice laid a long, feathered item on the desk. "This looks like an earring, but there's only one."

"It's a belly button ring," Ainslee said.

"Takes all kinds I guess," Ida Belle said from inside the closet. "Now these are some nice cowboy boots. No one in her right mind would leave these behind. Too bad they're not my size."

"That's exactly what I thought," Ainslee exclaimed. "She wouldn't leave all this stuff behind if she'd left voluntarily, would she?"

Ida Belle gently closed the wardrobe door.

"Miss Ainslee, what was this missing girl to you?"

Ainslee took a moment to answer.

"She needed work, and I needed someone to help out. She would fill in with the rooms when one of our regular staff called in sick, and she'd watch Bethany for me when there was a school holiday."

"Did you know her before she came here looking for work?" Ida Belle asked.

"I might've seen her around," Ainslee said vaguely.

A sharp rap on the door interrupted them. Ainslee opened the door to Fortune, who looked a little sweaty.

"Okay, I've established that someone could have made a getaway going across the roof. The drop down to street level is a little tough, but doable. I know, because I just did it. Now, you mentioned your boss doesn't know about this—"

"No, please don't get Mr. McCully involved," Ainslee pleaded. "Please. He depends on me to take care of things. The last thing I want to do is drag him into this."

# CHAPTER 4

"We have to talk to McCully," Fortune said as they soon as the women were in the elevator.

"But we don't want to get the young lady fired," Mary-Alice said, just as the doors slid open at the lobby.

"Don't worry." Fortune strode up to the registration desk and said something to the clerk. Ida Belle and Mary-Alice followed her.

"She'll know how to handle it," Ida Belle assured her. "We haven't gotten anyone fired yet. That I can recall."

The clerk disappeared through a back door, and out came Lionel McCully.

"Howdy ladies." He was trying to put on cheerfulness, but his eyes were tired. "Y'all enjoying your stay at the McCully Inn?"

"Mr. McCully, I'm Fortune Morrow." Fortune put out her hand in greeting. "These are my colleagues Ida Belle and Gertie. We're here on behalf of a client who prefers to remain anonymous at this time."

Recognition dawned in his eyes.

"Oh, my goodness, y'all are the ones who helped us out when that gentleman from New Orleans...well now."

He lowered his voice to a whisper and leaned across the counter.

"We're trying to upgrade our image. More family-friendly. Your discretion in this matter, whatever it might be, would be most appreciated. I'm not trying to tell you your business, you understand."

"Oh, we're discreet," Ida Belle interjected. "You'll hardly know we're here."

"Do you know an employee by the name of Solange Smith?" Fortune asked. "Early twenties, dark hair, slim build?"

Mary-Alice thought she saw a shadow pass over Lionel McCully's face. But all he said was,

"I'm sorry. I've never been good at remembering folks. Names and faces and such. My daddy was much better than me. You might could talk to Miss Ainslee, the head housekeeper. She's a wonder, Miss Ainslee. I'm not ashamed to say that she's the one who keeps this place going, and that's the truth. Did you say Solange?"

"Solange Smith. Yes."

"I can tell you she's not on my payroll records."

"You're sure about that?" Fortune persisted.

"Sure as I can be. I would've remembered. Solange is a beautiful name. Sorry I couldn't be more help. Let me know if y'all need anything else." Lionel's engaging smile disappeared the moment he turned away.

While they had been talking with Lionel McCully, Manny, the handyman, had set up in the lobby. He was on his knees, working on an electrical outlet. He looked up as the women walked by.

"Afternoon, ladies," he said. "How's it going? You find her yet?"

Fortune stopped abruptly. Ida Belle bumped into Fortune, and Mary-Alice bumped into Ida Belle. Starting with Mary-Alice, the three women backed up.

"Find who?" Fortune asked.

"Well, Solange. That's who Ainslee's looking for, right? Isn't that why you're here?"

"When's your lunch break?" Ida Belle asked.

Manny stood up He was about Fortune's height, nearly six feet tall. He towered over Ida Belle and Mary-Alice.

"I can take my break now," he said.

"You like the Waffle House?" Ida Belle asked.

"I wouldn't say no. Give me five minutes to put my tools away."

On the way into the restaurant, Mary-Alice bought a copy of the local paper. Mary-Alice preferred small-town papers to the big-city ones. The local papers featured good news, like high school valedictorians and award-winning pumpkins. The big newspapers showcased all the worst explosions, fires, famines, and murders from all over the world. Mary-Alice didn't think human beings were intended to take on all the world's misery at once. One town's problems were surely enough.

"I never did figure out what Miss Solange's job was supposed to be," Manny said, once they'd settled in and ordered. "She must've been meant something to Miss Ainslee, though. You shoulda seen her when she found Miss Solange's room empty. She was really upset."

"Have you been at the McCully Inn long?" Fortune asked.

Manny shook his head.

"Just started this month. And I'll tell you right now, I'm grateful to Miss Ainsley for taking me on. I moved down here from Oklahoma for a construction job. Well, I worked there about six months before it went belly-up. You seen that abandoned housing development just north of here?"

The women shook their heads.

"It was called Townehouse Downes. It was one of Old Man McCully's projects, coincidentally enough. Mr. Lionel's father. I guess there the old man tried to pull a fast one on the bank.

None of us knew nothing about it till they just stopped construction one day, and that was it. None of us got our last paycheck, and there was nothing we could do. Some people were saying the old man coulda gone to jail for it. He never did, though. Like I said, I got lucky when Miss Ainslee hired me. I'd like to say it was my amazing skill, but I think it was 'cause I was Army. Like her husband."

"Ainslee is married?" Ida Belle asked.

"Widowed. I don't know how she does it. Single mother, always working. Well, you know what, she's trying to improve the McCully Inn's image. Make it more of a family place."

"That's gonna be an uphill battle," Ida Belle remarked.

"If anyone can do it, Miss Ainsley can."

Manny glanced at his watch.

"Oof, speaking of that, thanks for the lunch, ladies. I'm much obliged. Any time y'all wanna talk."

# CHAPTER 5

The women sat at the booth and watched through the glass door as Manny sauntered back toward the McCully Inn.

"What do you think?" Fortune asked. "Could he be a person of interest?"

"You bet," Ida Belle said.

"We think Manny is a suspect?" Mary-Alice exclaimed. "Oh, dear, why, of course he is. How silly of me. He knows the motel and he must have keys to everything. And the young lady did disappear just after he started working there. What a shame. He seems so sweet."

"A lot of serial killers seem sweet," Ida Belle retorted.

"We'll want to see where he goes," Fortune said. "In case he's concealed the girl somewhere. There's also Lionel McCully. He seems preoccupied. Secretive."

"Yeah, kinda weird for someone who works in hospitality," Ida Belle said.

"Well, he did inherit the business," Mary-Alice said. "Running a motel wouldn't necessarily have been his first choice, now would it have? But I do have one question. Here we are, interviewing folks and buying them waffles and such, but have we agreed to take the case? I mean to say, I don't wish to assume the worst, but if we don't have a signed contract, I mean, I'm not saying she'd do this, but Miss Ainsley could have us do a lot of her legwork for free. Why, she could even turn around and have us arrested for trespassing if she'd a mind to."

"Well that's about the most cynical thing I believe I've ever heard," Ida Belle exclaimed.

"Why, I do apologize, Miss Ida Belle—"

"Listen, that was a compliment. This is a tough business, and it looks like you're learning a thing or two hanging out with us."

"Indeed I am," Mary-Alice agreed. In fact, Mary-Alice got most of her ideas from the mystery books she read, but she did not wish to rain on Ida Belle's parade.

"No private investigator guarantees results, Fortune," Ida Belle said. "It's right in the contract. If we only take cases we know are a sure thing, we might as well hang it up now."

Fortune set down her coffee cup.

"I see what you're both saying. We want to make money, and we don't want to give away our hard work. But I don't want to take Ainslee's money if it looks like we can't do anything for her. And the other thing is, if I'm going to do this professionally, I need to rack up some early wins to build my reputation. I don't want to be known as someone who takes your money and doesn't get results. How about this: we're here already here, so let's at least give it till the end of the day and see how we feel about it. If we don't like it, we walk away."

"Your idea sounds quite fair to me, Miss Fortune," Mary-Alice said.

"Sure," Ida Belle agreed. "I guess we can spare a few hours. Okay, so where do we start?"

"If we do decide to take this on, what do we need?" Fortune asked. "I think we start with tracking the handyman and the owner. Probably Ainslee too, just to be on the safe side. Now from what I could see, I'd guess the switchboard... Mary-Alice, you might not want to listen to this part."

Ida Belle and Fortune launched into a somewhat technical discussion of the merits (many) and legality (dubious) of various kinds of tracking and eavesdropping devices. Having been given permission to tune out of the conversation, Mary-Alice leafed through the scant pages of the Lemon Tree Herald-Tribune-Gazette.

Then she let out an involuntary "Oh!" And lowered the newspaper.

"What is it, Mary-Alice?" Ida Belle asked.

"It's our chance to observe the reclusive Mr. Lionel in the wild."

# CHAPTER 6

As Mary-Alice signed her name on the Elks Lodge attendance sheet, she did her best to project a calm exterior. But her hands trembled with excitement and nerves, rendering her signature illegible.

"Good job," Ida Belle whispered behind her. "No one would guess that's you."

Mary-Alice sucked in a deep breath and stepped away from the registration table. The plan was to sit at separate tables to maximize the chance of seeing something important.

The lodge interior was gussied up for the occasion, festooned with fairy lights. A banner proclaiming Welcome Friends of the Lemon Tree Public Library hung on the back wall, above a stuffed elk head. Mary-Alice felt a little like a spy; it didn't seem that long ago that the organization was off-limits to women. But the transgressive thrill evaporated when she realized that the hall was packed with women, mostly mature ladies like herself. The few men in attendance wore string ties and cowboy hats. Fortune, who had already signed in and seated herself, was surrounded by a cluster of cowboy hats.

It was possible they wouldn't see Lionel McCully or anything else of interest. But the Library Friends Annual Fundraising Dinner was underwritten by an endowment from the McCully Company. And according to the Lemon Tree Herald-Tribune-Gazette, the McCully family attended every year. Mary-Alice thought Fortune would be excited to attend, seeing as how she was a librarian too, but strangely, she wasn't. In fact, out of the three of them, Fortune seemed the most nervous about the event. It's probably bittersweet for her, Mary-Alice thought, now that she's just about settled on changing careers.

Mary-Alice found a vacant seat at a table occupied by a group of agreeable-seeming ladies. It turned out they were not only pleasant and welcoming, but they had excellent literary taste as well. Soon Mary-Alice found herself in a discussion of Susan Wittig Albert's China Bayles mysteries. So engrossed was she that she nearly missed the morose young man plodding through the alcove in the direction of the bar.

Mary-Alice stood and excused herself (with genuine regret) and headed to the doorway through which she'd seen Lionel McCully disappear. She found herself stuck in a crowd clustered around the bar. For a moment she thought she'd lost Lionel. But then she spotted him at a small table next to a bay window, sitting across from a young lady.

Fortunately, Mary-Alice saw another table with a single vacant chair right behind Mr. Lionel. People in this part of the lodge apparently preferred to stand if it meant being close to the bar. The line for the drink tickets was too long, so Mary-Alice wouldn't have the excuse of nursing a drink. She'd have to sit and observe.

She skirted the edge of the room and approached the table with Lionel facing away from her. As absent-minded as he seemed, he had just seen her earlier that day and was likely to recognize her. Mary-Alice had a clear view of the mystery woman but would have to observe her in glances; she couldn't very well sit and stare.

The woman wore her auburn hair in an upsweep. She was young, not yet forty, but she'd already had what Mary-Alice recognized as "work" done. Her lips were pillowy, her eyebrows immobile. The womanly contours showcased by her plunging neckline looked like they'd been bolted on to her rib cage. Mary-Alice noticed that her ring finger was bare, with a faint indentation where a wedding ring used to be.

Divorced? Cheating?

The body language didn't seem flirtatious, however. Far from it.

Mary-Alice strained to hear the conversation, but the murmur of the crowd was too loud. Just as she was about to give up, she heard the woman say,

"Lionel, honey, you did promise him. You're not a man who goes back on his word, are you?"

The remark was not well-received. Lionel stood abruptly and stalked off.

Mary-Alice was about to follow him when a tall man in a black cowboy hat approached the table.

"Brandi-Lynn, sweetheart," he boomed, "where ya been?"

So the woman had a name. Mary-Alice pulled her writing journal and her sunflower pen out of her handbag. Quietly, and quite unnoticed by the crowd, she sat at the little table and wrote down everything she'd just witnessed.

# CHAPTER 7

"Well, what do you think?" Fortune asked.

"I guess we've made some progress," Ida Belle said. "We know Lionel McCully lives alone in the house he shares with his father. The fact that his sister was invited to speak at the event tells me she's more respected in the community than he is. And thanks to Mary-Alice, we know he's on the outs with a woman named Brandi-Lynn."

The ladies were sitting in Fortune's Jeep in a far corner of the parking lot of the McCully Inn. She had the fan blowing, but the weather had cooled down to where they didn't need air conditioning. Gertie was in on the conversation via Ida Belle's cell phone.

"That's good enough for me," Gertie said. "I think it sounds interesting. I'm starting to wish I'd come out there with you."

"I'm not used to answering to someone," Ida Belle said. "We've always done things our own way, and on our own time. There are too many unknowns here. I feel like I'm working with one hand tied behind my back."

"You're just feeling a little shaky 'because I'm not there in person to help you out," Gertie retorted. Ida Belle rolled her eyes.

"And don't roll your eyes, Ida Belle. We discussed all this. We knew it was going to be different doing it for money. The jobs might not be interesting to us. We'd have to answer to other people. We'd have to keep track of expenses."

"Well when you put it that way," Ida Belle said. "Why did we agree to do this in the first place?"

"Because Fortune is considering retiring from her…er, librarian job," Gertie explained with exaggerated patience."

"True," Fortune agreed.

"She'd like to stay in Sinful, and private eye is the only job there that fits her unique skill set."

"Couldn't have put it better myself," Fortune remarked.

"This is a business, now, Ida Belle. Just like brewing Sinful Ladies' Cough Syrup is a business. We have to persist, even when we don't feel like it."

"Speaking of that, how'd the acai berry experiment turn out?"

Gertie was silent for a moment.

"I don't think I'd make the acai berry cough syrup again."

"What do you mean?"

"It ended up tasting like Dr. Morgan's pinworm medicine. Don't worry, we don't have to throw it out. If you mix it with fruit punch it does a pretty good job of hiding the taste. Now, this is a real missing person case? You don't think the girl just picked up and left?"

"There were signs of a struggle," Fortune said. "And she left clothing and jewelry behind. Ainslee says the police took her report, but it didn't seem like a top priority for them."

"What if Miss Ainslee made it look like a struggle?" Mary-Alice asked. "She had plenty of time to rearrange the room before we arrived."

"My goodness, Mary-Alice, you do have a devious mind," Ida

Belle said admiringly. "But then why would Miss Ainslee call us in and act so worried about the girl?"

"Well…" Mary-Alice's active imagination, nourished on a steady diet of murder mysteries, immediately came up with a number of explanations. "Perhaps there was a misunderstanding between the two women, and Miss Ainslee wanted to make things right. Or this Solange stole something, or someone, from Miss Ainslee, and Miss Ainslee wants it back. Or perhaps Miss Solange killed Miss Ainslee, and took her place, although I suppose someone surely would have noticed the substitution...well, there are so many possibilities, aren't there?"

"Well now, this case is sounding more interesting by the minute," Gertie exclaimed. "What are we waiting for?"

"I'm inclined to take it," Fortune said. "Gertie, I really wish you were here with us."

"I think it's best to stay out of Texas for the time being. Anyway, I have to stay here at least until this batch is bottled. But I'll be here if you want to call in. I think we should take it. Make sure to get half the money up front."

"Sounds like you're awfully eager to put us to work, Gertie," Ida Belle said suspiciously.

"Fine. Full disclosure, I just found out I need a new transmission. It's gonna to cost me five grand to fix."

"That rust bucket isn't even worth five grand!" Ida Belle objected.

"Yeah, so what are my options, Marie Antoinette? You think I can just waltz out and buy myself a brand-new car?"

"Fine," Ida Belle grumbled. "Looks like we're taking the case."

# CHAPTER 8

Fortune locked up the Jeep and the women went into the hotel to look for Ainslee. It was close to midnight, and the only employee in sight was the night clerk, a sullen young man with a tangle of green-black hair. He claimed not to know who Ainslee was, and when informed she was the head housekeeper, shrugged and suggested coming back the next day.

The women moved away from the desk, out of earshot.

"I'll text her," Ida Belle volunteered. "That way we won't wake her up."

Within seconds, Ida Belle's phone rang. Ida Belle motioned them outside.

"We've decided to take the case," Ida Belle told Ainslee.

"That's wonderful," Ainslee's voice said.

"Remember, we'll do the work, but we can't guarantee we can find Solange," Fortune added.

"I guess that's all I can ask for," Ainslee said.

"And you have our rate sheet," Ida Belle added.

"Yes, I was looking it over. I only had a thousand dollars saved up for this. I thought it would be enough. Can you just do whatever you do until you use it up?"

Fortune and Ida Belle looked at each other.

"I suppose we can do that," Fortune said.

"Guess Gertie's gonna be hitchhiking for the foreseeable future," Ida Belle remarked.

"Just one thing," Fortune said. "You have to be honest with us. And tell us what you know."

Ainslee was quiet for a moment.

"But you won't tell anyone else, right?" she said, finally.

"If there's evidence of criminal activity we're required to report it to the appropriate authorities," Fortune said.

More silence.

"You still with us, darlin'?" Mary-Alice asked.

"Yes, I'm here," Ainslee said finally. "Yes. Let's do this. I mean, if I want to find her it's really the only way, isn't it? Okay, first things first. I'm gonna set you up with a room."

Their new "command center" (as Mary-Alice liked to think of it) was an unused room on the second floor, a few doors down from where Solange had been staying when she disappeared. Inside were two double beds and a couch. Fortune immediately volunteered to take the couch, and no one argued with her. That was one of the advantages of age, Mary-Alice thought. No one expects you to sleep on the fold-out.

While Mary-Alice got ready for bed, Fortune and Ida Belle went to work. They disconnected the room telephone and in its place plugged in a tan plastic box about the size of a deck of cards. Then they pulled out a similar box and hooked it to a laptop.

"Are those little hard drives y'all are setting up?" Mary-Alice asked.

"They're listening devices," Fortune explained. "This one is an International Mobile Subscriber Identity-catcher. It's like its own little cell phone tower. If Solange's kidnapper calls someone in the area, we can not only hear the call, we can trace the location of the phone."

"We should be able to hear anything that comes through the switchboard too," Ida Belle added. None of it's admissible in a court of law, and might not even be legal, but this setup's pretty useful."

Mary-Alice came over to take a closer look. Fortune slid under the desk to do something with wires and cables.

"Are there headphones?" she asked. "Will we be listening and taking notes?"

Mary-Alice imagined herself wearing big studio-style headphones for hours on end and wondered whether her ears would get sore.

"Thankfully, no," Ida Belle said. "That's how they did it back in my day. I mean, in spy movies. But now they can record and transcribe the conversations."

"That way we can actually get some sleep," Fortune said from under the desk. "And the voice recognition has some problems south of the Mason-Dixon Line. It can't tell the difference between 'oil' and 'all'."

"Well I'm gonna turn in," Ida Belle said as she headed toward the bathroom. "Mary-Alice, you should get some sleep too. We have a big day tomorrow."

The next day Mary-Alice went downstairs to do surveillance in the motel lobby. She sat, unnoticed, observing. She occasionally made notes in her journal, but Sunday seemed to be a slow day for adulterers, so Mary-Alice spent most of her time reading.

That afternoon Mary-Alice borrowed Fortune's Jeep and drove over to the Lemon Tree Public Library for their weekly book club meeting. She had managed to finish reading the book club's selection as she was conducting surveillance in the lobby. So by the time she showed up, she was ready to discuss The Last Chance Olive Ranch by Susan Wittig Albert.

Mary-Alice returned to the room that evening in good spirits. She had picked up some interesting gossip and was eager to share it.

"I brought some sandwiches for us," she announced as set the takeout bag down. "How was y'all's day?"

Fortune and Ida Belle looked up at the same time.

"Pretty good," Ida Belle said.

"Depressing," Fortune said.

"I don't know why you seem so surprised that men cheat on their wives," Ida Belle said mildly.

"I'm not surprised. I'm depressingly unsurprised. Mary-Alice, right before you walked in I listened to a guy call his girlfriend and tell her, I'm in room 209 and I'm naked. My wife thinks I'm out buying cat food so we have about twenty minutes."

"Isn't that romantic?" Ida Belle said drily.

"There's more. I guess he'd dialed the wrong number, because the next thing I heard was, Ew, Dad, it's me!"

"Long story short, someone's getting a new Mustang for her sixteenth birthday," Ida Belle said.

"Oh, Fortune, darlin'," Mary-Alice exclaimed, "don't you worry. Your deputy sheriff isn't anything at all like that man."

Fortune rubbed her temples and stood up from the computer.

"Thanks, Mary-Alice, but I wasn't thinking that."

"Yes, you were," Ida Belle said.

"Yes, I was. I need to take a break. What kind of sandwiches are those?"

"You find out anything at the book club?" Ida Belle asked.

"Bacon, lettuce, and tomato, and yes I did."

"Delishish!" Fortune exclaimed through a mouthful of squishy bread and crisp bacon.

"Well now." Mary-Alice sat down on the edge of her bed. "I don't know as any of this will be helpful for our case, but you can't say for certain until it's all over, can you? Anyway, I found that Brandi-Lynn, the woman who was with Lionel McCully at the Library Friends meeting last night, is his first cousin. It seems she's recently widowed. She got married only a few months ago, but her husband was quite a bit older and had heart problems. The ladies seemed to feel a bit sorry for Mr. Lionel. Always in the shadow of his father, and not exactly renowned for his sparkling personality. The ladies all seemed to agree it was his sister who'd inherited their daddy's charisma. Now what did y'all find out today?"

"Fortune already told you the most interesting part," Ida Belle said. "We didn't learn anything that would help us find the girl. But if we ever want to get into the blackmail business, we're set. Oh, and Fortune went out to Lionel McCully's house.

"Just to make sure he wasn't keeping the girl hostage," Fortune said.

"I suppose you didn't find anyone," Mary-Alice said.

"The cleaning service was there and they left the front door unlocked, so I was able to go in and take a look around. I scanned for heat signatures in the house, but there wasn't anyone tied up in a closet or anything like that. Not alive, anyway."

"Is there anyone else we should be following?" Mary-Alice asked.

"We already are," Fortune said. "Ida Belle went out this afternoon while you were at the book club and stuck trackers on people's cars. When people start driving home, we'll be able to see their cars moving on the map. Come take a look."

# CHAPTER 9

Hours later, Mary-Alice was still watching the computer screen, transfixed.

"That's Mr. Lionel's car right?" she asked. "That little red dot crawling on down the highway toward the Chili's?"

"Yes, that's right." Fortune leaned in to peer over Mary-Alice's shoulder. "He's the only one who's still out and about. Manny and Ainslee have both been stationary for a while. So unless either of them takes a bicycle out or something, we can assume they're both in for the night. Ainslee's staying in this apartment building and Manny ...looks like he's stopped near this closed subdivision.

"I wonder if he's sleeping in his car," Mary-Alice said. "Poor man."

"Yeah. Mary-Alice, you don't have to stay up. I've got it under control, and anyway, the computer's recording everything. It's getting late."

As if to second Fortune's suggestion, Ida Belle snorted in her sleep. Mary-Alice wondered how Ida Belle could sleep with those big plastic rollers in her hair.

"But it doesn't seem right," Mary-Alice insisted. "Look, he's stopped at the restaurant. I mean to say, Mr. Lionel simply doesn't seem like the type to go out gallivanting around after hours."

Fortune laughed.

"Maybe he's on a blind date."

"Maybe one of us should see what he's doing," Mary-Alice said. "In person. I can do it, Fortune."

Fortune braced her hands on the desk and frowned.

"You think something's off?" she asked.

"Well, yes. I do. From what I know of Mr. Lionel, I'd be very surprised to see him going out and partying."

"Maybe he doesn't like showing his wild side at work."

Mary-Alice glanced down at the computer screen.

"It's uncharacteristic behavior, Miss Fortune. I mean to say, the way the ladies at the book club talked about him…I believe someone should see what he's doing out there. I don't believe he's simply out having fun."

"I've had enough of going undercover at dive bars to last me a lifetime," Fortune said. "If you want to do it, be my guest. Do you want to go out now?"

"Yes! Do you mean it?" Although it was well past her usual bedtime, Mary-Alice felt wide-awake.

"Of course. I'll fit you with an earpiece so we can keep in audio contact. We'll call in law enforcement if you get in trouble."

"Why, Fortune, are you sure—" Mary-Alice began.

"You bet." Fortune stood up from her laptop and glanced at Ida Belle, gently snoring away in her bed. "But first, let's go over how to tail someone."

Mary-Alice caught up with Lionel as he was pulling out of the Chili's parking lot, and followed him on to the highway. She checked the gas gauge and reassured herself that the tank was full. When she looked up, Lionel was pulling off the highway. He led Mary-Alice along what she was starting to think of as a typical East Texas road—wide and flat, lined with tire stores, diners, motels, and the occasional trailer park. Mary-Alice wasn't accustomed to driving at night, so she focused on the distinctive single taillight of Lionel's Dodge Challenger.

Lionel drove on for about three miles, then turned up a side street, down a sparse residential road, and finally into the parking lot of a one-story honky-tonk. It was on the same model as the Swamp Bar back in Sinful, but instead of crushed oyster shells, the parking lot was bare dirt. And there was no bayou flowing out back—indeed, no sign of water anywhere nearby.

Lionel McCully parked, got out of his car, popped on a black cowboy hat, and headed to the building, glancing around at the other cars as he went in.

Mary-Alice waited a few moments and then quietly walked in behind him.

Inside it was noisy and packed with men and women in cowboy hats. Mary-Alice was surprised at how smoky it was inside. (Mary-Alice didn't spend much time in bars.)

At first Mary-Alice thought she'd lost him, but to her relief, she spotted him standing at the end of the bar. Mary-Alice took a position by the wall on the other side of the dance floor, where two-stepping couples would obscure her from Lionel McCully's view. He watched the crowd, and she watched Lionel. Three different women approached him and asked him something (for a dance, perhaps?) Judging from the body language, Mary-Alice inferred that he made a polite excuse to turn them down each time. After about half an hour, Lionel pushed away from the wall and walked out the door. Mary-Alice struggled to get through the crowd in time to follow him.

Mary-Alice watched as Lionel's car swung back onto the road, and then followed at a distance, as Fortune had instructed her. In the excitement, Mary-Alice nearly forgot that she'd been fitted out with audio, so Ida Belle's voice in her ear startled her so much she almost went off the road.

"So what'd you see at Texas Tommy's?"

"Oh, my goodness, Ida Belle, I thought you were asleep!"

"Well, Fortune told me you took the Jeep and now I can't get back to sleep for some reason. You see anything interesting?"

"It was the strangest thing." Mary-Alice followed the Charger's distinctive horizontal taillight as it made a turn. There were no streetlights on this stretch of road now, and it would have been easy to lose the black car. "He went inside, just stood there watching everyone, turned away all the pretty girls who asked him to dance, and then left. Now we're driving again."

"It looks like you're closing in on The Yellow Rose," Ida Belle said. "Not much else out that way. Man, the kid likes to party, doesn't he? This'll be his third stop tonight."

"Well, I certainly hope he manages to have some fun along the way," Mary-Alice replied. "That poor young man looked absolutely miserable at the last place we stopped. What was it called, Texas Tommy's? Oh, now he's pulling off the road. Why, Ida Belle, you were right. We're at the Yellow Rose."

"Okay, Mary-Alice. You go do your thing. Just press your earpiece if you need to talk to me."

The Yellow Rose had a line out the door. A mean-looking bouncer sat behind a tiny table, collecting the cover charge and checking IDs. Mary-Alice stepped into line three people behind Lionel McCully. So far he hadn't seemed to notice her at all. She was nervous about the bouncer, but he grinned at her, tipped the brim of his cowboy hat, and let her in for free.

"The Yellow Rose is always happy to have a classy lady visit us," he said as he waved her in.

Well, he doesn't think I'm going to stir up trouble, so there's a success, Mary-Alice thought as her eyes adjusted to the dark interior. She found Lionel McCully very much as he was earlier, leaning against a wall and observing the crowd. Once again, he seemed to be the only person in the place (besides Mary-Alice) without a drink or a cigarette in his hand.

As he had before, he watched the crowd for a few minutes, then walked out, got in his car, and drove off.

The next two stops—Billie's Ballroom and the Lucky Longhorn—followed the same routine, with one exception. As they were leaving Billie's Ballroom, Lionel McCully walked up behind a pretty blonde and touched her shoulder. When she turned around, the disappointment on his face was so obvious that she rolled her eyes and walked away before he could finish apologizing.

Finally, Mary-Alice followed Lionel McCully back to his house. When his garage door closed, she pressed her earpiece.

"Looks like our boy's safely home in his McMansion," Ida Belle said. "Does he have company?"

"No. He came home all by himself, Ida Belle." Mary-Alice watched as a light went on downstairs.

"I can't believe he struck out at four honky-tonks in a row. His game must be pretty weak."

"It seems to me he's looking for someone in particular," Mary-Alice said. "And I believe that person is a young lady with light blonde hair."

"Well, our missing girl's got dark hair. Anyway, if he doesn't know where she is, that means he's not the one who took her. Well, good work, Mary-Alice. Fortune's still asleep, so try to be quiet when you let yourself in. Aw, what am I saying? You're always as quiet as a mouse. See ya when you get here."

# CHAPTER 10

The next morning the women met Ainslee MacEntire in the borrowed motel room. It wasn't a particularly comfortable place for a discussion, but at least it was private. Fortune and Ida Belle had artfully concealed the listening apparatus by piling laundry on it.

"I'd rather have her think we're slobs, not spies," Ida Belle had explained to Mary-Alice as she draped a worn brassiere over the top of the pile.

"Any progress?" Ainslee asked eagerly when she came in.

She looked around at the faces of the women and her own expression dropped. "Uh-oh. This doesn't look too encouraging."

"We've made some inquiries," Fortune said. "But you haven't given us much to work with. Are you sure you don't have any kind of photograph of the missing girl? Even a selfie would help. Anything."

"Sorry," Ainslee stammered. "I mean, if I'd known this would happen I'd have...I don't know what I would've done actually. Solange was kind of paranoid about social media."

"And you're certain you don't know anything about her family," Ida Belle said.

Ainslee shook her head.

"She never talked about 'em. I got the feeling she didn't have a great relationship with them. I didn't want to be nosy."

"And you haven't heard anything from her?" Fortune asked. "Even something like, don't contact me, don't tell anyone you heard from me. If she doesn't want to be found, you need to let us know."

"I'd tell you right away if I heard anything. I'm so worried she's dead. How many more days do we have left?"

Ida Belle and Fortune exchanged a glance. Mary-Alice suspected they were thinking the same thing she was: they'd probably keep looking even after the client's money ran out. As long as the client cooperated, in any case.

"The fact that you're comping us the hotel room is really saving on expenses," Fortune said. "It's helping your money go a lot further. And you're sure your boss doesn't mind our staying here?"

"As long as I'm not kicking out paying customers, Mr. McCully's totally fine with it. We're trying to improve the image of the hotel, you know. Fix it up, make it more family-oriented. He's put a lot of trust in me to make it work. You know, we lost a lot of business when we got rid of the half-day rates. That was my idea. He could've fired me when our daily receipts went down. But Mr. McCully backed me up."

"How well do you know Manny?" Ida Belle asked.

"He came here looking for work after the Townehouse Downes development got shut down. He'd spent all his savings on a brand new truck he drove down here for the job. So he was flat broke when he showed up. He was Army, like my late husband, and I guess that was in his favor as far as I was concerned. I'm not sure that answers your questions."

"And did he have any interaction with the missing girl?" Ida Belle asked.

Ainslee shook her head.

"Solange really didn't socialize much. That's how she was. I let her have her privacy."

"Miss Ainslee," Mary-Alice spoke for the first time. "If we were to ask Mr. Lionel about this arrangement, with your friend Miss Solange staying on at no charge, would he tell us he'd approved of it?"

Ainslee cleared her throat.

"Well, he didn't pre- approve the arrangement, exactly, as such, but as long as I wasn't hurting anything, he let me run things as I pleased. I mean, he's not a micromanager. That's what's nice about working with him."

"You'll find that we are micromanagers, when it comes to the truth," Ida Belle said sternly. "If you want us to have a chance at finding your friend, you can't keep anything from us."

Ainslee nodded sheepishly.

"Of course."

"One more thing, darlin'," Mary-Alice added. "Is Mr. Lionel in the habit of going out on the town? Would you call him a party animal?"

Ainslee started to laugh and then became serious.

"A party animal? Hardly. As far as I know, Mr. McCully just works and goes home. He's the farthest thing from a party animal."

# CHAPTER 11

The next night, Mary-Alice gassed up the Jeep and went out once again to follow Lionel McCully. It was the same routine as the night before, only in reverse order. Lionel started out at Billie's Ballroom first, then moved on to the Yellow Rose, so on. As he had the night before, he stood to one side and scanned the crowd, an island of determined joylessness amid the Stetson-topped revelers.

When she returned to the hotel room just after midnight, careful to be quiet lest she wake anyone, she found Ida Belle and Fortune wide awake, sitting on opposite sides of the desk.

"Any news?" Fortune asked Mary-Alice as she walked in.

"Nothing new, I'm afraid," Mary-Alice replied. "But I'm more convinced than ever he's looking for a particular young lady. Why, there were any number of pretty girls who came up to him, and he was simply as uninterested as could be. I had half a mind to walk up to him and offer him the services of the Sinful Ladies' Detective Agency. I mean to say, we're already here looking for one missing girl. Why not two?"

"It'd be great if we could get McCully as a client," Ida Belle said. "I bet he can pay a whole lot better than Ainslee. Although come to think of it, McCully might not be looking for a lady at all. Maybe he's looking to buy one of those honky-tonks. And he's going to each one at different times of night to check out how many customers they have."

Mary-Alice plumped down on the edge of her bed.

"Have y'all heard any calls come in about a real estate deal, Ida Belle?"

"No, but he might just be thinking about it at this point."

"Well, maybe I'll follow him one more night," Mary-Alice said. "And if I don't find out anything new, I'll come back here and help you all go through the transcripts."

"That would be helpful," Fortune said. "We're already behind. I think McCully's a distraction. I don't think he knows where the girl is."

"No, I must say I agree with you on that point, Miss Fortune," Mary-Alice said. "But I do wish I knew what Mr. Lionel was looking for."

# CHAPTER 12

The following evening, Lionel McCully worked later than usual. Then another break in his routine: instead of going out, he drove directly home. Mary-Alice parked halfway down the block, shut off her lights, and determined to wait half an hour to be certain he was in for the night. She was glad she'd stuck it out when after twenty minutes the Charger pulled back out of the garage. Keeping Fortune's instructions in mind (the things that young librarian knew!), Mary-Alice followed him at a distance.

This time, he did not drive in the direction of his usual haunts. Instead, he headed east.

Mary-Alice pressed her earpiece to activate the voice link.

"He's pulling onto the Interstate," Mary-Alice said.

"Yeah, we see it," Ida Belle replied. "You're gassed up, right?"

"Yes, the gas gauge says full."

"That'll be good for about two hundred thirty miles. Although if you're on the freeway, you might get a little more. Oh, man, did you say he's driving a Charger?"

"Yes, he is. Ida Belle, is that a problem?"

"Dang. I hope it isn't one of the ones with the eighteen-and-a-half gallon gas tank. He'll be able to go twice as far as you without stopping."

"Oh, dear. How terribly inconvenient. But if I do have to stop, you'll be able to tell me where to find him. Won't you?"

"As long as he stays with his car. Hey, you just crossed back into Louisiana. Can you feel how much more civilized it is?"

Mary-Alice followed the Charger as it drove on for about an hour and a half straight on. Then the car turned south.

Mary-Alice spotted a gas station at the interchange that looked like it was still open, and pulled off.

"You're losing him," Ida Belle said into Mary-Alice's ear. "Are you stopping for gas?"

"Yes I am. I'm getting low and I don't see where I'll have another chance."

"Man, this better be worth it. If we're burning a day and a tank of gas just to follow this guy to some booty call…"

Ida Belle directed Mary-Alice back onto Lionel McCully's trail, and she caught up to him quickly. She followed him as he exited the highway and drove through what Mary-Alice guessed was a reasonably big town (based on the fact that they passed a Walmart Supercenter and a Lowe's).

Mary-Alice had to follow the horizontal taillight at quite a distance now as there was hardly anyone else on the narrow road, and she didn't want to be obvious. Clouds obscured the sliver of moon, and there were no streetlights. Mary-Alice started to feel a little nervous. She wasn't in the habit of driving at night, and she didn't know where they were headed.

"Ida Belle," Mary-Alice clicked in, "do you have any idea where we're going?"

"You're heading southeast, along Bayou Lafourche," Ida Belle said. "Wait, he's slowing down."

The taillight abruptly disappeared. Following Ida Belle's directions, Mary-Alice slowed down, thankful that there was no one driving behind her. When she had reached the point where

Lionel McCully had left the road, Mary-Alice pulled off onto the shoulder and shut off her lights.

"There's nothing here," Mary-Alice said to Ida Belle. "Just a bunch of trees and bushes."

"Right past those trees and bushes is a bayou, and the satellite image shows there's some kind of building there. Look for a driveway."

"I'm exiting the Jeep now," Mary-Alice whispered. She opened the door to a cacophony of nighttime critters and stepped carefully down onto the grass. Immediately she felt the humid air close around her.

"I can hear you're outside now," Ida Belle said into Mary-Alice's earpiece. "Watch out for gators."

Mary-Alice closed the Jeep door quietly and slowly walked back along the grass shoulder.

"I see it," Mary-Alice whispered. "It's a very narrow drive. I don't want to take the Jeep in. It'll make too much noise. I'm going on foot."

"You're almost there," Ida Belle reassured her.

Mary-Alice stepped quietly along the overgrown driveway, hugging the side to avoid stepping on the crushed oyster-shell paving. She followed the cracking noises of an engine cooling down and quickly arrived at a clearing.

She paused to take in the situation. Directly in front of her was an abandoned-looking one-story camp, beyond which she could see the sluggish black water of the bayou. Lionel's black car was nearly invisible, but Mary-Alice could hear it ticking as it cooled. After a few moments, Lionel McCully himself rounded the building, mounted the steps to the rotting front door and knocked. He stood, listening. There was no answer. He disappeared around the side. Through the window, Mary-Alice watched the beam of a flashlight playing around the front room.

Lionel came around again, shining his flashlight around as if he were looking for something. Whatever it was, he didn't find it.

Mary-Alice watched him start his car and drive away.

"What just happened?" Ida Belle demanded.

"Mister Lionel just left," she said. "Should I follow him, or should I have a look around here?"

"Check out the building!" Ida Belle urged. "See what he was looking for."

"Do you think it's safe, Mary-Alice?" This was Fortune now.

"Well, there don't appear to be any people around," Mary-Alice said. "I suppose that's a good thing."

Mary-Alice carefully stepped up onto the porch and shone a flashlight through the front window, the one that wasn't boarded up. The circle of light played across a forlorn shag carpet that had probably been a shade of avocado green when it was new.

"I don't see much here." Mary-Alice turned her flashlight up to the bare ceiling. Wires sprouted where a light fixture used to be. "I believe this place has been abandoned for a while. It looks like there have been scavengers."

"What kind of place is it?" Ida Belle asked. "Can you describe it?"

"Just a little camp by the bayou." Mary-Alice took another long look and then made her way back to the Jeep. "It's rather remote. I don't see any other buildings around. It looks like it used to be quite nice, but one of the windows is boarded up, and it's clear no one's been there in a couple of years. It's a shame, really. It seems like it could be a nice home for someone. But there's something else I need to tell you. It's quite remarkable—"

A loud crashing sound pulled Mary-Alice's attention. Just in time, she spotted a dark shape muscling swiftly through the underbrush. Before she knew it she was inside the Jeep, propelled by her survival instincts. She gunned the motor, pulled a sharp U-turn, and sped off in the direction of the Texas border.

"Mary-Alice!" Ida Belle exclaimed. "What on earth just happened?"

"Oh, nothing of importance." Mary-Alice's heart was pounding, and her voice wavered. "Just a friendly little gator. Y'all try to get some rest now. I'll holler if I need anything."

In the excitement, Mary-Alice forgot to tell Ida Belle something important: that she was certain she had seen that house somewhere before.

# CHAPTER 13

Dawn was breaking when Mary-Alice pulled up to the McCully Inn. She was bone-tired. Manny, the handyman, was atop a ladder in the lobby when she walked in, working on a fluorescent light fixture.

Mary-Alice hoped the chatty handyman wouldn't see her. She'd have to stop and talk, and she wanted nothing more than to fall into bed.

But Manny did see her, and Mary-Alice, exhausted as she was, resigned herself to a quarter-hour at minimum of conversation with the garrulous handyman.

"Miss Mary-Alice." He climbed down the ladder. Oh, no. This was going to be a while. Mary-Alice wished she could find a way to sit down, at least.

"I was hoping to talk to one of you ladies," Manny said. "And I knew it was too early to knock on your door. Do you have a minute? Maybe we could sit down."

"Sit down? Why, of course," Mary-Alice was relieved. At least she wouldn't have to stand. Mary-Alice in her sparkly tee and white capris, and Manny in his coveralls, sat across from each other on the lobby chairs with a glass coffee table between them.

"Well now, you know Miss Ida Belle told me to keep an eye out for anything that was worth observing."

"Yes indeed," Mary-Alice stifled a yawn. "And we do so appreciate your vigilance."

"Now, I don't know it this has anything to do with the missing young lady. But I thought it was worth passing along."

"Of course, darlin'." Mary-Alice dug her peach-colored nails into her palms to jolt herself awake.

"Miss Brandi-Lynn was here," Manny said, in a conspiratorial tone. "Mr. Lionel's cousin."

"Why, is that unusual?"

"Well now, I haven't seen her here before. I just happened to overhear a little of their conversation. Not that I was listening in, of course." Manny was drawing the story out for maximum effect. If Mary-Alice were as direct as Ida Belle, she would simply tell him to get on with it. But it was not in Mary-Alice's nature to do any such thing. She would have to suffer and be patient.

"So what did you hear?" Mary-Alice pasted on a patient smile.

"Well now, it seems Miss Brandi-Lynn was none too happy with Mr. Lionel."

"And why would that be?"

"Well now, I couldn't say for certain, Miss Mary-Alice. I'll let you be the judge. She was in his private office, and like I said, I'm not one to eavesdrop, but she was just about hollering at the top of her lungs. This is what she said: 'How could you, Lionel. Our family name is the most precious thing we have. And now you've associated it with a terrible crime…' and that's the honest truth. 'A terrible crime' is what she said to him."

"Crime?" Mary-Alice prompted, feeling a little wider awake. "What kind of crime was she referring to?"

"Well, now I couldn't tell you that. Mr. Lionel said something to her, real quiet like, and I couldn't hear any more than that."

"Now Manny, darlin', did you hear anything else at all? Any names, or possibly an indication of what kind of crime, particularly?"

"No, ma'am. I truly don't have any more information than what I just told you, Miss Mary-Alice. But I did want to pass it along."

"Well thank you so much. Every bit helps. If you find out anything else, please do let me know."

Several disturbing possibilities were stirring in Mary-Alice's mind.

# CHAPTER 14

Fortune and Ida Belle were still asleep when Mary-Alice let herself into the room. Ida Belle was in one of the beds, and Fortune had the couch. Mary-Alice's bed was undisturbed, and looked extremely inviting.

But before she could rest, she had one more thing to do.

"Fortune! Ida Belle! I have some news."

Ida Belle sat up in bed so fast it set her giant hair rollers bouncing.

"You find the girl?"

Fortune did not sit up. Instead she muttered something and pulled her pillow over her head.

"No, but that nice young fellow Manny overheard something." Mary-Alice pulled out the chair and sat at the desk where Fortune's laptop lay under a stack of folders and papers. A cold, half-empty coffee cup completed the tableau.

"As I was coming in this morning, Manny told me that Mr. Lionel's cousin came by and gave him a piece of her mind, and you'll never guess about what. Well, I'll just tell you. She accused him of associating their family name with a terrible crime."

Fortune sat up slowly, and swung her impossibly long legs

onto the floor. When she had finished rubbing the sleep out of her face she asked,

"Can you remember exactly what Lionel McCully did out there? Did it look like he was hiding something for someone else to pick up later? Did he bury anything? Dig anything up?"

Mary-Alice thought hard.

"No indeed, Miss Fortune. It didn't look like he was dropping anything off. He just went up and knocked on the door, and when no one answered, he had himself a look around, and then he drove away."

"Did you have eyes on him the whole time?" Fortune was wide-awake now.

"I did lose sight of him for a moment. Right after he parked and got out of the car."

Mary-Alice slipped off her tennis shoes and sat on the edge of her bed. "My goodness, this feels lovely. I'm sorry, I don't see what you're getting at, Miss Fortune."

"I'm saying maybe the house wasn't empty," Fortune said. "Maybe the knock was a signal."

"Who drives six hours to knock on a door?" Ida Belle called from the bathroom. "He can't sent a text message or make a phone call?"

"He could've been leaving food or supplies for a hostage," Fortune said. "Mary-Alice, did you see any indication of that at all?"

"I didn't see him drop off anything," Mary-Alice said. "But do you know, it's odd. The building looked familiar. I felt I'd seen it before, back when it was in better shape. I wonder whether there isn't a picture of it around here somewhere. Miss Fortune, are you saying Mr. Lionel might have abducted the missing girl? Why, that might be why Miss Ainslee doesn't want us to talk to him about it. She suspects him and she doesn't want to admit it, not even to herself! Should we call the police?"

"And tell them what?" Ida Belle asked.

"Ida Belle's right," Fortune said. "All you witnessed was Lionel McCully knocking on the door of what looked like an abandoned house, and then you saw him drive away. There's nothing to report. We should've sent you out with night vision. Then you could've seen if there was anyone hidden in the house."

"We could ask Gertie to check it out." Ida Belle emerged from the bathroom, brushing her white hair into waves. "The place they went to last night was only about an hour's drive from Sinful. I'm sure Gertie can talk her way into borrowing someone's car."

Ida Belle placed her hairbrush on the night table, picked up her phone, and called.

"Oh, there you are. Well, you're up now, aren't you? Because we have an assignment for you, that's why. What do you mean, finally? Okay, you know where I keep the NVDs? Now listen and take notes. No, I don't trust you to remember. Go get a pen that works. I'll wait."

Ida Belle filled Gertie in on the case to date, read off a set of coordinates, and set a time for Gertie to call her back. When she'd hung up, she said,

"I'm glad we did that. Gertie was going nuts back there, knowing we were having all the fun out here. Okay, where are we?"

"Miss Ida Belle," Mary-Alice asked quietly, "is there a particular reason Miss Gertie didn't join us? Aside from helping out with the cough syrup?"

"She has a gentleman friend out here. Mister Tran. They've been friends since—I guess it's going on fifty years now. He's started making noises about how it's time for them to get married, and Gertie wants none of it. She's happy with the way things are. She's giving him a wide berth till he comes to his senses. Smart choice, if you ask me. Anyway, Gertie's gonna check out the house again."

"Oh, Ida Belle," Mary-Alice asked, "did you remember to tell her about the gator?"

Ida Belle shrugged.

"Gertie's armed. I'm more worried about the gator than about her."

"Mary-Alice," Fortune asked, "do you think you can remember where you saw that house before? It might be important."

"Do y'all mind if I just lie down for just a moment?" Mary-Alice crawled up to the head of the bed and rested her head on the delectably soft pillow.

"Not at all," Fortune said. "You've been driving all night. Ida Belle, let's try to think this through. Okay, number one. Ainslee MacEntire lets her friend, Solange Smith, stay in a vacant room at the hotel. It sounds like Ainslee was doing a favor for a friend. Although she's been pretty evasive about why Solange Smith needed the favor."

"Maybe she was running from someone," Ida Belle said.

"Yeah, I'll buy that. Okay, so Solange goes missing, and her room shows signs of a struggle. Ainslee is so worried that she's willing to spend her own savings to find her. She also doesn't want us to alert Lionel McCully."

"So you think Ainslee suspects Lionel McCully," Ida Belle said.

"Uh huh. And like Mary-Alice said, she might not even realize she suspects him. Who wants to think they're working for a monster? Let's talk to Ainslee again tomorrow."

Mary-Alice was half-listening and drifting off to dreamland when a realization jolted her awake.

"Miss Ida Belle. Miss Fortune. I know where I've seen that house before!"

# CHAPTER 15

It was clear to Mary-Alice that Ainslee MacEntire was not a good liar. What was not as clear was this: what was she lying about?

Mary-Alice, Ida Belle, and Ainslee were sitting at a booth at the Waffle House. Fortune was two booths down with little Bethany, Ainslee's daughter. Bethany seemed perfectly happy to supervise herself, and was watching videos on her little pink mobile phone as Fortune attempted to engage her in conversation.

"There's no way Mr. McCully has anything to do with Solange disappearing," Ainslee was insisting. "I'm a hundred percent sure he doesn't know anything about it."

"Ainslee," Ida Belle said, "You hired us, now trust us. The quicker we find Solange, the better her chances. You know that."

Ainslee shot an anxious glance back at her daughter. Fortune gave Ainslee the thumbs-up. The girl continued to play on her phone.

"Listen." Ida Belle brought Ainslee's attention back. "If you want us to find this girl, we need to know everything you know."

Ainslee was quiet for a long time.

"Okay," she said, finally. "But when you talk to Mr. McCully, I want to be there. I want to explain."

"Ainslee, darlin'," Mary-Alice said gently, "you ever watch any of those police shows on television?"

"Not really. Why?"

"Well, because whenever someone on those shows says they have important information that they're not gonna talk about until later, they always end up dead before they can tell. Now I don't want to scare you or anything, but whatever you're planning to explain to Mr. Lionel, you should tell us now. It won't do to wait."

"Well then, let's go talk to him right now," Ainslee said. "If I get fired, I get fired. There's other jobs out there."

Ida Belle motioned to Fortune, who said something to Bethany.

"But I'm not done with my paaaancakes!" the little girl wailed.

"You go ahead," Fortune called over. "We'll catch up. Where should we meet you?"

"Mr. Lionel's office," Ainslee called back, to Fortune's obvious surprise.

Lionel McCully opened his office door to the three detectives from Sinful, accompanied by his head housekeeper and her little girl.

"Is everything okay, Miss Ainslee?"

"I hope so."

Ainslee stood aside to let Fortune, Ida Belle, Mary-Alice, and finally little Bethany file in. Ainslee came in last and pulled the door shut behind her.

"How may I help you ladies today?" he asked.

"We'd like a word," Ida Belle said.

Lionel McCully's office was not set up for visitors. It contained a small desk and a single chair, and no other furniture. He glanced from Ida Belle to Mary-Alice and back, not sure to which of the older ladies he should offer his seat.

"I believe I'm the senior member of this gathering." Ida Belle plopped into the chair. "So. Let's not beat around the bush. Mr. Lionel, we were brought in to investigate the disappearance of one of your employees, a young lady."

He glanced over at Ainslee, who nodded.

"One of my employees? What happened?"

"Well, that's what we're trying to find out," Ida Belle went on. "We have a few questions."

"I'll help you in any way I can," McCully said earnestly.

"Wonderful. Why did you visit the former home of two escaped convicts last night?"

Lionel McCully fidgeted and reddened.

"Well now, Miss…"

"Ida Belle," Ida Belle prompted him.

"Miss Ida Belle," he stammered, "I do admire your tenacity in collecting information, but I don't see how my comings and goings are germane to your, uh, situation."

"Escaped convicts?" Ainslee's eyes widened.

"They're gonna get the chair!" Little Bethany exclaimed, her eyes fixed on her phone. "They're gonna fry!"

Ainsley patted the little girl's shoulder distractedly.

"Bethany, honey, let the grownups talk. What's all this now?"

Ida Belle swiveled the chair in Ainslee's direction.

"You hear about Willa and Wilfred Woodham? Also known as Ma and Junior? They broke out of prison, killed a couple of guards, and now there's a big reward out for 'em."

"I saw it on live TV when they captured them," Mary-Alice said. "I believe everyone in Mudbug was watching. I mean, it wasn't that far from us. But that's where I'd seen the house before."

"How did you…did you follow me all the way out there?"

"I did," Mary-Alice said, with some pride. She had tailed

McCully halfway across Louisiana and he hadn't even suspected!

"Let's review what we know," Fortune said. "Ainslee came to us to report that your employee had disappeared during the night. She was so worried about the missing girl that she signed a contract to pay a thousand dollars that she probably couldn't afford. There were indications that the girl didn't leave willingly. Mainly that her stuff is still there. Now you, Mr. McCully, were just observed driving across state lines to visit an apparently-abandoned building that used to be the home of two individuals wanted by law enforcement. We also know your cousin confronted you about your involvement with some kind of crime."

"Sounds pretty suspicious to me," Ida Belle chimed in. "Maybe you should tell us where the girl is. Or we call the police right now."

"No!" Ainslee cried. "It's not like that! Mr. McCully, there's something you need to know. I'm so sorry, and if you fire me I completely understand."

"Miss Ainslee? Why ever would I fire—?"

"The missing girl was Solange."

Ainslee's words silenced the room. Even fidgety Bethany, who had been yanking on her mother's arm, fell still.

Lionel McCully stared at her for a few moments.

"Solange?" Lionel's eye were so wide they looked like they would pop out of his head. "Solange was here?"

# CHAPTER 16

"You know who she's talking about?" Fortune demanded. "Miss MacEntire, there's no point in hiring a private investigator if you're going to withhold important information. It's a waste of my time and your money."

"Some things weren't mine to share." Ainslee drew her daughter into a defensive embrace. "And I swear to you, Mr. McCully knew nothing about any of this."

Bethany squirmed free of her mother's arms and turned her attention back to her phone.

"Miss Ainslee," Lionel pleaded, "why didn't you tell me? When was she here? What did she say?"

"She came to me about a week ago," Ainslee said quietly. "She told me she was out of options. She needed work, and she still... she was hoping, Mr. Lionel, but she was afraid. She had no assurance that you still—"

"Miss Ainslee, if you had let me see her—"

"Mr. McCully, I asked her to come downstairs with me and talk to you. I swear I did. So many times. But she was afraid. As long as she could put off seeing you, she said she could imagine you still loved her and missed her. But she was afraid once you'd seen her, you'd tell her to leave, and then she said she'd have nothing. No job, no place to stay, and no hope."

"Well then what was she waiting for?" Lionel cried.

"She was waiting for something from you," Ainslee said quietly. "Some sign that you hadn't forgotten about her."

"Could someone tell us what's going on?" Ida Belle demanded. Mary-Alice was glad Ida Belle asked the question, because she too was dying to know. "Who is this Solange Smith?"

"Smith?" Lionel asked Ainslee.

"That's the name she was using," Ainslee said defensively.

"Mr. McCully," Fortune asked, "do you know the missing person by a different name?"

"Yes. Her name, as far as I know, is still Solange McCully. She's my wife."

Mary-Alice could see the muscles of Fortune's jaw tense up.

"Miss MacEntire." Fortune's voice was deadly calm. "Did the fact that your missing person was married to the owner of the motel from which she was abducted not seem important enough to mention?"

"Mama," Bethany wailed, "that lady is meeeeean! Make her stop talking!"

"Excuse us, please." Ainslee pulled the girl out of the office and closed the door behind her.

# CHAPTER 17

"Ladies," Lionel McCully pleaded, "I swear, I don't know any more about this than you do. I had no idea any of this was going on. And to think my Solange was right here, under this roof—"

"Why was your wife hiding from you?" Ida Belle interrupted.

As Ida Belle seemed to have no intention of giving up Lionel McCully's chair, Fortune and Mary-Alice perched on the desk on either side of her. Lionel sighed and leaned against the wall.

"Y'all got some time?" he asked.

"Take all the time you need," Fortune said.

"I'm sure y'all have heard about my daddy," he said. "Put the town of Lemon Tree on the map. Or so he liked to say. McCully Motors, this here McCully Inn, the apartments downtown—"

"And let's not forget that big unfinished housing development," Ida Belle cut in. "Did you know after construction stopped, the workers didn't get their last paychecks? He ripped off everyone from the bank on down."

Lionel nodded sadly. "Winning was everything to him. Making sure you got ahead, took every advantage. That's why he had his heart set on me marrying Brandi-Lynn."

"Your cousin?" Fortune blurted out.

"Yes ma'am."

"Your father wanted you to marry your first cousin? I mean..." Fortune glanced around at her companions. "Is that usual in Texas?"

"No ma'am." Lionel looked miserable. "It's not even legal in Texas. Nor in Louisiana, for that matter. My daddy didn't care. His plan was for Brandi-Lynn and me to get married in New Mexico, and then come back here."

"Wait, Texas and Louisiana don't let you marry your first cousin, but New Mexico does?" Fortune cleared her throat and fidgeted. "Sorry, it's just that...I mean I would've thought... never mind."

"Well now, how did Miss Brandi-Lynn feel about this plan?" Mary-Alice asked gently.

Lionel shrugged.

"Didn't bother her none. Brandi-Lynn's a lot like my daddy. Very ambitious, and not too worried about the ethical fine points. I didn't want to have anything to do with it. That's why as soon as I was out of college I told my daddy I needed some time to travel. I went the opposite direction from New Mexico, over to Louisiana. I just wanted to spend some time on my own, do some fishing, and get my head on straight. Well, I was on the road, the weather turned bad, it turned out to be a hurricane, and I pulled over and stopped at the first house I could find. Little camp right on the bayou. I knocked on the door and who do you suppose opened it? Solange. I knew she was the one for me, right then. Love at first sight, just like in the storybooks."

"And so you married?" Mary-Alice asked.

He shook his head.

"No. Not then. I stayed the night. Solange was an angel, but her brother made me nervous. And her mama was even worse. I don't know, it was something about 'em put me on edge. I didn't know at the time they were robbing banks. Well, credit unions, if you want to be precise about it."

"You stayed the night with Ma and Junior Woodham?" Mary-Alice gasped.

"Yes, ma'am. I left the next morning when the weather'd calmed down enough. I thought about Solange every day from then on, though. Even though I knew there wasn't a chance of me being with her. Well, a little while after that I went over to New Orleans for Mardi Gras, and it was like a miracle. Up on a balcony, there was my Solange. She had all these beads. She looked like a goddess..."

Lionel brought himself back down to earth.

"Well, now, I need to give y'all some background here. My daddy had fallen ill, and he'd started to make plans for when he was gone. So the car dealership and the apartments went to my sister. He told me I could have the McCully Inn because he said the place practically runs itself and any jackass could do the job. And that's when he told me I was to marry Brandi-Lynn. That way the money would stay in the family, he said, and she'd make certain I didn't make any stupid decisions. Well, when I met up with Solange out there in New Orleans, it was like fate had given me a second chance. I wasn't gonna let her go this time. We got married then and there. I figured after that my daddy couldn't make me marry Brandi-Lynn. Solange was my wife, and he couldn't do anything about it."

"Still waiting to find out why she was hiding in one of your rooms," Ida Belle said.

"Ma'am, you didn't know my daddy. Not that it's any excuse for the cowardly way I behaved. I brought Solange back here to the Inn and put her up in one of the rooms. I didn't dare introduce her right away. I figured the time had to be right. Well, my daddy took a turn for the worse and the doctor called me in. I figured it was my last chance, so I brought Solange over, and had her wait outside the sick room while I went in to soften him up, you see. But he started in right away about Brandi Lynn having another suitor and how I needed to get moving before she was off the market. So I said, well, it may be as Brandi-Lynn is happier that way, and speaking of that, I have some news, but before I could go on, my daddy roared that if he got a whiff of disobedience from me, he'd cut me right out of his will. Well, I didn't care about myself, but I wanted Solange to have a comfortable life. So I thought I'd just say what I had to say to calm my daddy down. I told him, fine, I'll marry Brandi-Lynn. I never meant to go through with it. I was just saying it to make him happy."

"And Miss Solange overheard you?" Mary-Alice asked.

Lionel nodded.

"I came out of that room to explain what had just happened. And tell her not to worry. But she was already gone. I never saw her again. I've been looking for her ever since."

"Did you suppose you might find her at Texas Tommy's?" Mary-Alice asked. "Or The Yellow Rose?"

Lionel nodded. "I've been looking in a few other places too, that she liked to go to. I was never one to go out much, but she did love to go out dancing, and I was happy to oblige her."

A soft knock on the door was followed by Ainslee's head poking in.

"Sorry about Bethany. She's doing her homework in the lobby, and Manny's keeping an eye on her. I thought Mr. McCully might have some more questions for me."

"Come in," Ida Belle commanded. "Miss Ainslee, there is one thing I'd like to clear up. Now in observing Mr. McCully's movements, it appeared that he was looking for a blonde. Is that correct?"

"It is," he said. "Solange had the most beautiful hair. Like the color of sunlight."

"But you told us your missing girl had dark hair," Ida Belle said to Ainslee.

"She dyed it," Ainslee said plainly.

"May I see where she was staying?" Lionel asked.

# CHAPTER 18

They all went trooping up to the second-floor room that Ainslee had shown them earlier. Lionel went over to the dresser and opened the drawers one by one. Mary-Alice noticed him holding the turquoise belly-button jewel which she had mistaken for an earring. He hastily wiped an eye and set the item down when he saw her watching.

"Solange was staying here." It was a statement, not a question.

Ainslee nodded.

"This is the room she was staying in before. When I first brought her to Lemon Tree." He walked over to the closet, slid open the door, and ran his hands over the tiny jeans and tank tops hanging there. "She left without taking her things. Miss Ainslee, I thank you for taking such good care of her. But I must admit to being rather vexed that you didn't share her whereabouts with me."

"I consider her a friend, Mr. McCully," Ainslee said. "We got to know each other pretty well when she was staying here the first time. And I'm sorry, but I had to respect her wishes. She wanted to take it slow. I feel responsible for her going missing. That's why I brought the ladies in."

"Miss Ainslee, don't you pay a penny of your hard-earned money for this," Lionel declared. "All this mess is entirely my doing."

"Too late," Ida Belle said. "She already paid us."

"Well then, Miss Ainslee, I'll pay you back. Ladies, are y'all any closer to finding her than I am? Because I haven't had much luck at all."

"We might have made more progress if we'd been given all the information," Fortune said pointedly.

"Am I fired?" Ainslee asked fearfully.

"Not at all, Miss Ainslee. This is entirely my fault. You were out of the room with Miss Bethany when I was telling the ladies about it, so perhaps I should explain. I told my father I'd marry Brandi-Lynn, but the only reason I did that is I wanted to get the inheritance so I could support Solange the way she deserved. Now I have the danged inheritance and I don't have Solange. I can't blame anyone but myself."

"She told me what happened," Ainslee said quietly. "She heard everything."

"We were looking for a Solange Smith, Ainslee," Fortune made no effort to hide her exasperation. "That's why I couldn't find her. I should have been looking for a Solange McCully."

"But she wasn't going by McCully anymore," Ainslee defended herself.

"You might have let us know her maiden name," Mary-Alice said. "My goodness, I can't say I admired Ma Woodham exactly, but it's so unusual, isn't it, to have a woman in charge. I mean to say, bank-robbing is such a male-dominated profession."

"I don't know why anyone robs banks these days," Fortune added. "You can make so much more money defrauding people online, and it's not nearly as risky."

"Why are we talking about robbing banks?" Ainslee looked confused.

"Just another small detail you omitted about your missing person," Ida Belle said pointedly. "The fact that your friend's immediate family was a pair of armed and dangerous escaped convicts."

"What? Solange's family?"

"You didn't know?" Fortune asked.

"No. You have to believe me," Ainslee fought back tears. "I'm sorry. I didn't know anything about her family. I didn't even know her maiden name. She told me she was going by Smith, so that's what I told you. I just knew she was sorry she ran away from Mr. McCully, and she wanted to make things right with him. I was only trying to help."

"They have her," Lionel McCully said quietly, still gazing at the closet full of abandoned clothes. "Her mama and her brother. I was worried sick when I heard they'd broken out of prison, and now I know I was right to be."

Fortune stood up.

"I think we're done here. My advice to both of you is to call the police and tell them everything. We did the best we could, but there's only so much we can do if we don't have all the facts."

Mary-Alice and Ida Belle had no choice but to follow Fortune out of the hotel room and back to Sinful.

# CHAPTER 19

"I wonder whether either the hotel owner or the housekeeper really cared about the girl at all," Gertie mused as she tucked the bills (two hundreds, two twenties, and a ten) into her giant handbag. "Or if the whole thing was a ruse to get close to the Woodhams, and then get the reward money."

The women were sitting around Fortune's kitchen table, enjoying blueberry cheesecake squares from Francine's Diner

"Miss Ainslee didn't appear to know that the missing girl was related to the escaped convicts," Mary-Alice said.

"Not that she let on," Ida Belle added.

"I realize I kind of lost it back there, and I'm sorry if I embarrassed anyone," Fortune said. "But not telling us about her relationship to Ma and Junior Woodham—not knowing that could've gotten us killed."

"You were pretty upset," Ida Belle agreed. "I don't believe I've ever seen you so mad about anything."

"Am I wrong?"

"Nah, I get it." Ida Belle picked the last crumb from her plate then helped herself to another cheesecake square.

"Ida Belle, that's your third helping," Gertie pointed out. "We've gotta stay in shape now that we've gone pro."

"Don't you worry about me," Ida Belle said with her mouth full. "Hey, you get your new prescription yet for the night vision goggles? Doesn't do much good to have 'em if everything's a green blur, now, does it?"

"Oh yeah, thanks for sending me all the way out to scope out a totally abandoned house," Gertie retorted. "That was exciting. And by the way, Ida Belle, I could see well enough to know that there was nothing alive in there. Unless you count that big gator."

"Now, I'm new to all of this detecting," Mary-Alice ventured, "and perhaps I need to learn how to keep from getting too emotionally involved, but aren't y'all still worried about Miss Solange? She's still missing, after all."

"You have to detach," Fortune said, not meeting Mary-Alice's gaze. "If you get too close, you can screw things up. Worse than you know."

The women were saying their good-byes when Ida Belle's phone rang. She answered it as the other three women watched.

"Lionel McCully," she mouthed to them as she listened.

"Is that so," Ida Belle said, and then, "what time was this?" and finally, "tonight? Okay, we'll be there soon."

Ida Belle clicked off.

"Time to do some speed-packing, ladies," she announced. "Let's meet back here in twenty minutes."

"What happened?" Fortune asked.

"The other shoe dropped," Ida Belle said. "Solange McCully's being held for ransom. And Lionel swears he'll give us any information we need."

# CHAPTER 20

The four Sinful ladies, Ainslee MacEntire, and Lionel McCully were gathered around the computer in Lionel's tiny office. They were watching what Mary-Alice thought was the most disturbing thing she'd ever seen.

A woman—heartbreakingly young—sat against a white wall, her eyes wide with terror, her mouth sealed shut with two strips of silver duct tape. Her dyed-black hair had grown out and her natural pale blonde roots were coming in, giving the illusion that her hair was floating above her scalp.

A computer-generated voice assured the viewer that Solange was still alive and would continue in this state as long as instructions were followed. Lionel McCully was to make a deposit into a certain bank account. Fortune wrote down the account number as they listened. When the funds cleared, the robotic voice explained, Solange Woodham would be released unharmed.

Fortune started to say something, but was drowned out by Ainslee's sudden sobbing.

"I'm sorry," she sniffled. "I can't watch any more. Fortune, Ida Belle, Mary-Alice, Gertie, I'll meet you up at your room."

"Please don't tell anyone what you saw here," Ida Belle instructed her sternly.

"Not even your handyman," Fortune said.

"Oh, goodness, no," Mary-Alice agreed. "That young man simply loves to talk."

Any admiration Mary-Alice had once held for Ma Woodham had vanished. The woman was treating her own daughter like a disposable bargaining chip. Outlaws might seem glamorous in the movies, Mary-Alice thought, but when it came down to it, in real life they were generally quite disagreeable.

"Forward the email to Ida Belle," Fortune said, when the short clip had ended. "We'll see what we can do about narrowing down their location."

"You won't contact the authorities, will you?" Lionel asked, genuinely afraid. "The voice said not to contact the police."

"They always say that," Fortune replied. "But think about it. What kind of result do you think you're going to get if you don't call the police? But don't you call, Mr. McCully. Let us handle it."

Ainslee was waiting for them on the second floor of the motel.

"I saved your old room for you," she said. "And I put in another rollaway so the four of you will be comfortable. Gertie, so pleased to make your acquaintance."

"Likewise," Gertie said.

"I'm so glad you agreed to come. I'm just sick about Solange."

"Well, yes, we'll certainly do our best," Gertie said. "You two must have been very close."

Ainslee nodded, waited to make sure the keys worked, and then hurried off.

Once inside the room, Ida Belle quickly set up her laptop and opened the ransom video Lionel had forwarded.

"Is there any way to tell where it was filmed?" Mary-Alice asked.

"There might be," Fortune said. "Ida Belle, may I?"

Ida Belle got up and let Fortune take her place at the computer.

"I may be able to call in a favor…" Fortune muttered as she tapped on the keyboard.

"It's getting late," Gertie said, "and I never got to have dinner."

"Me neither," Ida Belle echoed. "Just the cheesecake squares back at Marge's—I mean, Fortune's house."

"It's okay," Fortune said, not looking up. "I still think of it as Aunt Marge's house too. I try to make her proud every day. Even though she never met me."

"Ally's baked goods are wonderful," Mary-Alice said, "but they aren't a proper meal."

"Unless you eat four of 'em in a row like Ida Belle," Gertie said.

"Why don't you all go to the Waffle House across the way," Fortune said, eyes still fixed on the computer screen. "I'll stay here."

"May we bring you back something?" Mary-Alice asked.

"I'm not hungry. Thanks anyway."

When they returned to the hotel room half an hour later, it was obvious something had happened. Fortune stood up as soon as they came in, and Mary-Alice would have sworn she was tucking something into the waistband of her jeans. A gun?

"Harrison got the location," Fortune said. "Townehouse Downes."

"What the heck kind of name is Townhouse Downs?" Gertie demanded as she dug in her suitcase and brought out two preposterous-looking pairs of goggles.

"It's an abandoned housing development up the road," Fortune said. "Huge eyesore. Lionel McCully's dad is the one they can thank for it. He scammed the bank, probably should've gone to jail over it, but of course never did."

"So is it time to call the police yet?" Mary-Alice asked.

"Yes," Fortune said. "Now is the time. Go ahead and call emergency, Mary-Alice. Tell them we have information about Ma Woodham and her son and we believe they have a hostage."

As Mary-Alice talked to the dispatcher, she wondered how Fortune could tell where the video had been taken. This "Harrison" person must be a librarian friend of hers who had access to some kind of fancy database.

When Mary-Alice hung up, she asked,

"Are we certain the Woodhams have Miss Solange? We know they escaped, and we know Miss Solange disappeared shortly afterward. But didn't you say the handyman, Manny, was staying in Townhouse Downes?"

They were interrupted by a knock on the door. Ida Belle opened it to find Lionel standing there, looking haggard.

"Is there any news?" he asked.

"The police have a lead on their location," Ida Belle said.

"Where is she? Do you know?"

Ida Belle, Fortune, and Gertie all shrugged convincingly.

"They said the fugitives are armed and dangerous," Fortune said. "This is no job for amateurs. If your wife is still alive, they'll bring her back. By the way, where's your handyman? Manny?"

"I don't know who that is," he said. "I'm terribly sorry, but Miss Ainslee takes care of all the hiring. Now isn't there anything we can do?"

"We can wait here, and do whatever the police tell us to do," Ida Belle said authoritatively.

Lionel straightened up.

"I'll stay here with you, then, and wait for news. I can have supper brought up for us."

"Nice of you to offer, but we just ate," Gertie said.

He glanced around at the four women who were clearly

waiting for him to leave. His upbringing would not allow him to intrude on a party that clearly didn't want him there.

"I'll just go on down to my office then," he said. "Please let me know if you hear anything."

# CHAPTER 21

A steady "whup-whup" sound signaled a helicopter overhead. The helicopter's searchlight swept the flat area in front of them, occasionally lighting up the abandoned housing development ahead.

"Roadblock," Ida Belle said. Two police cars, lights flashing, were parked sideways to block the road into Townehouse Downes.

"Turn off here," Ida Belle commanded, and Fortune swerved onto a dirt path. "Don't worry. Marge's Jeep's taken worse than this."

"Are you sure we should be here?" Mary-Alice asked from the back seat. Fortune had pulled off the road onto a narrower street. It was paved, but cracked and overgrown. To their left, hulking, half-built McMansions loomed in the dark. To their right were acres of scrubby, undeveloped land. In the distance Mary-Alice could see headlights and taillights moving on the highway.

"Keep going," said Ida Belle. "Stay on the access road going north."

Mary-Alice hadn't been to Townhouse Downes before. The

dark husks of houses looked more desolate than she could have imagined. It broke her heart to think of the workers like Manny, who must have been so proud to be part of building something so grand, until it all came crashing down thanks to the greed of Lionel McCully, Senior. She remembered a poem she had learned in school.

Look on my works, ye Mighty, and despair! Nothing beside remains.

A flicker of motion in her peripheral vision made Mary-Alice turn around. Through the cloudy back window of the Jeep, she saw the glint of a car in the moonlight. Its lights were off.

"Someone's following us," Mary-Alice said.

"Cover 'em, Gertie," Ida Belle said calmly, and to Mary-Alice's astonishment, Gertie pulled an enormous handgun out of her bag, held it with both hands, twisted around and slid the gun just out the window, pointed at the car behind them.

"Two NVDs, right?" Fortune asked.

"I can't put on the goggles while I'm trying to cover this guy," Gertie said. "Mary-Alice and Ida Belle, you two should put 'em on. You should be able to see adults at two hundred yards, and distinguish male and female at a hundred fifty."

Ida Belle reached back and helped Mary-Alice put on the goggles.

"It feels weird at first but you'll get used to it pretty fast," Ida Belle explained.

"Well now, I thought these night vision doohickeys couldn't see through walls," Mary-Alice said as she turned to take another look at the car that was still following them. This time, she saw a glowing body in the driver's seat, and the hood was lit up like a furnace.

"These aren't available to the general public," Fortune said.

"We got 'em on eBay," Ida Belle added quickly. "Probably some kid's science fair project."

As Mary-Alice's eyes adjusted, she was able to see that the "abandoned" housing development was teeming with life. Four-legged creatures slunk, scurried, and strutted around the empty buildings. And then Ida Belle cried,

"Stop!"

Mary-Alice saw right away what Ida Belle was talking about. In the house to their left, a human figure paced.

"Why, I see it," Mary-Alice exclaimed. "Walking around on the second floor!"

Fortune pulled the Jeep to the edge of the dirt road and stopped.

"Can I see?" she asked. Mary-Alice lifted the device from her head and handed it to Fortune.

"She's holding still now," Ida Belle said.

"Our friend stopped a ways back," Gertie said. "I've still got 'em covered."

Fortune adjusted her headset.

"Anything?" Gertie asked.

"Not up here. How about our friend back there?"

"Nothing. Just parked, waiting."

They sat for a few minutes.

"Why, this is just awful," Mary-Alice remarked. "I mean, the kidnapping is terrible, of course, but these houses. Why, these look like they could have been perfectly good homes, and there are so many people out there without."

"That looks like the girl," Fortune said. "She's small, just like Ainslee said. I wish I knew where Ma and Junior were. Not knowing makes me real nervous. Maybe if we carefully—"

"Willa and Willard Woodham," blared a male voice from a loudspeaker somewhere. "Come out with your hands up."

"She's moving," Ida Belle said.

A figure passed by the window, barely visible in the moonlight.

"Whoa," Gertie exclaimed, "our friend's getting out of the car."

Mary-Alice looked back, just as the helicopter's spotlight made a sweep of the area.

"Why, it's Mr. Lionel!" Mary-Alice exclaimed.

"Idiot," Ida Belle muttered.

Lionel McCully had seen the figure in the window. And recognized her.

"Trade places with me, Mary-Alice," Gertie ordered as she climbed over Mary-Alice to get to the left-hand seat. Mary-Alice was more than happy to comply, especially as Gertie was still holding her handgun.

They watched Lionel walk onto the weed-infested dirt behind the house.

"Solange, darlin'," Lionel cried out. "It's me, sweetheart. I'm here for you."

The helicopter passed low overhead, kicking up clouds of dust. The spotlight swept across the abandoned houses and scrubby fields.

"I said no cops," a woman's voice yelled.

The spotlight swept past again, lighting up a skinny girl with black hair. She was raising a shotgun to her shoulder, pointing it right at Lionel McCully.

Gertie pulled her trigger. The girl flew backward, and the shotgun tumbled to the ground.

Lionel didn't move. He stood on the bare dirt, stunned.

"I think it's time for us to go." Fortune gunned the Jeep as the sirens got louder and the police closed in on the scene.

# CHAPTER 11

Solange Woodham sustained a small injury to her wrist where Gertie had shot the gun out of her hands, but was otherwise unharmed. Faced with the prospect of spending the rest of her life in prison, she made a deal, and ratted out her mother and brother. Ma and Junior Woodham were apprehended in Brownsville, right before they were able to cross into Mexico.

Lionel McCully was devastated to learn that not only had Solange faked her own kidnapping, but the entire scheme had been her idea. She figured if she simply asked him for money, he might say no. Staging a kidnapping would yield better results. He wanted nothing to do with the reward money, and let the Sinful Ladies' Detective Agency have it all.

"So the girl, Solange, was deceiving poor Ainslee as well?" Gertie asked.

The ladies were safely back in Sinful, gathered around Fortune's kitchen table and savoring their triumph (along with a platter of chocolate-chip cookies).

"Looks like it," Fortune said. "They'd become friends when Solange was hiding out at the hotel before, and Solange took advantage. Ainslee had no idea. She really thought that she was like a fairy godmother, helping to bring the two young lovers back together."

"The poor thing. She must have been lonesome," Mary-Alice mused. "A widow, working all hours like she did…I can see how Miss Ainslee would have been happy to help out someone she thought was a friend."

"Well, Lionel McCully got over Solange pretty quickly," Gertie said. "Harriet down at the bookstore told me he's already filed to annul their quickie Mardi Gras wedding."

"How does Harriet know that?" Ida Belle demanded.

"Someone in Harriet's bookseller's group has a cousin out in Pinehurst. It's been the talk of the town," Gertie said.

"By the way, don't mind me." Fortune was paging through a stack of envelopes. "I'm still behind on bills. Help yourselves to tea and cookies. Oh, look at this."

Fortune drew a large manila envelope from the stack, tore the end open, and pulled out a paper with a check attached.

"Nice. Here's our payment. From McCully Partners. For services rendered."

"Did we actually bill him after all that?" Mary-Alice exclaimed. "I mean, we did get the reward money."

"Well of course we billed him," Ida Belle declared. "We're a business, not a charity."

"And here's a note." Fortune lifted a Post-It and read,

"To the Wonderful Ladies of the Sinful Ladies' Detective Agency,

Thank you for your great work on this case and for helping me to find some important answers to questions I didn't even know I had.

With gratitude,

Lionel."

"There's something else in there." Gertie shook the envelope and a smaller, cream-colored envelope fell out. Fortune picked it up.

"Open it!" Ida Belle urged, although it was already clear to everyone what was inside.

"The honor of your presence is requested," Fortune read, "at the marriage of Ainslee MacEntire to Lionel McCully. Whoa. I did not see that coming."

"It does make sense, the two of them," Gertie said. "She obviously adores him, and he needs her to help him keep his head on straight."

"Well I think it's very romantic," Mary-Alice said.

"Now I have an important question," Ida Belle interrupted. "Should we invest in some new equipment? I think we could use an electric van. They run real quiet, you know. And gas isn't about to get any cheaper."

And from there the ladies spent an agreeable evening discussing how they were going to spend their money.

# VAMPIRE BILLIONAIRE OF THE BAYOU

Stock art: Pixabay, Freepik, Vecteezy

# CHAPTER 1

Mary-Alice Arceneaux marveled at her good fortune. If she were still living back in Mudbug, the high point of her week would be Crafting Circle or Bingo Night. But since she had moved to the town of Sinful, Louisiana (population 253), her life had become far more exciting. Her new friends, Fortune, Gertie, and Ida Belle, had led her into all kinds of exciting adventures. Even better, the four had recently combined forces to form the Sinful Ladies' Detective Agency.

Like Mary-Alice, Ida Belle and Gertie were on the sweet side of seventy. This was an advantage in the world of detecting, as people tended to let their guard down around harmless-looking old ladies.

Young Fortune Morrow, the leader of the agency, claimed to be a children's librarian and retired beauty queen, although Mary-Alice had her doubts about that. Fortune looked like Barbie, but she walked, shot, and swore like G.I. Joe.

"And here we are." Fortune pulled off the road and parked on the patchy grass underneath a spreading oak. "The haunted Polk Plantation. At least according to the Sinful Sprits Ghost Tours website. Everyone have your client files?"

"Now, don't make fun, Fortune," Gertie chided. "Lots of folks around here genuinely believe there are ghosts here. Do you know, back when I was still teaching, I tried more than once to take my class to the Polk Plantation for a field trip. It would have been a fascinating history lesson. But so many of the parents refused to sign the permission slips that I could never manage it."

"My daddy always said that ghost stuff was a bunch of superstitious nonsense," Ida Belle said. "Although he never would eat both ends of a loaf of bread, and practically had a stroke one time when a bird tapped on our window. Mary-Alice, did you ever come here for the tour when you were a girl?"

"I never dared ask. My parents believed it wasn't proper for a good Catholic girl to take an interest in ghosts and spirits." Mary-Alice did not mention that her father was too busy chasing the help to be bothered to take his daughter anywhere. And her mother did take an interest in spirits, but only the kind found in a Sazerac cocktail.

"Alright. Are we ready to leave the air conditioning and brave the mosquitoes?" Fortune opened the door and swung her long legs out for an effortless dismount. She then went around the Jeep and helped the three others down.

"Gotta love eccentric billionaires," Ida Belle said. "Of all the places this guy could live, he decides to hole up at an old tourist trap in the middle of nowhere."

Unlike the movie version of Tara from *Gone with the Wind*, the Polk Plantation's big house was not particularly impressive. It was white with gray railings, and two dormer windows sticking out of the shake roof. There was no grand, pillared entrance. Only upper and lower floors of equal height, with wooden stairs connecting the two.

"I think having too much money turns your brain," Gertie

said. "Like Howard Hughes. Oh, my goodness, we're not going to walk into a house full of pee bottles, are we?"

"I doubt it," Fortune said. "Blood bottles, maybe."

Mary-Alice had never met a billionaire before. She trailed behind the other ladies, tugging her sequined t-shirt straight and wondering whether she was underdressed. Then again, Fortune was wearing jeans, Ida Belle had on a track suit, and Gertie was strutting along in an oversized off-the-shoulder tee and slightly baggy leopard-print leggings. As Fortune lifted her hand to knock, the doors swung open.

"In here," a man called out from somewhere in the back. "Behind the workout station."

"Oh my!" Gertie pressed her hand to her chest. "Now this is what I call an extreme makeover!"

The inside of the house had been gutted and painted stark white. In the center of the sparsely-furnished, warehouse-sized room stood an assembly of workout machines with a mirrored wall behind it. There were no visible light fixtures; instead, the entire ceiling glowed.

"It could do with a bit of color," Mary-Alice whispered. "Maybe some nice throw pillows."

"Should I close—" Fortune started to call out, but the doors snapped shut behind them.

"SLEMCO must be making a fortune off this guy." Ida Belle muttered as they made their way to the back of the house. "It feels like a freezer in here."

They made their way around the gym, past an open kitchen with stainless-steel fixtures, to a wide doorway that opened into a compact office.

"Come in," Raymond Fosca called out. He sat behind a cluttered desk as a young man in a white Hemo-Vital jumpsuit ministered to Fosca's extended arm. Mary-Alice caught a glimpse of the crimson tube snaking into Fosca's vein and quickly looked down at her sneakers.

Fosca leaned back and closed his eyes.

"Ah, DeVonne," he murmured. "You do have a way with the cannula. Ladies, make yourselves comfortable."

This was an empty invitation, as Fosca occupied in the only chair in the room.

"Feels like your climate control's on the blink, Mr. Fosca," Ida Belle said.

Fosca opened his eyes.

"Not at all. Cold thermogenesis is an effective anti-aging adjunct to the transfusion treatment series."

Fosca himself seemed perfectly comfortable, although he wore only a t-shirt and jeans. The false daylight from the glowing ceiling illuminated his bruise-blotched arms. Some of the marks were fresh and purple, while others had faded to yellow.

Fosca's anti-aging regime appeared to be only partly successful. At first glance, he looked to be around thirty; his hair was lush and his face unlined. But something about his eyes indicated a much older man.

Finally, the medic swabbed and bandaged Fosca's arm, packed up, and left. Fosca watched the young man walk away, then rolled his chair up to his desk.

"Now. Down to business."

# CHAPTER 2

"You are familiar with Hemo-Vital?" Raymond Fosca asked.

Fortune nodded. "Your company sells elective blood transfusions. Like the one we just observed. Claimed benefits include improved muscle strength and cognition. You made a killing on the IPO, you maintain a controlling share in the company although you've largely removed yourself from day-to-day operations, and you don't care for the vampire jokes."

"You've done your homework. Good girl."

Fosca picked up two manila folders from his cluttered desk and handed them to Fortune.

"Thomas Williams," she read. "And Terry Poindexter. Why am I looking at this?"

"I want you to watch them. Follow them. Where do they go? Who do they talk to? What do they say to each other? Can you do that?"

"You're talking twenty-four-seven surveillance?" Fortune asked.

"I can afford it," Fosca replied.

"Why do you want to surveil them?"

"That's my business."

"If we're going to take the job, we need to know that we're not party to stalking or harassment."

Annoyance flashed on Fosca's face, but he quickly controlled it.

"I have reason to suspect that one or both individuals are involved in a plan to steal my intellectual property. Trade secrets. That is why I want a report of their actions. I want you to devote your full attention to this case."

"Now, Mr. Fosca, what you're asking—" Fortune began.

"I understand you have other clients clamoring for your services. And I assume your standard fee does not include a provision for exclusivity. So. I am offering to pay a surcharge."

When Fosca mentioned the sum, Mary-Alice held her breath. Gertie emitted a squeak of excitement, then clapped her hand over her mouth. Ida Belle folded her arms and frowned, as if to demonstrate how unimpressed she was. She was probably calculating how many new motorcycles she could buy with her share.

Fortune kept a poker face as she leafed through the files.

"We can commit to one week," she said, finally. "You'll get daily reports via secure email."

"There is no such thing as secure email."

"What do you suggest instead?" Fortune asked.

"A status meeting at midpoint, and a hardcopy report to be delivered seven days from now."

"Fine." Fortune kept her face perfectly neutral. "We'll commit one week at this point. If at that time you're happy, and we're happy, we can see where we want to go from there, and we can see what we can do about our other commitments."

"I'll put it on the calendar." Ida Belle pulled her phone out. "Hey, there's no signal."

"No, there is not," Fosca said. "This is the secure room."

"Secure from what?" Fortune asked.

"Signal leakage. A precaution."

"Speaking of precautions," Ida Belle said, "We'll need half payment up front."

"Do you accept TaggertCoin?" Fosca opened his desk drawer.

"Cash or check," Fortune replied.

"Cash it is, then." He pulled out a bulging tan envelope and offered it to her. She handed it to Gertie, who deftly riffled through each roll of bills to confirm the amount.

Mary-Alice was glad to see their meeting was wrapping up. Not only was Fosca's house freezing, the tiny office had no windows. The blank white walls were making her feel claustrophobic.

"I guess we have what we need," Fortune said. "Was there anything else?"

"Yes, there is." Fosca stood and ran a hand through his unnaturally thick hair. "Sinful Spirits."

"The bus tour company?" Fortune asked.

"I have made it abundantly clear that the Polk Plantation is no longer open to the public. But that bus drives by nearly every day. It would be bad enough if they simply passed on, but they stop and let out all the looky-loos and tire-kickers. They peer in my windows, try the doors, and leave trash everywhere. The tourists are a nuisance, but beyond that, it would be all too easy for someone who wished me harm to hide in a crowd. Trying to go through official channels has gotten me nowhere."

"Do you have footage from your security cameras?" Fortune asked.

"There are no security cameras. I have yet to find a system that is completely hacker-safe."

Fosca placed his hands on his desk to steady himself. "I do not believe in fear. But I will admit to a touch of what one might call informed paranoia."

"Do you have family or friends you're worried about?" Fortune asked. "As far as a kidnap risk?"

"Yes. I have Angela."

Fosca pressed a button under his desk and immediately a gleaming cage descended from the ceiling. Angela cocked her head and hopped from her perch to the side of the cage, where her feet gripped the slender steel bars.

"Angela is a European starling." Fosca gazed with affection at the plump little bird. "True, her beauty is not of the ostentatious sort. But in this garish age, I find her modesty quite becoming."

"Well, Raymond Fosca takes the prize for creepiest client ever," Gertie declared as they climbed into the Jeep.

"I must say, I'm impressed by his commitment to his decor," Mary-Alice declared. "Even his little pet bird doesn't have any color."

"Careful." Ida Belle buckled herself in and turned to the back seat. "He can probably hear us talking, somehow."

"If he doesn't like what he hears, he doesn't have to hire us." Fortune gunned the engine and sped off. "But honestly, I've worked with worse than Son of Dracula back there. For a lot less money, too. Hey, we're going to have an easy case this time. No murders, no missing people. Kind of a nice change of pace, don't you think?"

# CHAPTER 3

Thomas Williams and Terry Poindexter seemed like unlikely corporate saboteurs. The surveillance targets appeared to have better things to do than steal anyone's company secrets. When they weren't in their hotel room, they were out hiking, paddling, and snapping selfies on their phones.

"I must say, Miss Gertie," Mary-Alice ventured during one of their tedious nights .of surveillance, "I felt nothing but sorry for Mr. Fosca when I met him, and you may laugh at me if you like, but I feel even sorrier for him now."

Mary-Alice glanced at the passenger seat in time to see Gertie's head fall forward.

"Miss Gertie, you're falling asleep again!"

"What?" Gertie snapped her head upright and lifted the binoculars to her eyes.

Mary-Alice reached over and gently turned the binoculars around the right way.

"They turned the light out half an hour ago, Miss Gertie. May I pour you a cup of coffee?"

"No, I promise I'll stay awake. If I drink any more coffee I'll be prowling around in the bushes all night looking for a place to pee. Now what were you saying, Mary-Alice?"

"I was saying I feel terrible for Mr. Fosca. He's a very lonely man."

"Don't feel sorry for him," Gertie retorted. "He's a creepy control freak, and he has way too much money to deserve anyone's pity. And he's using a fake name, so he probably has a criminal background. How much do you want to bet he's got bodies buried all over that house?"

"Do you really think so?" Mary-Alice gasped.

"Nah, not really. Well, there was that body that turned up on the property right after he moved in, but it was just some poor hobo who probably died of alcohol poisoning."

"I read the book he got his name from," Mary-Alice said quietly. "It's called *All Men are Mortal*. In the book, there's a man named Raymond Fosca who is cursed to live forever. He's doomed to witness humanity's failures and disappointments, one after another, through history. And he only wants to make the world a better place, but it never works out."

"I don't see how spying on a pair of newlyweds is making the world a better place," Gertie retorted. "All it's doing is reminding me how long it's been since I've had any action."

"Well, it's three nineteen," Mary-Alice said brightly. "Less than four hours to go on our shift."

"And then we get to come back and do it all again tomorrow night." Gertie stifled a yawn.

At the four-day mark, the ladies returned to the Polk Plantation.

This time, the meeting took place in the spacious living room. Raymond Fosca had some color in his face, and his movements were energetic. He was wearing the same jeans and t-shirt uniform as before, only this time the shirt was dark blue instead of dark green. A fresh violet bruise in the crook of his arm marked the site of his recent transfusion.

Fosca paced as he leafed through the surveillance report. Ida Belle, Gertie, and Mary-Alice huddled on Fosca's couch, shivering. Fortune stood and paced, acting as if the cold didn't bother her at all. Perhaps it didn't.

"We didn't observe anything to support the idea that your targets had any intention of stealing from you," Fortune said. "Or that they even know who you are. There wasn't a single mention of you or Hemo-Vital. We don't think there's anything there. My assessment? You're barking up the wrong tree. If you want to stop the surveillance today we can prorate the fee."

Mary-Alice hoped Fosca would take up Fortune's offer of an early exit. She was bored with the assignment, and exhausted from her night shifts.

"Hm." Fosca leafed through the slim document. "They spend all their time together?"

"Yes, during the time we observed," Fortune replied.

"Do they seem happy?"

"Do they seem…what? Happy?"

Fosca stopped pacing and looked up from the report.

"Did you see tension? Was there contempt? Were there tears?"

The women looked at each other.

"I guess they seemed like they were having fun." Fortune was clearly mystified by Fosca's question.

Fosca snapped the folder shut.

"What about the tour buses? I've endured four separate visits from Sinful Spirits Bus Tours in as many days."

Ida Belle raised her hand. "I looked into it. As long as they stay off your property and on the road, there's nothing you can do."

"The passengers ignore my no-trespassing signs."

Ida Belle shrugged.

"You could probably get away with shooting one or two of 'em. Otherwise I don't know what to tell you."

"So Mr. Fosca," Fortune interjected, "what do you think? Would you like to close out now?"

"No, I would not. I would like to hold you to our initial contract. I find your work entirely satisfactory. Please continue to surveil the targets as we originally agreed."

"But we stuck to them like ticks and we didn't find anything," Ida Belle protested.

"I disagree. You will continue your thorough surveillance of these two individuals. We will meet Sunday, at eleven o'clock. You will bring the final report at that time."

Fosca turned his attention to the French doors at the front of the house. Right on cue, the doors swung open, and the meeting was over.

# CHAPTER 4

Sheriff Robert E. Lee, Sinful's senior law enforcement officer, was thinking about retirement. That blonde beanpole Fortune Morrow had brought along a minor crime wave when she'd moved in, but that had died down. Lately there hadn't been much going on in Sinful, crimewise. To his surprise, Lee found he missed the excitement. Worse, he had been getting daily calls from that loudmouth Yankee fellow who'd bought the old Polk Plantation and turned it into his private residence. It was bad enough that the man had closed the historic site to the public. But he seemed to believe he was entitled to keep traffic from driving past his house on the public roads.

So when Lee's dispatcher transferred an outside call to his desk phone, he wasn't exactly eager to answer it. But both of his deputy sheriffs were out of town, so there was no way to avoid it.

"This is Lee," he said warily into the receiver. Then he perked up.

"Now, slow down, boy," he instructed the caller. "The Polk Plantation? Are you there now? Oh, I see. You didn't witness any of this yourself. Ah. Can you describe her? Sparkly? Sparkly in what way, exactly? Uh-huh. And what's your name, young man? No, I suppose you don't have to if you don't want to. I'll be out there presently."

An hour later, Sheriff Lee tied his burro to one of the Polk Plantation's massive oak trees, and dismounted cautiously (Lee had had both knees replaced three times, and his hip twice). The grounds were still and quiet, with not a soul in sight. There was certainly no sign of an emergency. Lee wondered whether he had been pranked. He went up to the French doors and tried to peer in, but when he leaned in to see the interior, the glass quickly clouded into milky opaqueness. He stepped back, and the glass cleared, but the reflection of the oaks behind him obscured his view of the interior. He rapped on the door, but no one answered.

"Sheriff's department," he called out.

He pressed down on the door handle. The door swung open so easily Sheriff Lee nearly fell face-first into the house.

Lee paused and glanced around. It might be a trap, he thought, but for the life of him he couldn't imagine who would want to ambush him. Most of his enemies were long dead. That was one consolation of old age.

"Sheriff's department," he called out again as he entered.

It was rumored Fosca had made his workmen sign nondisclosure agreements, and no wonder. What the man done to the Polk Plantation was nothing short of desecration. He'd ripped out the wainscoted walls and stamped tin ceilings, leaving a bare, warehouse-like expanse. Gone was the antebellum clutter of rugs and ottomans and overstuffed chairs draped with antimacassars. The place looked like an empty freezer—and felt like one too. The chill air cut through Lee's shirt sleeves.

Lee made his way slowly down the space between the workout area and the kitchen, turned left, and then he saw something that made him draw his gun. A dark bundle lay in a doorway. But as he got closer, Lee holstered his gun. There was no point in calling an ambulance.

A scrolled silver knife handle protruded from the side of Raymond Fosca's neck. Blood soaked the collar of his dark t-shirt and pooled on the gleaming maple floor beneath him. On Fosca's chest lay a delicate gold chain with a small gold cross about an inch in length. It was grotesquely fitting for the man the local paper had dubbed "The Billionaire Vampire of the Bayou."

Lee stepped over the body to examine the cramped office. It contained a cluttered desk and a single chair. The far wall was a windowless blank. Whoever stabbed Fosca did it so quickly he didn't see it coming. There was no sign the man had fought back.

Or perhaps the killer had managed to incapacitate him. But how?

Lee pulled out his radio to call back to the sheriff's station, but couldn't get a signal inside the room. And there was no telephone in sight.

*What kind of dang fool plasters over the windows?* Lee thought.

Lee was about to step over the body when he paused. The wooden baseboard near the doorway looked like it had been gouged, then painted over. Whatever it was, the damage had happened some time ago, and it wasn't worth risking his knees to bend down for a closer look. Lee stepped over Fosca's body again. Once he was out of the small office and in the main room, he was able to radio his dispatcher. As he described the scene, he noticed a glint on the floor next to his foot.

This, he couldn't ignore, no matter what his knees thought about it.

# CHAPTER 5

Mary-Alice, Fortune, Ida Belle, and Gertie sat around Mary-Alice's dining room table, refreshing themselves with sweet tea.

"My goodness," Mary-Alice exclaimed. "My hands are still shaking so badly I can scarcely pour. I'm certain I've never been so close to a dead body before. And we were just talking to Mister Fosca the other day. I still can't believe it!"

"It's funny," Gertie said. "Fosca thought of himself as immortal, with the name, and the weird temperature control, and all those blood transfusions...I realized I'd started thinking of him that way myself. Why, Mary-Alice, I half-expected you to tell us he'd turned himself into a bat and fluttered away."

"I know that technically it wasn't our responsibility to protect him," Fortune said. "That's not what he hired us for. But I still feel like this is my fault. I missed something."

"I agree, Miss Fortune," Mary-Alice said. "The poor man trusted us. Perhaps we should offer to help Sheriff Lee find out who killed him."

"I'm not sure we want to get mixed up with this one." Ida Belle helped herself to an oatmeal raisin cookie. "We don't know what we're up against here. With that much money in play, people can lose their minds. Mary-Alice, good job getting that kid to make the call for you. Now you're sure no one saw you at the house?"

"About as sure as I can be, Miss Ida Belle."

"I do wonder, though," Fortune said. "He knew those two meant him harm. Otherwise, why have us watch them? Why didn't we see it?"

"If they were the ones that did it," Gertie said. "I mean, we looked into their backgrounds and watched them for nearly a week, and we didn't see anything amiss. They were just as ordinary as they could be."

"Well we obviously missed something," Fortune said. "We didn't have any indication that they knew Fosca, but they went right to his house."

Mary-Alice shook her head.

"I have trouble believing those two young people are murderers. I saw their faces when they came out of the house. I mean, y'all know they weren't weaklings with all their hiking and paddling and all. But they walked out of there looking like they were about to faint."

Mary-Alice stood up to refill the tea pitcher.

"Well, there's no shortage of other suspects," Gertie said. "I mean, we're talking about the most hated man in the parish."

"I think that's a little bit of an exaggeration," Ida Belle said.

Gertie held up the newspaper she'd been reading to show Ida Belle the headline:

*Most Hated Man in Parish: 'I got mine, now git.' Newcomer Fosca won't consider reopening Polk Plantation to public.*

"Honestly," Gertie said, "If I ran the Sinful Spirits tour company, I'd be hopping mad too. It's not like we have a whole lot of other haunted plantations around here."

"It is interesting that there was a tour bus at the house when you got there," Ida Belle said. "Mary-Alice, did you—hey, you're shedding!"

Mary-Alice placed the tea pitcher on the table.

"I'm sorry, Ida Belle?"

Mary-Alice looked down at her sequined shirt to see a loose thread hanging.

"She's right!" Gertie cried. "You're dribbling sequins everywhere, Mary-Alice! You look like you've been cursed by a drag queen."

"Oh, dear, when did that happen? I'm so sorry. I'll just be a moment."

Mary-Alice disappeared into her bedroom and then reappeared, wearing a sparkly blue-and-green floral t-shirt in place of the sparkly red-and-purple floral t-shirt she'd just dropped into the mending basket. (She couldn't decide which color scheme she preferred, so she had plenty of both in her wardrobe. She liked the red because it picked up her bright red hair, but she was also partial to the blue-green because it contrasted and made her coif look even more vibrant.)

"You didn't drop any of those shiny things at the crime scene, did you?" Fortune asked.

"I'm sure you mean to say sequins, Fortune." Gertie shot Fortune a stern look that Mary-Alice couldn't decode. "Of course, you already know what they're called, with all the sequined evening gowns you've doubtless worn as a beauty contestant."

"Sure," Fortune replied quickly. "The word slipped my mind, that's all. Mary-Alice, you didn't drop any *sequence* at the crime scene, did you?"

Ida Belle smirked, and Gertie buried her face in her hands.

"Why, I don't believe so," Mary-Alice faltered. "I mean to say, I certainly hope not."

"Oh, don't worry about it," Ida Belle assured Mary-Alice.

"Even if you did, this is Sheriff Lee we're talking about here. He'll never think to trace it back to—"

A knock on the door interrupted Ida Belle before she could finish her sentence.

# CHAPTER 6

"Why Sheriff Lee! What a delightful surprise!"

Mary-Alice's heart was pounding so wildly she was sure Lee could see it beating under her shirt. "To what do we owe the pleasure? Oh, please come in."

Lee removed his campaign hat and entered.

"Afternoon, ladies. I'm afraid I've come with some sorrowful news."

"Well now, Sheriff Lee, let me get you a nice cold glass of tea, and let's all make certain we're sitting down. We're in the dining room enjoying the air conditioning as it's a little too warm outdoors." Mary-Alice busied herself getting the refreshments set out, then sat down once everyone was served.

"Well now." Lee cleared his throat and took a sip of tea. "This is very nice, Miss Mary-Alice. I thank you. It is my unpleasant duty to report that a man has lost his life at the Polk Plantation. It appears to be a case of murder."

"Well that's terrible news," Ida Belle said sincerely. "Who was it?"

"A man named Raymond Fosca. Do you know him?"

"Why, we've just been reading about him." Gertie held up the paper to show Lee. "The most hated man in the parish!"

"Yes indeed," Lee said. "Now ordinarily I'd have the help of my deputies on a case like this, but as it happens I had to send them to a records management software training session in New Orleans. And if they don't stay for the whole session our office will lose a good bit of funding."

Lee didn't seem put out by the lack of help; in fact, one could detect a gleam of excitement in his eye. "Now, Miss Mary-Alice. I pray that you forgive my breach of modesty, but it has not escaped my attention that you favor these ornaments."

He pulled out a handkerchief and unfolded it to reveal a clutch of red and purple sequins. They were an exact match for the glittering flower-and-parrot pattern on the shirt that Mary-Alice had just changed out of.

"Those don't match the shirt she's wearing, Sheriff," Fortune said.

"No, that is correct, Miss Fortune." Lee leaned over and plucked something from the floor. "But they appear to be an excellent match for this sequin I just picked up from your floor, Miss Mary-Alice. Now, I must ask you. Were you ladies at the Polk Plantation recently?"

"It was only me, Sheriff," Mary-Alice said truthfully. "These ladies weren't there. I went up by myself this morning."

"Well now." Lee settled back in his chair. "Maybe you can start from the beginning, Miss Mary-Alice. When did you drive up to the Polk Plantation, and why? And as it's no longer open to the public, how did you gain ingress?"

Mary-Alice realized she had to tell the truth, or at least enough of it to appease Sheriff Lee. The other three women watched her carefully, which made her quite nervous.

"Oh, dear. The whole thing was so unpleasant, Sheriff. You see, I was out for a drive. (Following Terry Poindexter and Thomas Williams, Mary-Alice didn't mention.) I saw the sign for Polk Plantation, and I thought I'd have a little look-see. When I got there, well, there was a Sinful Spirits tour bus and a whole lot of people milling around. (These things were true.) So I thought I'd wait in my car until the crowd cleared up a little. Now, when all the tourists finally got back on the bus and left, I saw a car still parked there. (The one that she had followed there to begin with.) Now, what do I see next but a man and a young lady coming out of one of the doors, and it seemed to me something was very wrong, they looked so upset. When they left, I suppose I went in to the house to make sure nothing bad had happened. And of course, something very bad had happened."

Lee's bushy white eyebrows drew together.

"Miss Mary-Alice, y'all can't just go into a man's house uninvited when you've a mind to. Why, there are laws about criminal trespass."

"But the two young people looked so distressed," Mary-Alice blurted out. "I knew something was wrong. I do apologize, Sheriff, from the bottom of my heart, and I take full responsibility for my actions."

"Sheriff, you're not going to arrest Mary-Alice for trying to help, are you?" Gertie pleaded.

"Not at the moment, no. I'm more concerned with getting to the bottom of all this. Now, Miss Mary-Alice, do you have a description of this unlucky pair?"

Of course she had more than that—they had names, photos, and a dossier of their activities over the past week.

"Well, the young lady was around five foot, I'd say, and she had black hair. The man was taller, closer to six foot, with brown hair and one of those little scruffy beards that they like to wear nowadays. Oh, and I happened to see the license plate number of their car."

"Well now that's very useful information, Miss Mary-Alice." Lee wrote down the number she gave him. "One more thing.

When I received the call, it wasn't from you. It was from a young boy who refused to give his name."

"That is true, Sheriff," Mary-Alice confessed. "I didn't want to get mixed up in it, you see. On the way back I stopped by the high school and offered a boy twenty dollars to make the call for me. (Mary-Alice had borrowed this trick from a murder mystery she'd recently read.) You're right. I shouldn't have gone inside the house. I do hope you can find it in your heart to forgive me, Sheriff Lee."

Lee braced his hands on his knees and heaved a moustache-rattling sigh.

"Well, Miss Mary-Alice, I do appreciate your honesty, however belated." He stood up slowly. "And at least you didn't touch or move anything. You didn't touch or move anything, did you?"

"Oh no, certainly not," Mary-Alice assured him. Not on purpose, in any event.

# CHAPTER 7

Sheriff Lee rode back up to the Polk Plantation two days later, to examine the house at his leisure. Raymond Fosca's body was at the medical examiner's office; the preliminary verdict was that Fosca had been stabbed in the neck with a letter opener.

The house looked much as it had before Fosca's death. Lee had made the decision not to put up crime scene tape. The incident wasn't in the news yet, and Lee wanted to keep it that way for the time being. The fact that Fosca was such a recluse was a help.

Unfortunately, searching for next of kin to notify presented a problem. "Raymond Fosca" not only had no living relatives, but he apparently had only existed for about a decade. There was no record of where Fosca had grown up or gone to school. The man had been working under an assumed name, and Lee hoped the key to his identity lay somewhere on the grounds of the Polk Plantation.

The interior of the house was still freezing when Lee walked in. It was not clear how one might go about turning the A/C off. In fact, the entire house seemed to be controlled by some remote system. The downstairs doors were unlocked, and there was no obvious way to lock them.

Lee went back to the study, snapped on gloves, and examined the contents of the desk. There were business magazines, a stack of Wall Street Journal issues, a pile of what looked like unopened bills, and stacks of file folders. Lee opened one of them to find a stapled magazine article, about a woman who recovered from cancer. Underneath that was a clipping from a Montana newspaper from five years ago, about a young woman who was the valedictorian of her high school class. The next item was a birth announcement.

Lee continued to page through the folder. There were computer printouts, newspaper articles, and glossy magazine pages. They were arranged in chronological order. Most of the subjects were women or girls.

Lee picked up the next folder. It was the same thing. Then it dawned on him. He picked up a third folder. Then went back to the first one.

Every item was about someone named Angela.

*Most peculiar,* Lee thought. *Now what was the name of the girl Miss Mary-Alice observed at the house? Terry. Not the same name at all.*

Lee opened the desk drawer, expecting more clutter, but instead it held only two objects: One, a large, brown envelope, and two, a lined yellow legal pad.

Lee pulled out the pad and read the note scribbled in blue pen:

*My dearest John:*

*How does it feel?*

*Do you miss her?*

*Warmest regards,*

*Felix*

Lee pulled out his own notepad and wrote,

*John. Felix. Who is "her"?*

Lee sat in the chair, and swiveled around to face the blank wall. Then he stood and knocked on it. It was solid. *With all that money,* Lee thought, *Fosca could afford to buy something nice to hang there. Maybe an antique map of New Orleans, or one of those paintings of dogs playing poker.*

A glint of stainless steel under a folder caught Lee's eye. He moved the folder aside to see a panel of buttons. They were unlabeled; he took a chance and pressed one.

The room immediately took on a blue cast. Lee looked up to see that the entire ceiling was glowing blue.

He pressed another button, and heard a humming and then a twittering sound. It took him a few seconds to realize what was going on: A cage was descending from the ceiling. Inside was a drab little brown-and-black speckled bird, chattering with alarm at having been disturbed.

"Well hello there," Lee said. "My word, I do wish you could tell me what happened here. It's quite a conundrum. All this gadgetry, yet there are no surveillance cameras that I can see. I suppose I'll just keep on pressing buttons until I find something useful."

Lee pressed another steel button. It looked just the same as the others, and Lee didn't suspect anything was amiss, until he felt the subsonic grinding. By the time he saw the steel door sliding shut, it was too late.

He got up and pushed the door, but it was a solid slab of metal, and did not budge. He pounded on it, with no effect.

His eye traveled to the scratch marks on the baseboard. Maybe Fosca or the previous owner had owned a dog, and kept it locked in this room. Still, there should be some way for a human being to get out.

He went back to the desk and pressed the rest of the buttons on the panel. At first he tried one at a time, and then he tried combinations of two or three. The light in the room changed from blue to red to white to green, and the bird cage went up and down, but the door remained shut.

And there were no windows to climb out of. Lee went over to the blank wall and pounded it, then kicked it, but it was as solid as before. It felt like plaster over brick.

There was no choice but to call back to the office and get someone to break him out. He pulled out his radio.

There was no signal.

Lee realized there was no computer in the room, in addition to there being no telephone.

With rising alarm, Lee realized that the room had no plumbing. How long could a person survive without water? Deputies Breaux and LeBlanc were due back in a few days, but even then, would they know where to look for him?

Lee sank down into the chair and stared at the steel door sealing him off from the world. He would die here, in this crazy rich man's office. There was no way out.

And was it his imagination, or was the air feeling unusually close? Lee could see no air vents in the room. He closed his eyes and tried to slow his breathing.

A grinding sound made him open his eyes again.

And as he watched, the door began to slide open.

Amazed, he rose from the chair.

"Miss Mary-Alice?" he exclaimed. "Miss Ida Belle? Miss Gertie? Miss Fortune! What are y'all doing here?"

"Interfering," Gertie said. "Just like you told us not to."

"There's a button out here that controls the door," Mary-Alice explained. "But it seems there's no such thing inside the room. It certainly seems dangerous not to have any way to escape in case of an emergency."

"I'd like to see the permits for this remodel," Fortune said. "There's definitely something weird going on with this house."

"Oh!" Mary-Alice cried. "Angela!"

"Did you say Angela?" Lee exclaimed.

"No," the women chorused in unison, and three of them glared at Mary-Alice.

"I said, what about that adorable little bird?" Mary-Alice declared brazenly. "Does it have a home?"

Sheriff Lee knew he shouldn't let Mary-Alice walk off with part of the crime scene, but neither did he want to deal with the bird himself. He pressed the button to lower the cage, then unhooked it and brought it over.

"Very well, Miss Mary-Alice," Lee said, "you may take the bird into your custody. But if we need to take him back for any reason, we will do so."

"Her," Mary-Alice mentally corrected him, but wisely said nothing.

"Now ladies, I'm extremely grateful for your assistance," Lee said. "And I hope I have not seemed to be dismissive in any way. Er…may I entreat you to keep this incident a private matter?"

"Sure," Ida Belle said. "I think we can make a deal."

# CHAPTER 8

The four ladies and Sheriff Lee sat on Mary-Alice's back porch, sipping sweet tea and watching the bayou roll by. Ida Belle wasted no time with small talk.

"We'd like to assist in the investigation," she said.

"We want to be good citizens," Gertie added. "And we think we can really help."

Lee sighed heavily, setting his white moustache aflutter.

"Well now I do find myself shorthanded until my two deputies are back in town. And I must admit that y'all have been moderately helpful to our efforts in the past, if a touch overbearing."

"And we rescued you from starving to death in that room," Ida Belle reminded him.

"Actually, Ida Belle, he would've died of thirst or suffocated before he starved," Gertie chimed in helpfully.

"But it is most unusual to involve private citizens in this way. I mean to say, what if y'all turn out to be suspects?"

"Why don't we cross that bridge when we come to it?" Gertie suggested. "Besides, Sheriff, you've known us for seventy years, give or take. Have you ever known us to kill anyone?"

"Well, now, I don't believe I have."

"So, there you go."

"We'll get further if we share information," Fortune suggested.

Sheriff Lee closed his eyes and was quiet for such a long time that Mary-Alice feared the sheriff had passed away. Fortunately, she was spared having to deal with two corpses in a single week.

"Very well," Lee said finally. "I suppose I could use some assistance."

"Okay," Ida Belle said. "Who would want to kill Raymond Fosca?"

"Not us, of course," Gertie declared. (Because he still owes us the other half of our money, Gertie did not add.)

"Sheriff Lee," Fortune asked, "there was another death on the property recently, wasn't there?"

Lee nodded.

"A John Doe. Couple of the Guidry kids were out there on a dare, and they found him."

"Do you remember what he looked like?" Fortune persisted. "Could someone have mistaken him for Raymond Fosca?"

Sheriff Lee leaned back and rubbed his moustache as he tried to recall the scene.

"Well now, begging your pardon, ladies, but the poor man had been out in the elements for some days. I mean to say, from what I recall, I suppose the two men were of similar size and coloring."

"That's an interesting angle," Ida Belle said. "So maybe someone tried to kill Fosca but got some hobo instead?"

"How did the poor man die?" Mary-Alice asked. "Was he stabbed like Mr. Fosca?"

"No, Miss Mary-Alice, he was not. The poor man died of exposure, best as the coroner could tell."

"Fosca must've popped a gasket when he found out someone was inconsiderate enough to die on his property," Ida Belle said.

"Not at all," Lee replied. "Mr. Fosca was very gracious about it. He even paid to get the man cremated."

"Fosca was gracious?" Ida Belle exclaimed. "That doesn't sound like the Fosca we…have read about in the newspaper."

"Maybe he felt guilty that an innocent man died in his place," Gertie said.

"Do you know whether Fosca fired anyone recently?" Fortune asked. "Or does he have an ex out there somewhere?"

"Well, there certainly was no love lost between Mr. Fosca and Odile Beaumont," Lee said reluctantly.

"Oh, that's right," Gertie said. "My goodness, I certainly hope it wasn't Odile. I can understand her being frustrated. Sinful Spirits Tours was her entire livelihood. I do hope you have some other leads, Sheriff."

"Leads are exactly what I don't have," Lee groused. "I can't even find the man's next of kin to notify them. And I do thank you for the license plate number, Miss Mary-Alice, but when I followed it to the address on the registration, I found the owner had moved out and left no forwarding address. At the moment, I find myself at a loss."

"Oh, we can help you there," Ida Belle interjected.

"Yes, that's true, Sheriff Lee," Gertie added. "We've been doing a little investigating on our own, haven't we? Mary-Alice, do you happen to recall where Miss Poindexter and Mr. Williams were staying?"

"Why, I believe I do, Miss Gertie," Mary-Alice answered cheerfully. "Let me just go get my notebook."

# CHAPTER 9

Mary-Alice drove Sheriff Lee out to the Robichaux Suites, where Thomas Williams and Terry Poindexter were staying. It was a little too far to take the burro.

The couple seemed willing to talk. But although Mary-Alice and Sheriff Lee spent nearly an hour sitting in the lobby with them, plying them with overpriced gourmet coffee served in paper cups, they got very little useful information. They were newlyweds on their honeymoon, they explained. They had already hiked around the forests and paddled the bayous, and wanted to see the famous Polk Plantation. They didn't know it had been closed to the public. The travel review sites didn't mention it.

Lee wondered how they got into the house. Although he addressed his questions to both, it was the husband who did most of the talking.

Thomas Williams told Sheriff Lee that the door was unlocked, so they walked in. Once inside, they looked around a little, saw no one was there, and left. And no, they didn't see anything unusual at all.

"What about you, Miss Terry?" Sheriff Lee asked. "Did you notice anything out of the ordinary?"

"No," Terry said.

"Y'all looked awfully upset when you left," Mary-Alice chimed in. "It seemed to me y'all had seen something tremendously upsetting in there."

"No, I sure didn't," Thomas Williams said. "Did you, honey?"

"No," Terry said.

It was all very frustrating, and only confirmed Sheriff Lee's assessment of the younger generation as entirely useless. Disappointed, he bid them a good afternoon and dismissed them.

Mary-Alice was certain they weren't telling the whole story. They coincidentally happened to show up at Raymond Fosca's house right after he hired the Sinful Ladies' Detective Agency to follow them? No. Mary-Alice, who normally gave people the benefit of the doubt, didn't buy it.

Unfortunately, Sheriff Lee was sitting right there, so she couldn't come out and ask them "why was Mr. Fosca paying us to follow you?" That was one piece of information the ladies had decided they didn't need to share with Sheriff Lee.

But she did have an idea.

"Sheriff," she whispered, when the couple had gone, "Do you have any evidence bags with you?"

"Why no, Miss Mary-Alice, I don't. But I daresay a plain paper bag will do in a pinch. Why do you ask?"

Their next interview was with Odile Beaumont, owner and operator of Sinful Spirits Tours. This wasn't terribly informative either, although it was therapeutic for Odile. She freely admitted —one could even say bragged—that she'd "dragged" Fosca on "Twitter." Sheriff Lee did not know what this meant. Odile and Mary-Alice explained to him that Mrs. Beaumont had made uncomplimentary statements about Raymond Fosca in a public online forum. Odile reminded Lee that she was within her First

Amendment rights to share her views in this way, that Fosca was a public figure and therefore not entitled to a right to privacy, and if that cowardly carpetbagger didn't like it, he was welcome to return to whatever Yankee snakehole he'd crawled out of, and let decent, hardworking widows support their families in peace.

And yes, she had brought tourists out to the Polk Plantation on the afternoon Lee asked about.

"Why Miss Mary-Alice," Odile exclaimed, "didn't I see you parking your Oldsmobile behind me that day?"

"You did indeed, Miss Odile. You are very observant."

"Well, then, you can tell the sheriff here that I stayed on the bus and off that man's property. But there's no reason I can't drive out that way on the public roads paid for by my taxes. Why are y'all asking me all these questions about that afternoon anyway? Did something happen out there?"

Since Fosca's death was not yet public knowledge, Lee didn't have a good answer for her.

While Sheriff Lee and Mary-Alice were conducting their interviews, Fortune, Ida Belle, and Gertie were crowded into the sweltering records room at Sinful's City Hall. They found that the paperwork for the Polk Plantation remodel was incomplete, and that was putting it mildly. The file was full of long-expired applications for extensions. The drawings and permits that should have been there were not. The ladies discovered only one new piece of information: the name and phone number of the Lake Charles architect who had supervised the remodel.

Gertie called the phone number of Herve Semmelweis Design, and found it had been disconnected.

"Well, now what?" Fortune asked.

"Guess we pack it in for today." Ida Belle glanced at her watch.

"Let's hope Mary-Alice and Sheriff Lee found out something useful."

That evening found the four ladies, Sheriff Lee, and one little European Starling on Mary-Alice's back deck. The starling hopped and pecked cheerily in her cage; the humans stared glumly out onto the bayou. They had updated each other on their progress, such as it was, then lapsed into pensive, tea-sipping silence.

And then the bird peeped something that sounded like,

"Angela!"

Tea glasses were quickly set down; heads turned to the steel cage.

"My dearest Angela," the bird repeated. This time the words were unmistakable.

Sheriff Lee stared. Gertie clapped her hand over her mouth. Ida Belle scowled. Fortune jumped up, pulled a gun out of the back of her jeans, and pointed it at the bird.

"My goodness," Mary-Alice exclaimed, "Angela can talk!"

"Angela can talk!" the bird repeated.

"Well, what do you know." Fortune tucked her nine-millimeter back into her waistband (had she been keeping it there all along? Mary-Alice wondered) and calmly sat back down.

"Angela," Lee said. "Why, I completely forgot about that in the excitement of getting stuck in that man's infernal office."

"Forgot about what?" Ida Belle asked.

"Mr. Fosca appeared to be inordinately fond of the name Angela."

Lee told them what he had found in Fosca's manila folders. Article after article about Angelas young and old.

"Maybe he had an ex named Angela," Fortune said. "Not that that makes it any less disturbing."

"Perhaps he is acquainted with someone by that name," Lee conceded. "Although I have not been able to discover—"

"Let me out!" the bird cried. "Let me out! Angela! My dearest Angela! Help! Let me out!"

"Oh my goodness," Mary-Alice whispered. "I wonder whether that's a clue!"

But Angela the bird didn't say anything else that evening. Despite the humans' coaxing, Angela was content to hop around her cage and peck at her tray of bird seed. Even Gertie's attempts to teach her Cajun swear words had no effect.

"It's no use, Gertie," Ida Belle said, finally. "Old birds can't learn new words."

"We'll see about that," Gertie retorted.

# CHAPTER 10

Over the next few days the ladies lavished Angela with attention, hoping she would tell them something that would help them crack the case. The little bird would peep her name, or cry, "Let me out!" but she said nothing that got them closer to a solution. When Mary-Alice wasn't looking, Gertie would lean in and whisper *embrasse moi tchew* at the little bird. But Angela politely declined to repeat the phrase.

The ladies traveled to the Hemo-Vital office down in Lake Charles to speak with DeVonne Jackson, the young man who had administered Fosca's blood transfusion. But because Sheriff Lee still hadn't found Fosca's next of kin, the young man didn't know his client was dead, and the Sinful ladies were not at liberty to tell him so. Thanks to medical privacy laws, Jackson couldn't tell them anything about Raymond Fosca. He wasn't even allowed to confirm that Fosca was his client—even though the ladies had all watched Mr. Jackson giving Mr. Fosca his blood transfusion.

Sheriff Lee was similarly stymied; he still had no luck in his search for Fosca's next of kin. He had come to believe "Raymond Fosca" was an assumed identity, and the ladies agreed with him on that point. But that got him no closer to finding out who the man really was.

The letter opener that had struck the fatal blow had one of those fiendish textured handles that made it the very deuce to lift prints. It was possible—but by no means certain—that the handle had been wiped.

Lee felt like his brain was spinning in circles and getting nowhere, just like the ancient fan rattling away on his desk.

And then the phone rang. The coroner's office had a message for Sheriff Lee.

# CHAPTER 11

Thomas Williams and Terry Poindexter did not seem thrilled to see Sheriff Lee and Mary-Alice again. But they agreed to sit down for another chat in the lobby of the Robichaux Suites, and accepted Sheriff Lee's offer of coffee.

"I don't know how we can help." Thomas popped the plastic cap off his paper cup and blew on his macchiato. "But we'll tell you whatever you want to know."

"Same," Terry added, without making eye contact.

"You folks enjoying your stay here at the Robichaux Suites?" Lee asked.

The young couple exchanged a glance.

"Yes," Terry said.

"It's perfect for us," Thomas added, "cause there's a little kitchen in there. You don't have to go out to eat. Good thing too, cause it's not like there's a lot of restaurants around here anyway. Not that that's a bad thing. We wanted to come here. You know, get away from it all."

"Seems like a peculiar choice for a honeymoon," Lee said. "I mean to say, this place is more for business travelers, isn't it? Lots of oil and gas folks and such?"

"We wanted an extended-stay hotel," Thomas said. "To tell you the truth, we were planning to move here permanently. We gave up our apartments, sold everything on Craigslist, and came down here. So yeah, it's great. Well, except it seems local law enforcement isn't crazy about us, heh."

"Is this correct, Miss Terry?" Sheriff Lee asked. "You and your husband are planning a permanent move to the area?"

She nodded.

"Fair enough," Lee sat back and rubbed his moustache thoughtfully. "Now, we've established that the two of you went to Raymond Fosca's residence. Mr. Williams, I apologize if I'm repeating myself here, but what is your relationship to Mr. Fosca?"

Thomas Williams chuckled.

"Heh, I wish I was related to him. I mean, the guy's a billionaire."

Terry simpered nervously.

"Well then," Lee said complacently, "today's your lucky day."

"I'm sorry?"

Lee sat up.

"You are a blood relation of Mr. Raymond Fosca. He is your uncle, your grandfather, or your half-brother."

"Or your double cousin," Mary-Alice interjected. "I believe that's when your daddy and his daddy are brothers, and your mama and his mama are sisters."

"Thank you, Miss Mary-Alice," Lee said. "Yes, double cousin."

Terry had her hand on Thomas'.

"He's my half-brother," Thomas mumbled. "How did you know?"

"Y'all were careless with your DNA," Lee said. "It was all over your coffee cups. We tested it against the victim and got a match. Miss Mary-Alice here got the idea from one of her mystery books. May I assume it was no accident that you were at Mr. Fosca's home that afternoon?"

"He means the afternoon Mr. Fosca was found murdered," Mary-Alice added. "It's okay, Sheriff. I believe they already know the poor man is dead."

"Why don't you tell us what really happened?" Lee asked.

Terry's grip tightened on her husband's hand.

"Raymond Fosca's real name is Felix Williams," Thomas said. "He was from my father's first marriage. I didn't know him that well. When my father died, he didn't leave me much. There wasn't much to leave. But Felix had done really well with Hemo-Vital. When I met Terry, I thought he'd help us out. I mean, I didn't want a free ride or anything like that, but just a loan would've helped. And I kind of wanted to reconnect. I mean, after dad died it was just him and me left. He was kind of back-and-forth about it, so I thought, if I could bring Terry out and let him meet her, he'd see how great she was and how happy we were, and he'd want to help us out. I don't remember how, exactly, but it kind of turned ugly, and then all of a sudden he was like, 'you want my money? Take it!' and he picked up this letter opener from his desk and stabbed himself in the neck."

"Why didn't you call for help?" Lee asked.

"I tried," Thomas said. "Look."

He pulled out his phone and showed Lee his call history.

"See? I called 9-1-1 but it didn't go through."

"Were you in that little office of his?" Mary-Alice asked.

"Yes, we were."

"It's his secure space," Mary-Alice explained. "He has something inside the walls of that office to block phone signals so no one can spy on him. It's like a Faraday cage."

"You might've tried calling for help once you were outside," Lee said quickly, before anyone could ask him to explain what a Faraday cage was.

"It was obvious he was dead," Thomas said. "I'm sorry, we

panicked. We just wanted to get out of there as fast as we could. It was so horrible."

Terry was staring at the table, her hand now gripping her husband's so hard that her knuckles were white.

A tear plopped onto the table in front of Thomas Williams. Mary-Alice reached into her purse and handed him a tissue. He noisily blew his nose into it.

"Mr. Williams," Sheriff Lee said," I have one more question for you. You may be aware that your late half-brother was known in certain circles as The Billionaire Vampire of the Bayou."

Thomas nodded. "He was pretty sick of the vampire jokes. I might not have known him that well, but I did know that about him."

"Well, this is not a joke. When I examined the deceased, I found a cross on his chest. Who put it there?"

Mary-Alice knocked over her coffee cup. Fortunately, it was nearly empty and she was able to clean up the mess with the napkins on hand.

"I'm ever so sorry," she whispered.

"Do you remember him wearing a cross?" Thomas asked Terry. She shook her head. Mary-Alice kept wiping the table, even though it was already clean.

"I don't know," Thomas said. "It wasn't either of us. I'm sorry. I should have told you the truth."

"Are we in trouble?" Terry asked.

"We'll see about that," Lee said with a touch of irritation. "In the meantime, I'd advise you two to stay put."

# CHAPTER 12

That evening, Mary-Alice met the ladies at Fortune's house, the imposing dark-blue Victorian that Fortune had inherited from her great-aunt Marge Boudreaux. They sat around Fortune's sturdy kitchen table, dining on Francine's fried chicken and trying to make sense of what had happened earlier that day.

"So that's it?" Ida Belle demanded. "Case closed?"

"I believe Sheriff Lee was satisfied with the young man's explanation." Mary-Alice's tone implied that she herself was not so easily taken in.

"Fosca stabbed himself in the neck?" Fortune narrowed her eyes at Mary-Alice. "Come on, do you believe that?"

"Well now, Miss Fortune, I will frankly tell you that in my opinion, young Mr. Williams was not being entirely truthful."

"Is Sheriff Lee going to charge them with not reporting the suicide?" Gertie asked.

"There seems to be no legal requirement to do so," Mary-Alice replied. "If anything, they could get in trouble for misleading the sheriff the first time he talked to them, but I don't believe Sheriff Lee will pursue those charges. I believe he feels sorry for them."

"Is there anyone else we can talk to?" Gertie asked. "Any other avenue to explore? It may be that things happened just as you were told today, but I'd like to make sure."

"I agree," Fortune said. "I don't feel right leaving things like this."

"We never did find Mr. Fosca's architect," Mary-Alice suggested. "If you recall, his telephone had been disconnected. Perhaps he knows something about who might have wanted to harm Mr. Fosca, and why."

"I don't have anything better to do," Fortune said. "Who's up for a drive to Lake Charles?"

Herve Semmelweis Design had occupied the end unit of an unfashionable strip mall on the outskirts of Lake Charles. The signs were still in place, but the occupant was long gone. The unit was devoid of furniture and fixtures, and a faded For Lease sign hung in the window. It was too hot to stand around outside, so the ladies got back into the Oldsmobile. Mary-Alice turned on the air conditioning, and Gertie called the number of the property manager.

"Well?" Ida Belle demanded when Gertie had hung up.

"The last time they heard anything from Semmelweis was when his December rent check came in," Gertie said. "After that he just dropped off the radar. They didn't want to evict him, because he'd been a good tenant, but in the end, they didn't have a choice. Mary-Alice, you might as well drive us on home. There's nothing to see out here."

"Did he have anyone working for him?" Fortune asked.

"He was a one-man shop," Gertie said.

"Why did Fosca pick this guy?" Ida Belle demanded. "He's supposedly a billionaire, and he hires some nobody working at the butt end of an ugly strip mall."

Mary-Alice waited until the traffic was clear in both directions, then pulled out onto the wide street.

"Maybe that's precisely why Mr. Fosca chose him," she said.

"Remember when Sheriff Lee got stuck in Mr. Fosca's office and we had to rescue him? Well now, with all the rules and regulations we have nowadays, do you imagine anyone would be allowed to install a door that could trap someone like that?"

"Mr. Fosca's permits sure were a mess," Gertie said.

"Herve Semmelweis was willing to break the rules," Ida Belle mused. "And Fosca probably paid him enough so that Semmelweis could move to a tropical island and start a new life."

"But then why on earth would he burn his bridges with his landlord?" Gertie asked. "If Mr. Fosca was as generous with Mr. Semmelweis as he was with us, Semmelweis would most certainly have been able to pay off his lease."

"I have an idea," Mary-Alice said tentatively. "But I must say, I'm of two minds about sharing it with y'all. Oh dear, of course now I've told you about it, I suppose I have to fill in the details, don't I?"

"Yes, you do," Ida Belle said.

"It isn't terribly nice," Mary-Alice said.

"Mary-Alice, some of your 'not very nice' ideas have turned out to be pretty helpful," Fortune replied.

"Well, alright then. I was wondering, when did that poor man turn up dead on Mr. Fosca's property again?"

"Just after Christmas," Ida Belle said. "Wasn't it?"

"Mary-Alice," Gertie exclaimed, "are you saying the dead man was Mr. Fosca's architect?"

"Only because we have one man who disappeared around Christmas, and another who turned up dead around the same time. Both are connected to Mr. Fosca. And Mr. Semmelweis wasn't from around here. No one would've been able to identify him. Except for Mr. Fosca."

"But if Fosca knew him, he should have been able to recognize him, even after..." Fortune trailed off. "Unless there was a reason for Fosca not to identify him."

"Did anyone take photos when that poor man was found?" Mary-Alice asked.

"Well, there's one person we can ask," Ida Belle said. "Too bad it's the same person who's already decided we don't need to do any more investigating."

# CHAPTER 13

It wasn't hard to persuade Sheriff Lee to show them the death scene images. Lee was proud of the photos. He had taken the last few himself, after Deputy Kyle Breaux fainted and nearly broke the camera.

"Now, these aren't going to be too pretty," Lee opened the folder and spread out the photos. "Our John Doe'd been out in the elements for a while by the time we found him."

Fortune produced a computer printout and laid it next to the death scene photos.

"This is from the architect's website," Fortune said.

"Unfortunately, a regular photograph wasn't hip and trendy enough for his website," Ida Belle added. "So we only have this line drawing."

"Well," Gertie said, "I suppose it's possible they're the same man. I mean, clean-shaven, dark hair, narrow face, not terribly old nor terribly young."

"That could describe a lot of people," Ida Belle said.

"Including Raymond Fosca," Fortune remarked.

"Oh my," Mary-Alice exclaimed. "What happened to the poor man's fingernails?"

"Begging your pardon, Miss Mary-Alice," Lee replied, "But when a body's been outdoors for a few days, the critters get to them, and they often go for the extremities first."

"Yeah, I learned that at the body farm..." Fortune began, and then quickly corrected herself. "I mean, from reading about the body farm. In the library. The University of Tennessee's Forensic Anthropology Center. They put cadavers outside and observe how they decompose. The research they do there has really helped to advance forensic science. Or so I read."

"Miss Fortune," Mary-Alice exclaimed, "you have books about the body farm in your children's library?"

"Oh yeah, kids love that stuff," Ida Belle said quickly.

"Now, how will we know whether this is the same man?" Gertie asked. "Mary-Alice's DNA trick won't work this time."

"Now ladies," Lee said, "I realize that y'all are still interested in the Raymond Fosca case, or whatever the deuce that fellow's real name was, but it's over. The man killed himself and there's no evidence to say otherwise."

"Now sheriff, we understand that," Mary-Alice said. "And we absolutely respect your judgment in this regard. But now we're talking about a different case. The unexplained death of the John Doe who turned up on the grounds of the Polk Plantation."

"Wasn't unexplained," Lee said. "The man died of natural causes."

"What natural cause, specifically?" Mary-Alice asked innocently.

"Well, you see..." Lee cleared his throat. "there was no finding, as such, per se...I mean to say, they didn't find..."

"It's still unsolved, you mean," Ida Belle said flatly. "And no one cares because it was just some homeless guy. Or so you thought."

"Sheriff, you have to question Thomas Williams and Terry Poindexter again," Gertie pleaded. "They knew Ray Fosca or whatever his name was. They might know what happened to the man who did his remodel. I think they aren't telling the whole truth."

"Of course they aren't telling the whole truth," Ida Belle interjected. "I mean, this billionaire just up and stabbed himself in the neck? And then wiped his own prints? Right."

Lee raised his palms in resignation.

"The letter opener handle was textured, Miss Ida Belle. There may have been prints but we couldn't lift them. I'll admit the whole thing seems peculiar, but without any additional evidence, I fear our investigation is over. Unless there's something you know, and haven't told me."

It was time to come clean.

"Sheriff Lee, there is something," Fortune said. "Raymond Fosca hired us to follow Thomas and Terry. We were working for him when he died."

Lee didn't say anything. Instead, he turned a deep shade of red and then purple.

"Y'all were working for the victim?" he sputtered, when he had regained his power of speech. "I must say, it would've been very useful to know that a little earlier."

"We told you everything we knew that had a direct bearing on the case," Ida Belle said.

"And you must admit, Sheriff, our information was helpful," Gertie added.

"So, Miss Mary-Alice." Lee was fading from purple back to red, which the ladies took as a good sign. "You did not simply happen to be out at the Polk Plantation that day."

"You are quite correct, Sheriff," Mary-Alice conceded. "It was my turn to follow Mr. Thomas and Miss Terry. But as Miss Ida Belle has pointed out, we did share all of the salient facts."

Lee took a few more deep breaths.

"Well now. This does put things into a whole different perspective. That young miscreant Thomas Williams has come up with a different story each time I've talked to him. And now you tell me the man we know as Raymond Fosca was concerned enough about him to have him followed. Well, what did you find?"

"We've told you everything we know, Sheriff," Ida Belle said. "They really are newlyweds, and we didn't catch them doing anything nefarious."

"Well, not until they visited the Polk Plantation," Mary-Alice added.

"Since you ladies seem to be well ahead of me," Lee huffed, "what do you propose we do next? I suppose you'd like me to go question that young couple a third time?"

"Not yet," Fortune said, completely missing Lee's sarcasm. "First, I'd like us to take another look around the scene of the crime. Then we can bring them in."

# CHAPTER 14

"Miss Fortune, I must say, this is highly irregular. I mean to say, with all due respect, you are not an officer of the law."

Lee and the four ladies were huddled in the tiny observation space adjoining the interrogation/meeting room at the Sinful sheriff's department. Through the one-way glass, they could see Terry Poindexter and her husband Thomas Williams seated at the table, holding hands so tightly it seemed their lives depended on it.

"Sheriff Lee," Fortune pleaded, "I realize it's unorthodox, but I do know a little bit about interrogation. As a librarian, I've… read lots of books about things. Let me do it."

Lee sighed. His deputies Carter LeBlanc and Kyle Breaux would be back in Sinful in another couple of days. Sheriff Lee looked forward to showing the young men he wasn't ready for the glue factory quite yet. If solving the case quickly meant bending the rules a little, well, why not?

"Very well," Lee said. "But let's not make a habit of it."

Mary-Alice, Ida Belle, Gertie, and Sheriff Lee watched through the semi-transparent mirror as Fortune walked into the room.

She was holding two bottles of water, which she placed in front of the interviewees.

"What happened to the sheriff?" Thomas asked.

Terry unscrewed the bottlecap and gulped.

"I'm an associate of Sheriff Lee," Fortune replied smoothly as she seated herself. "Now, I'm not here to ask about your half-brother's death. I just want to know about his house. Specifically, his office. Did you notice anything unusual about it? Like a door that he could close and trap someone inside?"

Terry swallowed her water the wrong way and started to cough.

"Like I told the sheriff, I didn't know my half-brother that well," Thomas Williams said. "I didn't grow up with him. He was the son of my dad's first wife. The guy was old enough to be my dad, honestly."

"I see." Fortune spoke softly, but her manner was that of a cobra ready to strike. "Did you know about the surveillance cameras Mr. Fosca had placed around his home?"

"*Cameras*?" Terry knocked her water bottle off the table. Fortune reached out and caught it in mid-air, and calmly set it upright.

"She's bluffing!" Gertie whispered excitedly. "Go Fortune! Sheriff, Mr. Fosca told us he didn't like having cameras around his property because he thought they could be hacked!"

"Well now, isn't that clever," Lee mused. "I daresay Miss Fortune might get something out of those two yet."

"Tell us about Angela." Fortune fixed her gaze on Thomas Williams.

"Those two look like they're about to die of panic," Ida Belle remarked.

Terry tightened her grip on her husband's hand. Thomas looked like he was about to be sick.

"Should we ask for a lawyer now?" Terry whispered.

"Sure, if you want to make it official, spend the weekend

locked up here while we figure out how to set your bail..." Fortune's tone was breezy, but she was watching them closely. "Or, you can explain what we saw on the surveillance video."

"It was self-defense!" Thomas cried. "Maybe you couldn't see it, but it was!"

"Tell me about it," Fortune settled back in her chair, as if to say, "convince me."

"None of this is Terry's fault. I swear. You can't blame her for any of this."

"It's okay." Terry patted her husband's hand, looking miserable.

"It's a long story," Thomas warned.

"I have all day," Fortune assured him.

"Okay. This is the truth. My dad and this guy John Poindexter were friends back in the day. They were both finance guys, and they were kind of creative about making money, I guess you could say. Well, my dad got caught and got two years in federal prison. My mom had passed away by then, so Poindexter said him and his wife would watch my half-brother and my half-sister until Dad got out. They were like fourteen and fifteen at the time. This was way before I was born. Anyway, Dad gets out of prison, goes to get his kids, and he finds out my half-sister is dead."

"I'm sorry to hear it," Fortune said.

"Her name was Angela."

"Ah."

"Yeah, it gets worse. She'd stolen a bunch of pills from Poindexter's wife and killed herself. Poindexter gave my dad this big story about how no one saw it coming, and he didn't tell my dad 'cause he didn't want to make my dad's time in prison any harder than it had to be."

"But your father blamed his friend for his daughter's suicide," Fortune said.

"It wasn't suicide. Felix, my half-brother, told my dad that

Poindexter had been going into Angela's room at night. She'd told Felix about it, but made him swear not to tell anyone, cause she was afraid they'd both get thrown out and have nowhere to go. Old Poindexter got her pregnant, and she tried to fix the problem herself by taking Mrs. Poindexter's pills. She wasn't trying to kill herself. But she died all the same. Anyway, once my dad heard that, he wanted revenge."

"I see. And John Poindexter's last name is the same as your wife's. Is that a coincidence?"

Terry stared into her lap. Thomas shook his head.

"When my dad and my mom—my mom was his second wife—had me, right about then my dad heard the Poindexters finally had a kid."

"Me." Terry raised her hand.

"So my dad and my half-brother came up with a plan for revenge," Thomas continued. "And I was going to be the one to carry it out for them. It sounds crazy now, but you have to understand, I was young, and they totally sold me on it."

"What was the plan?" Fortune asked.

"I was supposed to ruin Terry's life."

# CHAPTER 15

Williams glanced at his wife, who was staring at the table.

"The plan was for me to ruin her life as payback for how Poindexter ruined Angela's life. I mean, now I realize it was totally unfair. Terry never did anything wrong. I feel like an idiot for ever agreeing to go along with it. Dad made me promise when he was literally on his deathbed."

Terry shrugged dismissively.

"And exactly how were you supposed to ruin Terry's life?" Fortune asked.

"Get in a relationship with her, then break her heart. My brother set me up to take lessons in Terry's dojo. I mean, it wasn't her dojo, she just taught classes there. I'd taken fencing when I was at boarding school, so I did okay. I was kind of her star pupil."

"And you fell in love," Fortune said.

Thomas sighed. "I know it sounds corny, but I did. And I realized, she's a human being, a person with feelings, not a…a way for me to get revenge. Not only that, turned out she wasn't really that close to her father anyway, so even if I broke her heart or whatever, he probably wouldn't even care."

"He wouldn't," Terry muttered.

"When my dad finally died, I figured all that weirdness was over. Terry and I got married, and I called my brother and told him I was done with this stupid revenge plot. Well, he threatened to stop my allowance, and I said I didn't care. But later he called me back and said, bring Terry by, and her father too, and we'll talk. Maybe we can work something out. I said okay. I realize now, that probably wasn't the smartest idea."

"So you went to visit him," Fortune said. "Was that the afternoon—"

"Yes. The first and last time we ever went to his house."

"I told him we shouldn't go inside," Terry interjected. "I had a bad feeling about it."

"Yeah, I should've known something was up. He'd built himself this weird fortress. He had these windows that turned white if you got too close. The doors opened and closed by themselves. And it was freezing cold inside. And my brother? No nice to meet you or anything like that, he just brings us back to his office and then boom. He tells Terry what her father had done to Angela, and how he deserved to suffer. Then he said he'd had us followed, and to prove it he told us everything we'd done in the past week."

"He'd had you followed," Fortune said.

"Yeah! Is that creepy or what? Then he says to Terry, 'Thomas is going to break your engagement, and consequently, your heart. You can go back to your father and tell him you were not good enough for Thomas Williams. That you have been rejected and now you are damaged goods.' Terry looks at me and says, is he serious? And then I said to him, hey, guess what dude, Terry and I are already married, so forget about breaking our engagement, it's too late for that. Then he asks, 'Where is John Poindexter?' So I tell him, oh, whoops, I guess I forgot to invite him. Felix is just furious, like his lips go all white and he looks like his head's gonna explode. He goes over and unhooks the bird cage and he says, 'I thought this might happen. That is why I have a backup plan. You see there are no exits from this room. You can shut the door from inside. But you cannot open it.' He presses this button on his desk, and this steel door slides out from the wall and starts closing. You know those kinds of doors that are hidden in the wall?"

"Pocket doors," Terry said.

"Yeah. We should've run out right then but you know how sometimes in a situation like that, you don't do anything 'cause you don't really believe it's happening? Anyway, he walks out with his bird cage while the door's closing, and I yell at him, 'you're going to kill all of us?' And he turns around and says, 'Not all of us. Just you.'"

"What happened then?" Fortune asked.

"I grabbed the letter opener from the desk and threw it at him," Thomas said.

"Really?" Fortune folded her arms and raised her eyebrows.

"They have the surveillance tape," Terry said. "Thanks for trying to protect me. But you already know I'm the one who threw the knife. Letter opener, whatever. I thought it was a knife. I panicked."

"Nice throw," Fortune said admiringly.

"Eight years of Hapkido training," Terry said modestly.

"She's not supposed to be complimenting the murderer," Lee blustered. Gertie patted his arm soothingly.

"Lucky for us, the door had a safety stop," Thomas went on. "You know, like a garage door? It hit his body, couldn't close, and then started opening again."

"Well no wonder those two looked so peaked when they walked out," Mary-Alice whispered.

"You left immediately?" Fortune asked.

"I tried to call 9-1-1," Williams said defensively. "Like we told the sheriff. There was no signal."

"You had time to put the bird cage back and wipe your prints off the letter opener."

"It was self-defense," Terry insisted. "I know all you saw on the video was me throwing the knife. But if you go back to the house and look at that office door, you'll know we're telling the truth."

"It would've saved us all a whole lot of trouble if you'd simply told us everything the first time," Fortune said.

Out in the observation area, Sheriff Lee mumbled,

"Amen to that."

# CHAPTER 16

"Gertie, stop giggling!" Ida Belle scolded.

"I can't help it," Gertie gasped, when she'd caught her breath. "It sounds kind of dirty."

"Everything sounds dirty to you." Ida Belle stabbed her fork into her biscuits and gravy. "Man, I've missed Francine's. How come we hardly go here anymore?"

"Because some of us need to fit into our jeans," Fortune said.

"*Intestate* simply means the man died without leaving a will, Miss Gertie," Mary-Alice explained. Gertie snorted, and Ida Belle glared at her.

"*I'm* listening, Mary-Alice," Ida Belle said pointedly. "You were saying, before you were so rudely interrupted, that Raymond Fosca, aka Felix Williams, died...without leaving a will. Right?"

"Maybe he really thought he was going to live forever." Fortune popped a forkful of fried potatoes into her mouth. "Mm, I forgot how heavenly the Seven Deadly Sins are."

"Now, why does Francine call her breakfast special The Seven Deadly Sins?" Mary-Alice asked.

"Eggs, bacon, sausage, biscuits, gravy, fried potatoes, and pancakes," Ida Belle and Gertie recited in unison.

"Not exactly a recipe for immortality," Fortune added. "But delicious. Okay, speaking of immortality. Since Fosca's plan to live forever didn't work out, what happens now?"

"Sheriff Lee told me that under Louisiana law, Thomas inherits everything as his only living relative," Mary-Alice said. "And the good news is, he wants to donate the Polk Plantation back to the parish. Miss Odile will be over the moon, now that she can run her ghost tours without anyone harassing her about it."

"What about Terry?" Fortune asked. "Is she in any trouble?"

"No, she isn't. Sheriff Lee won't bring any charges against her. He believes she acted in self-defense. He was trapped in that room himself, so he very much sympathizes."

"Good call," Fortune said. "I would've done the same thing in her place. Did you ask him about Semmelweis?"

"Sheriff Lee believes your theory fits the facts, Miss Fortune. Scratches on the baseboards of the office, the condition of the John Doe's fingernails...it seems Mr. Fosca wanted an escape-proof room, and he figured there was one way to test it. He trapped the architect inside. If there had been a way to escape, Mr. Semmelweis would have found it. The poor man, he had done his job too well. He tried to pull out the baseboards, but died before he could escape."

"Fosca locked the man in that room and let him die?" Gertie exclaimed. "Good heavens, that man was a monster!"

"Bonus, Fosca probably didn't even have to pay him," Fortune added.

"Well now wait," Ida Belle chimed in. "There's one thing that was never explained. Who left the cross on Fosca's chest?"

"Oh, that's right," Fortune agreed. "We never figured out how that got there, did we?

Mary-Alice's cheeks turned pink.

"It was mine," she said quietly.

"Yours?" Ida Belle demanded. "Mary-Alice, you don't really believe in vampires, do you?"

"I didn't know," she pleaded. "When I found Mr. Fosca, I bent over him to do CPR, but I realized he was past help. Later on, I couldn't find my necklace, and I was ever so distressed because it was real gold and all. It wasn't until Sheriff Lee said something about it being found on Mr. Fosca's body that I realized what had happened."

She avoided the disbelieving stares at her table, and concentrated on working her fork through a butter-soaked pancake.

"Did you get the necklace back?" Gertie asked.

Mary-Alice nodded. "Along with a very stern lecture from the sheriff. But I couldn't bring myself to wear it again, so I donated it to the church rummage sale. I am very sorry for not telling y'all sooner."

"Mary-Alice, you have to be careful with murder scenes. You can't just go in dropping sequins and jewelry all over the dead bodies. It confuses people."

"Ida Belle, she knows that," Gertie scolded. "She just said she was sorry. Go easy on her. She's a noob."

"Miss Gertie's right," Mary-Alice said. "I do have ever so much to learn. Oh, I nearly forgot. There is one more bit of news, I'm happy to say."

Mary-Alice reached into her bag and produced a bulging manila envelope.

"Where did you get that?" Gertie squeaked.

"I asked Sheriff Lee whether he'd found our money in Mr. Fosca's house. I showed him my copy of our contract and told him that Mr. Fosca still owed us the second half of our payment. Sheriff Lee had found the envelope, but he told me to talk to Thomas Williams to see whether we could keep it. Young Thomas said by all means, if his brother entered a contract, then he intended to honor it."

"Nice work, Mary-Alice," Gertie lifted her glass of tea in salute.

"I agree," Fortune added. "Great job."

"So do y'all forgive me for messing up?" Mary-Alice asked. "I promise to be ever so careful from now on."

"I guess so," Ida Belle grumbled. "But you're buying breakfast."

"And you're not allowed to get mad at any of us for at least a year," Gertie added.

"Now Miss Gertie," Mary-Alice exclaimed, "why on earth would I ever be mad at any of y'all?"

The next day, Father Michael stopped by Mary-Alice's house to pay a visit to his newest parishioner and to thank her for the generous rummage sale donation. As Mary-Alice was pouring tea, Angela hopped down from her perch, shook out her feathers, and squawked a hearty *embrasse moi tchew* at the shocked priest.

It turned out old birds could learn new words after all.

# FROM THE AUTHOR

Thank you for taking the time to read this book. If you enjoyed it, please consider telling your friends or posting a short review. Word of mouth is an author's best friend and much appreciated.

If you like the *Miss Fortune stories,* pick up *Trust Fall,* a free short story in *The Professor Molly Mysteries.* I wouldn't say the Professor Molly Mysteries are autobiographical, but they are close to my heart. Like Professor Molly, I work at a university in rural Hawaii. Unlike my protagonist, I am blessed with delightful students, sane colleagues, and a perfectly nice office chair.

Want to be the first to learn about events, promotions, give-aways, and new releases? Go to subscribepage.com/MissFortune to sign up for my newsletter.

# THE PAJAMA MURDER

## THE MARY-ALICE FILES BOOK 9

Buford Fontleroy Deale III, president and owner of Deale Properties, Inc., was scheduled to meet the private investigators at nine o'clock. This was a happy coincidence, at least for Deale. He had been stewing over his humiliation of the previous afternoon, and it had occurred to him that morning that the Sinful Ladies' Detective Agency could help him exact his revenge. He wouldn't even have to get his hands dirty.

The other matter could wait.

The investigators arrived five minutes early. A less worldly man might not have been impressed at the sight of them—a gangly girl and three old ladies. But Deale liked what he saw. Old ladies were nosy and unthreatening—a perfect combination for someone whose job was to poke around and dig up (or plant) dirt on people. The girl, he assumed, must be their assistant.

He was surprised when the girl stepped forward, reached across his desk, and dealt him a crushing handshake.

"I'm Fortune Morrow." She had the charmless, hard-edged diction of a Northerner. "You can call me Fortune. These are my associates Ida Belle, Gertie, and Mary-Alice."

Fortune wasted no time on small talk. Once they were all seated (and Gertie had managed to tuck her enormous purse out of the way) she produced a manila folder and slapped it on Deale's desk.

"Florentin Blaise Menard has been employed as bookkeeper for Deale Properties for twenty-three years," Fortune said. "He worked for your father, and when you inherited the company nine years ago you kept him on."

"That's correct." Deal felt a prickle of irritation at the reminder. Although it had been his grandfather who had started the business, Deale liked to think of himself as a self-made man. He believed his success was due to his own talent and hard work. (Just as his setbacks were entirely the fault of his enemies and detractors.)

"We believe your suspicions about Menard are worth following up," Fortune said. "His expenditures are way out of line with a bookkeeper's salary. He's made improvements on his house in the last five years that have doubled its value. And his automobile—"

"Yes, yes, we'll discuss that another time." Deale waved his hand dismissively and leaned back in his leatherette chair. "Something else has come up. Something much more important. Let's put aside Menard for now. In fact, Florentin Menard can help us."

Deale picked up the phone on his desk, summoning a small, middle-aged brunette.

"Regina, get Menard in here," he ordered.

"*Yes*, Mr. Deale. Right away, Mr. Deale."

Regina flashed a brief, unconvincing smile and stomped off.

Florentin Menard entered Deale's office with an innocent smile on his round face. If he had overheard any of the discussion about him, he didn't show it. He looked like a man who spent his life indoors, as pale and plump as a grub. With no chairs available in the crowded office, Menard stood and awaited further instruction. Florentin Menard seemed accustomed to standing in his boss's presence.

"Menard," Deale boomed, "These are some friends of mine. Miss Mary-Alice, Miss Ida Belle, Miss Gertie, and Miss Fortune."

Deale could tell the women were impressed that he had remembered their names. He always made a point of memorizing names, and he was good at it. He knew this skill would serve him later in life, when he would (he was sure) be called to run for public office.

Florentin Menard opened his mouth to greet the visitors, but Deale cut him off.

"Now, I understand we've had some unusual expenses recently."

"There have been repairs associated with the recent hurricane damage, Mr. Deale." Florentin Menard's tone was soothing, and his face remained as impassive as a cue ball. "We've lost several tenants to the new mall, as you know. We have been doing whatever we can to keep the ones we have happy. Admittedly it's a tough market right now, but we'll survive if we attend to our customer relationships."

"I've had a look at some of the repair bills myself." Deale leaned back in his chair and steepled his fingers. "They look high to me."

Menard swallowed, but maintained his serene expression.

"I appreciate your attention to these details, Mr. Deale. You must understand that taken in context—"

"And I believe I know exactly where the fault lies."

Menard gulped.

"Mr. Deale, I assure you—"

"Harriet Hamilton."

Menard's nervousness turned to astonishment.

"Harriet?"

"Yes."

"Harriet of Harriet's Books?"

The women stirred, apparently surprised by this development. Well, Deale prided himself on his unpredictability. It was how he kept his enemies off-balance.

"Harriet has been defrauding us," Deale declared.

"But—"

"I want you to help these ladies gather the evidence against her. I know she's guilty. It's just a matter of getting proof."

Florentin Menard opened his mouth and closed it again. He reminded Deale of a beached bluegill.

Fortune, the young, skinny one, stood up.

"We're not interested in taking this case," she said crisply. "We were led to believe we were here for something else entirely. Thank you for your time, Mr. Deale. Mr. Menard."

Florentin Menard nodded and scuttled out of the office.

Mary-Alice and Ida Belle stood to follow Fortune out. Gertie leaned over and tugged at her bag, which was stuck underneath her chair. She tugged again, but still the bag didn't budge.

Then she gave a mighty pull, and her overstuffed purse exploded.

A small, pink bottle flew up in a parabolic arc and smashed to bits against the wall, filling the room with a solvent stench. Ninja stars, brushes, books, and small firearms flew in all directions. Something that looked like a stick of dynamite skittered across the floor.

Gertie held up her purse and looked through it. Through the blown-out bottom, she met Deale's gaze. Deale scowled back at her. This was not at all how he had hoped this meeting would turn out.

Ida Belle was holding a goo-filled baggie between her thumb and forefinger.

"Gertie, do you even know what this is?" Ida Belle demanded.

"It's my egg salad sandwich." Gertie snatched it away from her. "I thought I'd lost it."

The ladies' dramatic exit had lost its momentum. They all pitched in to collect Gertie's things and clean up the mess as Deale glowered at them from behind his desk. He did not see any humor in the situation. He was angry with them for refusing to go along with his plan, and he wanted them out of his office. When they had finished gathering as much of Gertie's scattered property as they could find, they muttered halfhearted goodbyes and scurried out of the building.

"Well," Deale said aloud, when he was sure they had gone. "Time for Plan B."

Printed in the USA
CPSIA information can be obtained
at www.ICGtesting.com
CBHW051051210424
7298CB00013B/756